C000071234

INTRUSION

WWII,
Two boys,
A fateful rivalry

Rosalind Minett

Copyright © 2014 Rosalind Minett

All rights reserved.

ISBN: 978-0992716769

The right of Rosalind Minett to be identified as the
author of this work has been asserted by her in
accordance with sections 77 and 78 of the Copyright,
Designs and Patents Act 1988.

A CIP catalogue record of this book is available from
the British libary.

This book is a work of fiction. Names and characters
are entirely the product of the author's imagination.
Any resemblance to actual people, living or dead, is
entirely coincidental.

Uptake Publications
Kingswood Manor Cottage
Tedworth, Surrey KT20 7AJ

REVIEWS

"Minett weaves a powerful and compelling narrative with strong and relatable characters, and offers an evocative portrayal of England's war-time home front. . . The mounting tensions between Billy and Kenneth parallel the rising agitation in Europe The author is deft in capturing that sense of tightly controlled emotions in the parents' characters and the sense of social and familial obligation. This and the war's tension is offset by the humour that comes through when seeing it all through Billy's five-year-old eyes – it foreshadows the violence about to erupt in Europe ...
HARPER COLLINS

an enchanting trilogy written by Rosalind Minett who is a master of research. She has skillfully conjured scenes from the WWII era and the chaos and desperation of that time. She has managed to bring it to the reader's mind seamlessly and effortlessly with clever interpretations from a five-year old mind.
CMT Stibbe, USA

Like all great artists, Rosalind Minett paints vivid images with her words, drawing and colouring each character until you feel you know them. I lived through every page of this story, sharing Billy's emotions and imagining what it must have been like to live through those harrowing times.
Bee Aschmann, Spain

Minett's economic, yet powerful writing does a wonderful job at immersing the reader inside Bill's world. Her strength lies in the power of hints. These are all confusing to Bill, but perfectly clear to the reader, who can't help but feel for the hapless hero, victim to forces he can barely fathom, let alone control. Even better is the underlying, parallel narration of the events unfolding in Europe, mirroring the invasion of Bill's life by Kenneth. I have read many books on the war, yet few of them manage to capture so well the atmosphere of it all. All in all, a masterful tale by an obviously very talented story-teller.

Nicholas.C.Rossis, Athens

Minett writes beautifully with a deep understanding of a troubled boy's journey through trauma, disruption and invasion. I felt very much part of the landscape through the eyes of a remarkable boy whose story gradually unfolds and grips you from the very onset. I adore Billy's character and can't wait to read the next instalment I am officially hooked and highly recommend this unforgettable and exceptional well written story to everyone.

C.R.Putsche, Austria

The book is so beautifully scribed ...
Very strong writing this, a book pleading to become a film. Rosalind Minett is becoming an upper echelon writer. Highly Recommended.

Grady Harp, Los Angeles
Amazon Hall of Fame reviewer

A RELATIVE INVASION

A trilogy

Book One

INTRUSION

ACKNOWLEDGMENTS

My grateful thanks to Terry Cottle for wartime information, to Karen Perkins, editor, and to the lovely NEIL for his advice.

Very many thanks to the talented
Pradeep Premalal, for the cover design.

DEDICATION

To all those who struggled to survive
the emotional effects of the
Second World War

> *"In retrospect, though many were guilty, none was innocent."*

The Origins of the Second World War
A.J.P. Taylor

CHAPTER ONE
October 22nd 1937

*Today the Duke and Duchess of Windsor met
Herr Hitler at Berghof*

Kenneth. Until now he'd been just a name on a Christmas card written by someone else. Kenn*eth*. Billy felt his tongue thick against his lips. It felt the same when he said 'filth'. 'Filthy' was the word Mother used when he'd got dirty knees playing outside.

He bent down to his hobby horse's hard white head. The furry strip along the top of its neck was nice to stroke. He whispered into the leathery ear, 'Do you know? We're really, really going to have a boy to play with here, in our house! He's called a cousin.'

The horse's wheel was shiny red like a ripe tomato and when its head was pressed down, the wheel squeaked. Really that was the horse talking. Horsey always said it would be jolly good if Jim and Andrew could come over after school. But Mother said it would be too much to have a child here to play.

Now he would!

He smiled to himself. Yesterday, he'd felt really important at News Time. Miss Peake was kind and sometimes wore a pretty blouse. He'd put up his hand.

'Billy? Do you have some news for us?'

'I've got a cousin and he's coming to my house.'

'My cousin lives next door,' said Sonia.

Dick and Mick shouted out that they had UMPTEEN cousins not silly old ONE.

1

'No such number, *umpteen.*' Sonia was clever and she knew.

'Loads, anyway.'

'Yes, loads 'n loads.'

'Now twins, that's not very nice'. Miss Peake smiled, 'We're all happy that Billy has his cousin visiting, aren't we, children?'

'Yes, Miss Peake,' everyone chanted.

At home time, he'd told Mother, 'Miss Peake is ever so pleased that my cousin is visiting.'

Mother's mouth moved into something like a smile, only not as nice. 'Perhaps she'd like to entertain him, then.'

Now it was the very day the cousin was coming. He stroked Horsey's head. On Monday, he'd tell everyone what he and Kenneth had played.

'Billy!' Mother's voice calling upstairs made him start. 'Are you washed?'

He pulled Horsey away from the window where they'd been watching the children in the house over the road laughing and even shouting.

'Billy? They'll be here soon.'

He rode out of his bedroom and along the passage, past the big bathroom with its misty windows and the little lavatory with its long chain and white knob and down the stairs, being very careful not to catch the hobby horse wheel on the stair-rods as he went. At the bottom, it made a nice clickety-clack sound on the hall tiles.

Mother waved her arms. 'For goodness sake, child! Everyone can hear that for miles. People who live in Primley Road don't want your noise.'

The horse clattered into the hall-stand. Mother looked down with her *Don't* face. 'You'll have to behave when your relatives come, Billy. I'm sure Kenneth will, with that angelic face.'

A jelly face! He started to ask, 'Mother, why does—?'

'That horse in the umbrella stand, please. Look, here's your father home from Chambers.'

Horsey squeaked, 'Something big's going to happen.'

Father's shadow showed through the glass in the front door.

The galloping had made Billy's socks slide down to his ankles. They were a new pair but the elastic wasn't very strong. He pulled them up as neatly as he could before the front door opened.

Father came in with a whoosh of wintry wind, shaking raindrops from his gabardine. He shut the front door, leaving the dark outside with the empty milk bottles. 'Here I am, Marcia.'

Mother's shoes clippity-clicked forward as she went to collect his briefcase. 'You're quite late, Herbert. High tea is nearly ready. I'd have thought you'd be eager to entertain your relatives.'

'Indeed I am, dear. Family near at last. But what a day! Court sat late and then we were discussing this.' He tapped the newspaper under his arm. 'Ha! The Windsors' latest. Did you see it? I don't know what Frank's take on it will be. Judge Ware-Simpkins called it outrageous. I tend to agree.'

Mother nodded. She didn't answer but put his briefcase in its place and dabbed the raindrops off it. One dropped onto the hobbyhorse's mane, but it didn't squeak.

'Swanning over to meet Hitler, Marcia. Bavaria. H uh! The King surely won't like that— his brother mixing with the ruddy Huns.'

Mother shrugged. 'They must know what they're doing, I suppose. We don't want any nastiness, after all.'

The wireless voice often spoke about Nasties. Mother was afraid that Nasties would come here. Billy looked at Father to see if he was frightened of Ruddy Huns, but he was twirling his umbrella into a swizzle stick like a barber's pole. Billy smoothed his hands round the damp folds and stood it in the elephant's foot, his most favourite thing in the house. Horsey liked it too.

Father hung his coat on the hallstand where two hooks were still empty and lit his pipe. 'So, Billy. You'll have someone to play with at last, now that Uncle Frank has brought Aunty and Kenneth to live in Balham. Just across the common, you know.'

'Yes, I know. Mother's told me. Goody.' Billy hopped on one leg and then the other. 'Father, I want to see Kenneth.'

'I know you do. It's not such fun being an only child, is it?'

Billy shook his head hard.

'No. Now I grew up with an older brother and Mother with a younger one. It will be good for you to have Kenneth around.'

Mother put her head on one side. 'I'm not sure whether it will be good for him...'

'Marcia!'

Father's eyebrows were so big, like untidy caterpillars, while Mother's were so skinny and small, just a couple of dark dashes.

'-or good for me. Isn't one boy enough trouble?'

'After her—' Father dropped his voice— 'women's trouble, it's the only child they're going to have. You'll be such a support to poor Doreen. Natural they should spoil Kenneth a bit.'

It was a shame Kenneth was spoiled. When Billy had spilled tomato soup down his Sunday shirt it was spoiled and it was in the rag bag now. He'd got into terrible trouble.

'Boys can be such a blessed—'

'*Children are a Blessing and Our Future.*' Dad often said things to the ceiling or the sky. This time he talked to his pipe.

Mother's mouth gave that twisty smile again. She smoothed her apron and her shoes click-clacked back to the kitchen. Perhaps she'd made those lemon cakes that had the squashy tops with a blob of cream.

'Will Kenneth bring his toys, Father?'

'I shouldn't think so. You must share yours.'

'I'm going to, Father. I've set out my farm upstairs and the small bricks for building walls.'

'Good boy. Now, listen. I've been thinking. "Father" is rather formal, these days. Uncle Frank would think so. You can call me "Dad" from now on.

Billy tilted his head up and looked carefully. Father looked like the same man. *Father*– that was his name. Was he really called "Dad"?

'So, Billy. You say *Dad*, understand? Some of your friends at school probably use that name. So you practise saying it.'

It would feel ever so funny. "Dad" didn't feel like someone he properly knew. But Billy tried it, 'Yes – Dad.' It was like playtime at school. He'd been Teacher yesterday and banged his cane lots of times, and a fireman the day before. Now Father was joining in the game.

He scratched around his knees and up his arms. If only Mother hadn't made him wear his blue buster suit. It was a knitted one, and very itchy. She said it was dinky and he had to wear it for best. But it was worst! His hand couldn't get high enough to reach all the itches up his back.

'Stop hopping and wriggling, child. Go and sit in the front room until they get here.'

Billy looked at Horsey but thought he'd better leave it in the hallstand.

Dad's big hand moved him toward the front room door. 'You could get your new pencils and draw.' He pointed to the bookcase and the unopened pad and pencils upon it, Billy's birthday present.

'I don't really like drawing.'

Dad sighed and puffed at his pipe. A swirl of smoke rose up between them. 'When I was a boy, it was a treat to draw. Just sit then, and practise being quiet. Kenneth's a quiet child.'

'Yes, Fath— *Dad*.' Billy watched the smoke trapped in the closing door. The firm footsteps paced towards the kitchen.

The front room was like a foreign land, dark even on the sunniest days so the light had to be put on. It had a pale carpet to sail over and velvety seats with white clothy things which sat on their arms like silly gloves with no fingers. He perched on a webbing stool and bounced a bit, looking at all the things that might break or spoil. Mrs Donnington had been busy polishing in here all morning. There was a glass case with china teapots and vases, a picture of a sailing boat all alone on the sea, two low tables which shone and had a garden smell. There was a smashing glass thing on one, a bluey-greeny ball with bubbles trapped inside it. When he'd asked, Mother said that colour was called *turquoise*. The word sounded like a special animal so Billy always remembered it and told people it was his favourite colour.

He sat still watching for rain and listened to the Primley Road quiet. Until a huge knock on the door.

From the garden room, Mother's voice escaped. 'No question that's Frank. He knocks hard enough to startle the whole of Wandsworth.'

Dad strode to the front door, saying over his shoulder, 'All right, Marcia. Don't start before they've even stepped inside.'

He let the knocking person in.

Uncle Frank's voice boomed out, 'Here we are.' And behind him, a trilling lady voice, 'Hallo, Bert, hallo.'

In the background, Mother was saying, 'Why, welcome all of you,' in her nicest voice. 'Do come in.'

Another boom sounded. 'Where's that boy, then?' and the front room door flew open.

Billy looked up with a start. The doorway was filled by this man with high, wide hair, bushy like a squirrel but more bristly. He didn't have a beard so the dip in his chin showed. When he spoke, a gap between his front teeth came and went as his lips opened and shut; bark, snap, bark, snap.

'Ah, there he is! Right, Billy. Remember your Uncle Frank? Last seen before you were two.' Uncle's moist lips widened into an alarming smile. 'Made a pudding of your mother before we'd finished the wedding cake, you did.

Ha, ha, ha, ha, ha. Stand up and shake hands like a man.'

Billy looked at Mother to see if she was suddenly a pudding and whether he had to shake hands with Uncle but she was looking at the floor and her face was red. He took a slow step towards Uncle who immediately grabbed his hand and kneaded it like plasticine.

'Look. I've brought your cousin for you. Here he is,' and he brought the silky-haired boy forward. 'This is our Kenneth.'

Billy looked. Kenneth didn't wear a buster suit but shorts, with a harsh crease down each leg. His calves, so smooth in the silky grey socks, looked like the visitors' bathroom soap. Aunty Doreen, in a green suit and squat hat, trotted behind. She held the cousin by his hand.

Mother said, 'Oh, smart little boy! What a lovely fair-isle v-neck you've made him, Doreen.'

Kenneth smiled, new front teeth gleaming under the bright electric light. His face was not like jelly at all. It was like the obedient boy on the castor oil bottle.

People said it was good for boys, but it made Billy feel sick.

'Yes, here we are, everyone,' trilled Aunty on tippy toes. 'All moved in and snug as bugs.'

'I don't envy you the disruption, Doreen,' said Mother. 'It must have been a real headache.' She motioned to Billy, standing by the stool. 'Here's our one and only.'

Aunty let Kenneth's hand go. 'Ooh, Billy, you've grown big.' She bent to pinch his cheek. Her smell was like apple and custard. 'Can't call you Baba now,' and she giggled squeakily. 'So sweet, Marcia. You see, I told you it would grow on you, Motherhood.'

Mother fussed forward, her hand waving in front of her face like a fan. 'Yes, yes, do all sit down, please,' she said in a funny voice and pointed to a chair for Aunty.

Aunty sat herself down and removed her hat, placing it carefully on her bag not to dent its curled front. Billy looked at her rolls of beige hair, her squashy knees. Would she be nice?

Dad was very polite to her and got a cushion from the settee.

'Your manners were always better than your brother's.'

Dad pushed his hand around the edge of his beard.

'Shhh, Doreen!' said Mother as she sat down beside Aunty.

'So, Bert. How are the great bewigged?' Uncle Frank boomed.

Bewigged. Billy had seen that wig. It had its own special box and sat on the dressing table when Dad was home. He'd never seen Dad wearing it.

Dad said, 'We peg along, same as always, with the same rogues popping up on a regular basis.'

'Funny old job, yours,' Uncle bellowed, rolling back on his heels. 'Not that you get to decide anything, just being the clerk.'

'Clerk to the Court,' Mother put her right.

'And,' Uncle's voice got loud, 'hardly worth sending 'em down if they just pop up again. Still, someone has to do it, I suppose.'

Mother stretched out her hands, showing her shiny nails. She looked at Dad sideways.

He blinked and motioned to the chairs but neither man sat down. Uncle Frank's head was even nearer the ceiling than Dad's. Billy didn't come up to his watch chain and Kenneth only came up to his belt.

Dad walked over and put a hand on Kenneth's shoulder. 'Well then, Sonny.'

'Hello, Uncle Bert,' Kenneth smiled upwards.

Dad patted his shoulder again, then hesitated by the settee, waiting for Uncle to sit down. 'And how are things in the tax department, Frank?'

Uncle folded his arms over his wide chest. 'Magnificent.'

Aunty's eyes crinkled at the edges as she looked over at him. 'He's office based now, you know. Such a nice varied job, mixing with the right people.'

Mother's eyes went hard. 'It's not as if Herbert *mixes* with the riff-raff, Doreen! He has such a responsible post, advising the judge of the law.'

Aunty didn't seem to hear. 'So, isn't it lovely that Frank's been transferred, just where he wanted, right beside County Hall? I reckon they think well of him!' She took off her scarf and folded it on top of her bag.

Mother said, 'I'll make some tea in a minute.'

'Splendid,' said Uncle, spreading himself on the settee, his long legs out straight before him. Dad sat down on the edge and rubbed his knuckles.

Kenneth leant against his mother's knee while everyone looked at him. His shiny hair curled over his ears. Aunty Doreen stroked it and smiled at them all, her chin high and her lips pressed together as if she was holding back a chuckle. Billy often had to do that when people were very fat or dressed funnily and he mustn't say.

Kenneth's eyelashes were so long and curved. They were like the camel's at the zoo where Billy had gone for his birthday. It wasn't just the eyelashes, but the lips with their edges turned up.

'Displays calm, the camel,' Dad had said, 'but they can turn nasty.'

Kenneth was standing very still, looking at the pictures on the wall. Billy watched him, remembering not to kick to-and-fro or fiddle with his fingers.

Aunty got out her knitting from a flowered bag. There were four skinny needles with grey wool hanging in the middle of them.

Dad leaned forward, 'At work already, Doreen? You've only just sat down.'

'Mustn't waste a moment. Gloves for my men', she said with a little sigh, smiling at Dad. 'Winter's pretty well here.' Mother didn't knit. She bought their clothes in Arding and Hobbs, where the buster suit came from, or from Allders in Croydon and Billy had to wait by the clothes hangers while she tried things on for herself. She'd asked him to choose between a green and a blue blouse last time. He'd chosen the blue. It had little tiny buttons from top to bottom and white dashes round the collar. It was much prettier than Aunty's yellow knitted top that had lots of holes as a pattern.

Mother was looking at Aunty's click-clacking fingers with her polite face.

'You're so clever with your needles, Doreen, and look at Kenneth's lovely jumper. I'd like Billy to have one like that if I could knit, but a size bigger.'

Kenneth turned his camel face towards Billy, one lip curled. Did he know that Mother couldn't knit?

'You're quite a big lad, Billy,' Uncle Frank said in a disappointed tone.

Mother sighed. 'Yes, and boisterous with it. Strange, isn't it, when he's nearly a year younger than Kenneth?'

Uncle leaned forward. 'Come here, lad, put your fists up. We'll do a bit of arm wrestling.' He showed Billy how.

'Frank!' said Mother.

Dad put his hand on her arm, his big fingers nested in her sleeve as though they were hiding.

Billy did his best, but Uncle Frank's muscly arm soon had his bang flat on the coffee table.

'Ouch.'

'Just so as you know who's Boss, boy. Can't have you bullying my little lad, even though he's a bit older than you.'

Billy stared. 'I wouldn't!'

'He wouldn't,' said Mother, but Fath– *Dad* didn't say anything.

'That's all right then,' said Uncle Frank, a glint of light shining on his front teeth. 'Now, Kenneth, my lad, your Uncle is my younger brother. You can remember that if Billy gets uppity.'

Kenneth's eyelashes flickered. 'Yes, Daddy.'

Uncle turned back to Billy. 'So, now that's clear, you can take Kenneth upstairs to play. He'll like to see all your toys. Mind you share them. Not that he hasn't got plenty of toys himself.'

Billy moved quickly out of Uncle Frank's reach. Now he and Kenneth could build the brick pens and line up the animals.

Kenneth gave his smile to Aunty and then to Mother.

'Come on,' Billy said, holding the doorknob until Kenneth followed him out of the room.

'Play nicely, you two. Leave this door open,' said Mother.

Billy led the way upstairs. This would be fun.

'There's lots of doors,' said Kenneth when they got half-way up.

They leant over the banisters and Billy told him what each room was, downstairs and up. 'And my room's round the corner upstairs.' He padded up to the top. 'I haven't had anyone to play with here before. I've got my toys out ready.'

On the landing, Kenneth said quietly, 'I'm six. Are you six?'

'No, five.'

'Thought so. So I'm Boss, right? I choose things.' Kenneth went to stand by Billy's open door.

'They're my toys, though.'

'Not if you give me any. If you give me something, that makes it mine.'

'Then I shan't give you things.'

'You will.'

'But some of my things say William Wilson on them because I take them to school on Fridays.'

'I'll cross out the William and put Kenneth, then.'

'Kenneth Wilson! That's silly. That'll be wrong.'

Kenneth's voice raised. 'No it won't, I *am* Kenneth Wilson.'

Billy's raised his more. 'You can't be. Wilson is my name.'

'It's mine, anyway.' Kenneth ran to the banisters and called downstairs, 'Daddy, Daddy, I am Kenneth Wilson, aren't I?'

Uncle Frank shouted up, 'Of course you are, son. THE Kenneth Wilson.'

Billy glared and Kenneth glared back. Mother came to the stairs, 'It's all right boys. No arguing. You're both Wilson. Daddy and Uncle Frank are brothers, so they're both Mr Wilson.'

Both Mr Wilson! Billy stamped back from the landing. They'd said to share his toys, not to share his name. Everyone at school had different last names, although some first names were the same. There were two other Billys. That was bad enough. And now there was another Wilson.

Kenneth shut the bedroom door behind them. He looked down at the bricks and animals laid out on the floor. 'Bricks! Haven't you got anything decent to play with?'

'There's all different sizes and shapes. We can make walls and sheep pens.'

'Ughh. Baby stuff. I don't want to.' He pushed the cows and pigs over with one foot.

Billy picked them up and made a pig sty. Kenneth would join in soon.

Kenneth looked around and touched the little yacht on the windowsill. 'Who gave you this?'

'Nanny and Grandad.'

Kenneth frowned. 'My Grandad gives me big things like a car which goes. Your yacht doesn't go. It just stays there.'

'Yes, but I like it. You won't like it.'

'I will. I want it on my windowsill. Give it to me.'

'No.' Billy ran to rescue it.

'Yes.'

Kenneth held the little yacht by its tip so that if Billy yanked on it, it would break. He played with it a little while, then gave Billy a smile and pushed out of the bedroom. He pattered downstairs with Billy close behind him.

'Give it back, Kenneth.'

'Mummy, Daddy! Look what Billy's given me! It's because I'm his best friend. Look after it for me, Daddy,' and Uncle Frank took it. His hairy check jacket had bulgy pockets. They could be full of things Kenneth had taken from people. Billy wanted to tell but Uncle Frank's face was raw-looking, with big bones on the nose and the chin. Who could tell him anything?

'I think Nanny and Grandad might be upset,' Mother began just as Aunty Doreen said, 'How sweet, giving Kenneth his boat. They're such friends already. Kenneth's always so popular. Other children just give him things.'

Dad put in, 'I'm glad my boy can share despite being an only child.'

'So far,' said Aunt Doreen, and twiddled her fingers around her knitting.

Mother frowned at her and whisked from the room. She went down the hall to get the tea trolley ready. Soon, she called everyone into the garden room where there were little tables and not many ornaments. Billy led the way. Because of her dancing friends coming to tea, she'd taught him long ago how to hand round the plates and offer the cakes.

'That's nice, Billy,' Aunty Doreen said. 'Polite, like your father.' She spread a lacy napkin on her lap and put her head sideways at Dad.

Uncle Frank leant forward in front of her. 'What do you reckon to Halifax's trip, then, Bert?'

'Anything to avoid war. You know me.'

'You for appeasement? Where's your bottle? Lose it?'

Billy looked round but couldn't see it.

Dad said, 'Give the blighter what he wants. Then he'll be satisfied and stop grasping any new territory.'

Kenneth plopped down on Billy's special chair. He took three cakes and no-one said anything. He hadn't even had to ask first. Mother took her best apron off and tied it around him. 'We don't want you to spoil that lovely jumper, dear.'

Billy's wasn't lovely so she just said, '...and you be careful of your front, Billy.'

Uncle Frank was clicking his teeth and sighing. 'Impossible to have a conversation with nippers in the way.'

Although it was cold, the grown-ups sent the boys outside to get colour in their cheeks.

Billy rushed out. 'Topper. We can play football!'

Kenneth shivered. 'Rotten stuff. Boring. There's no outdoor toys.'

'Except my ball. Come on, catch!'

Kenneth missed but picked it up and threw it hard towards Billy.

'Ouch!'

'Your turn, dummy. Throw it, then.'

The ball kept going in Billy's face and it hurt.

'It's because you're only five. You don't know how to catch yet,' Kenneth said. 'Watch how high I can throw it.'

He threw it up higher than the fence and it came down the other side. He rushed indoors. 'Billy's thrown the ball over next door's.'

'Typical! How often have I told you to be more careful, Billy?' said Mother, in her annoyed voice. She flicked her black hair from her face like a piece of spare clothing. 'I can't face going next door to ask for it. I'll have to wait until I see them out shopping. You are a nuisance.'

'But I didn't!' Billy tried.

Dad said out of the side of his mouth, '*A lie never lives to be old*–Sophocles.'

Uncle Frank sniffed. 'So? I don't like the sort of lad that can't face up to what he's done. I'd give him the slipper if he was mine.'

Dad hesitated and turned a waxy face to Billy, his big hands hanging loose. They didn't look ready to grasp a slipper.

Kenneth stood close, his curls brushing Uncle's arm. 'It was an accident. Billy didn't mean to.'

The grown-ups made a soft murmur and Aunty put a hand on his curls, 'Bless him.'

Kenneth said, 'Billy, shall we play with your favourite things? We'll play nicely, Aunty. Upstairs. I think Billy wants to show me something.'

'Good boy, Kenneth. What a cherub you are,' said Mother in a breathy voice. 'Go along Billy, your father has let you off this time.'

'But it's not forgotten,' added Uncle.

Billy slid his fastest out of the door and up the stairs. Kenneth followed, humming.

Once they were in Billy's room, Kenneth stood with his back against the door. 'So. What are you going to give me for saving you from a thrashing?'

'You already took my yacht. And you threw the ball over. I'll tell, I will.'

'So? They'll only say you're blaming me.'

Billy sat on his bed hard. He mustn't cry. He found a wind-up car that didn't go very well. 'This is my bestest car. I'll be g-glad when you go home,' and he threw it towards Kenneth.

Kenneth picked it up, looking pleased. 'I haven't got one like this. I'll let you off this time.' He put an arm round Billy's shoulder. 'I do like playing with you, Billy. What's in that drawer?'

He didn't answer. His aeroplanes were inside. Kenneth opened it.

'Be ever so careful with these. They're my special things.'

But Kenneth got the whole lot out, whizzing them up in the air, crashing them into each other. 'There's going to be an aeroplane battle. Wheeeee splatttt zooom— that one's hit— and RIGHT down into the sea. Smaaashed! Drownded.'

Dad put his head round the door. Kenneth's hand stayed where it was, grasped around the plane. Dad's hand closed around it. 'It wouldn't be fun to see planes crash.' He lifted Kenneth's hand until the little plane was safe on a shelf.

Uncle Frank loomed behind Dad. 'And it won't be fun for you, Billy, if I catch you besting my little boy.' He wagged a finger, fat and hairy. 'You know, Bert, I had an odd feeling when we were coming here that your boy might pose a threat to mine.'

'No, no, Frank, he won't. My lad's mild-natured, but I'll look out for your Kenneth, never fear.' He put one heavy hand on each of their shoulders. 'Now boys, we've had enough of wars and fighting. You stay friends, because you'll be playing together every Saturday from now on.'

CHAPTER TWO
March 13th 1938

Annexation of Austria!
German troops march across the border

'It's certainly been a long winter.' Mother was wearing the pinny for when no-one was visiting. She got butter from the larder and put all the cooking things on the kitchen table. 'It'll soon be Easter and I suppose I shall be expected to make a Simnel cake.'

'Does it have icing?'

'No. Marzipan.'

'Kenneth doesn't like that.'

'Well, he can just have sponge fingers. He can't come today, by the way, he's very off colour.'

'Yippee!'

She tutted. 'You're very lucky not to be a sickly child. Aunty's had Kenneth in bed off and on ever since New Year.'

Billy smiled and winked at Horsey. At last, a Saturday with no Kenneth to hide his toys, break them or make him wait while he hogged them. 'M-Mother.' He'd better swallow so that the words would come out properly. 'Does Kenneth have to come S-Saturdays?'

'Yes he does.' She cracked two eggs into a bowl, 'and sometimes other days too because of Aunty's health. Since he's not here today, you can help me. Wipe up the breakfast things like I've shown you.'

While Mother bashed the butter and sugar like naughty children round and round the bowl, he wiped up the dishes, one by one, very carefully. He'd make sure Mother was pleased with him before he said anything. He piled up the plates just as she liked, humming the Hip, hip, hip hooray song.

'That's enough noise, Billy. You can play outside when you've finished the cutlery.'

He watched her sift the flour into the bowl, making a fairy snowstorm.

'Y-yes, Mother.' He swallowed as he picked up the first fork. 'I can play very quietly if I'm on my own. It's better when we don't have K-Kenneth.'

She didn't answer, so he pulled his jumper up to show the red marks on his side. 'Last Saturday, he t-trapped me in the Lloyd Loom basket.'

'You're both as bad as each other.'

'It jolly well hurt t-trying to get out.'

She looked at him over the bowl of creamy mixture. 'Don't you think it's a trouble for me, having two of you? But he's your cousin so—' she wielded the wooden spoon viciously round the edges of the bowl— 'we have no choice.'

Billy watched the nice sticky stuff for a long time as it went up the sides of the bowl then down into the middle where the spoon smashed it smooth. Sonia was allowed to lick the bowl after her mother made cakes. He watched until Mother scraped the sides of the bowl and spooned the mixture into the metal tin. Bits were left around the bowl. It would be ever so nice to taste it.

'What's *Wehavenochoice*?'

'It's Do What You're Told.' Mother plunged the bowl into the washing up water and ruined the scrapings.

He took Horsey into the garden, scuffing the toes of his shoes all the way down the path. 'She doesn't care. We'll ride right away, Horsey. Gee up.' He galloped to the end of the garden and pretended Kenneth was left far behind, like a slowcoach.

The back door opened. So Dad was home from his Conservative club.

'Billy! Come along indoors.' He was rubbing his hands in a pleased way. 'Bathroom. Now. We're going out. The Durbans have invited us over. Clean hands, knees. Jacket on.'

A quick, happy feeling squirmed inside Billy's tummy. He left Horsey by the big tree and ran indoors and up to the bathroom. He checked himself in the mirror and ran back into his room for his jacket. The Durbans were a father, a mother and a big girl. Mr Durban worked at Chambers with Dad and sometimes visited. He taught Billy the best way to catch a cricket ball and said he'd be a proper little sportsman. He let Billy sit on the arm of his chair to look at The Dandy together. Mr Durban was super-duper.

When Billy came downstairs, Mother had her red lips on and shoes with heels. She nodded to him. 'Good. We're all ready, Herbert.'

Outside, she held Dad's arm while Billy trotted beside them down to the end of the road where the trees were just stopping being bare and showing their green buds. There were three nice roads with flowers outside each house, then the horrid roads with no gardens, rickety bikes and fences squashed together. Children were shouting in the street, socks round their ankles and he wasn't supposed to look at them.

Dad was saying, 'So I thought we'd talk it over with the Durbans. It's not an easy decision.' They all walked more quickly until they reached the main road.

Mother held his arm closer to her, 'It doesn't really affect us, does it, Herbert?'

'It might. Hitler's amassing more and more power. That seems dangerous to me although the government is playing it down.'

Billy looked at Dad when he heard the Hitler word. Dad strode onwards, sucking at his pipe while Mother's steps got shorter and quicker.

'But the newsreel. All those Austrians waving and cheering, they're glad to have Hitler take over.'

'I'm guided by Judge Ware-Simpkins' opinion. He has friends in high places.'

Billy was having to trot to keep up. They were passing high houses with great trees showing their tops behind the roofs. He knew someone in high places. Mrs Donnington had to go to even the top rooms when she worked in big houses, she said. It would be funny to see her behind a high window with her feather duster.

Dad halted. 'Stop staring into peoples' windows, Billy. That's very rude. Now, come along and mind you show the Durbans your best manners.'

Billy nodded. Mrs Durban was very nice too. There would probably be cakes for tea. 'Mother, if they say, "Would you like another cake?" can I have one?'

'*May*, not can,' Mother corrected. 'If that happens, look at me and you'll see what my face is saying.'

Billy looked now and it said, *what a nuisance you are.*

The Durbans had a house joined on one side to another house, just like at home. Their sideway was much wider, though. It had a gate to it the colour of chocolate, same as the front door. The lace curtains were not as fancy as Mother's and no-one was fiddling with them as they arrived. Billy was allowed to pull the bell. It went ding, dong, ding instead of just buzzzzzz. He wasn't allowed to pull it a second time because that would have been rude.

When Mrs Durban came to the door, they all went into the front room where the big girl, Angela, was sitting at the piano ready.

'How lovely, Angela,' Mother said as the tinkling began.

Billy hoped she wouldn't play for long. He didn't fidget with his feet through the tinkling music, or when the grown-ups were chatting about Huns but he did feel a sigh come out of his mouth.

Mr Durban said, 'We'll discuss this later, I think. These young things will want their tea and then Angela can take Billy off to play.' Mr Durban looked over at him and winked.

Soon, Mother and Dad were sipping tea. Mrs Durban gave him orangeade and a buttered bun off the tea trolley. Then he was allowed to choose a cake. It had a great big blob of brown icing on the top. He didn't drop crumbs, so it was all very cheery.

Mrs Durban said, 'Angela. Time for children to be upstairs.'

Angela left her music open on the stand. She was nine, much older than him and had yellowy ringlets that bounced on her back as she led him out of the room. She spoke to him in a very kind voice as if he was ill.

'Look, Billy.' On the landing shelf was her Japanese doll with its little hands and bobbles of feet. It was so different from all the people he had ever seen. She let him touch it.

'Their eyes are all slitty. Are there really people who look like that? How do they see properly?'

'Of course they can see. You are cute.' In her bedroom with fairy pictures on the wall, she gave him a hug. 'You'll be handsome when you're a man.' She pointed at his reflection in her mirror. 'Now I'm going to show you all my things, my special things.

First, there's my Dutch Doll, Jane. Plain Jane, we call her.'

He looked at the hard wooden thing. Its arms swung to and fro and so did its legs but they didn't bend. You could see where all the bits were put together. Its lips were a thin red line.

'This is my box of handkerchiefs. They each have a different day of the week sewn on them. And here's my shell collection.'

He sat on the bed while she drew out one pretty treasure after another.

Angela nudged him after the last one. 'Do you like them?'

'Y-es. But they're girls' things. I like balloons and planes and swords.' He bounced up and down. 'Your bed's bouncy. Mine isn't.'

She looked at him. 'Shall I show you something really, really special –something important?'

'Yes, please,' Billy jumped from the bed.

She took him downstairs again, creeping along towards a closed door. 'This is Daddy's study,' she said, 'so Sshhh. And you mustn't tell. Promise.'

'Promise.'

Inside the room, shelves with lots of books went down to the floor as well as up high. There was a very big, shiny desk and a cupboard with shut doors. Angela opened these very slowly and carefully. 'Have to be careful or it'll squeak.' She put her hands inside and lifted out something very long and wrapped in rich brown leather.

He lifted a corner. 'I can see a red handle.'

'Hilt.'

He took a breath. 'Is that a sword inside?'

'A sabre, a kind of sword. Look, this is the scabbard.'

'Scabbard', he breathed. A wonderful word. It looked very old. Angela balanced the length of it on her outstretched palms and then pointed it to the floor. She held the magic thing in front of him so that he could see its full length, slightly curved. It was nearly as tall as he was, and everyone said he was tall. The handle was knobby, exactly right for fitting into a hand.

'Cor!'

Angela spoke just like a teacher, 'The knob and the hilt are silver and so are these studs down the sides of the scabbard.'

He touched halfway along where there was a circle of studded silver with a loop for hanging it on the wall, and the very tip had a silver sleeve.

After a few moments of stroking the leather scabbard, he asked, 'Can we take the sword out?'

'*Sabre*. Wait.' Angela put her head against the door, checking that the grown-ups hadn't moved from the front room. 'It's all right, they're still talking.'

She put the scabbard on the desk and waved Billy to stand away. Then, she slowly drew the sabre out. The metal was specky with brown, its grooved centre was softer, but its edges gleamed. Letters were dug along the length of the blade. Some were snake-like and others frilly. Billy's hand moved forward.

'No, you mustn't touch. It's very, very dangerous.'

His fingers itched to finger the blade and follow the pattern of the silver studs. Suppose it was out in the open in a battle, glinting in the sun, blinding an enemy! 'I do like swords, sabres. I haven't seen a real one ever.'

Angela said, 'It's *foreign*. Daddy got it when he was young. It belonged to a heroic Cossack soldier.'

'A Cossack.' The strange word sounded fierce. 'What's heroic?'

'Very very brave.'

'Was your father fighting him?'

'I don't know. I don't know how he got it. But he says this is the most valuable thing we'll ever have and it'll be mine when he dies. He was saving it for his son and we haven't got one. Only me.'

'Cor, Angela, you're so l-lucky. He could have had me for a son, then I'd have got it.'

'Shh. Don't be silly.' She carefully slid the sabre into its scabbard, then put it back in the cupboard. It was sad such a thing, the most thrilling thing he'd ever seen, was hidden away. If he could have a sabre everyone would be careful of him, even Kenneth.

'I'm going to have one l-like that when I'm a man.'

Angela put an arm round his shoulders. He rather liked that, something his parents never did.

'You're sweet, so I showed you the sabre as a treat. Did you like it?'

He nodded so hard his chin hurt his neck.

She wagged a finger. 'Now, we've got to creep out and pretend we've been playing in the garden, so they won't know. Mind you don't say anything. Not ever!'

'No I won't. I won't tell anyone.' He really really wouldn't. Then when Kenneth was horrible, Billy could think, 'I've seen a sabre' and Kenneth wouldn't know.

'C-can I come and see it again?'

She grabbed his arm. 'Perhaps. Come on. Quick, while they're still talking.'

As they crept towards the back door, the voices streamed out into the hall.

Mrs Durban: 'We don't know the possibilities.'

Mother's upset voice: 'Herbert won't join up if it comes to war.'

Mr Durban: '—too old but there's bound to be home defence against the Nazis. I shall—'

Angela put her hands over Billy's ears.

'What's defence? What are they talking about?'

25

'Grown ups' talk, Billy.'

'I heard them say *Nasties*. Is it nasty?'

'Probably. Come on.'

Billy was going to have a sabre like that when he grew up. He needed one. There were nasties. There was Kenneth.

'Billy, *come on*!'

They ran through the back door into the chilly garden.

CHAPTER THREE
March 18th 1938

Recruitment problem solved.
8,000 young men join the Territorial Army

It was good having a secret, and it was very very good that he had seen a sword for real and it had been a sabre and belonged to a Cossack and fighting had happened with it. Now, when Kenneth got him into trouble and he was sent to his bedroom, he practised being a Cossack and pulling out the sabre from its scabbard, holding it and watching out for its sharp sharp blade. It was a secret he wasn't going to share with anyone, especially not Kenneth.

On school days he didn't worry about big boys bashing him up. He ran round holding a piece of wood and knowing it was really a sabre. He didn't even tell Jim, the friend he liked best, because he would tell Reg and Reg would tell all of the others and then there wouldn't be a secret and it would be like not having a sabre any more.

At home, he had a sword picture to look at. It was in the book he'd found in the Boots' library. An olden times man had the sword stuck in a big rock.

'You won't be able to read that, silly child. Look at all the words!' Mother had said, 'but borrow it if you want. I suppose it's something you can look at with Kenneth.'

Billy had it spread out on his small bedroom table.

'You can't read that,' said Kenneth. 'You only read baby words.'

Billy smiled to himself. He could look at the picture and that was all that mattered. Kenneth didn't know anything.

He said, 'We're g-going to Nanny and Grandad's tomorrow. You don't go there.'

Kenneth stood on Billy's foot. 'We won't be friends.'

'Don't c-care. Ow.'

Kenneth pressed his whole weight down. 'Don't say anything or I'll tell Daddy you wouldn't share.'

'Ouch, ow, you're hurting my foot.'

Mother called up just then. 'Billy. Time for cubs. Uncle's going to walk you round.'

Kenneth got off quickly. 'Don't you dare *say*. I'm going to stay up here and draw while you go. Or I might play with your—'

Billy trailed downstairs. Uncle knew the cub master. They did Dib Dib Dibs together. If only Uncle didn't go to it, cubs would be fun.

Usually Sundays were happy, because they went to Nanny and Grandad's. Nanny's roast potatoes were crispy, not soggy, and she always found Billy interesting things to play with: buttons and conkers and coloured string. Grandad didn't go to work any more. He had a shed and a woolly waistcoat.

Billy skipped past Mother and Dad as they reached the green garden gate. He was going to tell Nanny and Grandad when no-one else was listening – not about the sabre, just in case they told Mother – but about Kenneth. Nanny sometimes gave Mother *advice*.

He was in his running position all ready, so Dad said, 'Go on, then.' Billy darted up the crazy paving path and patted the two friendly garden gnomes with their red caps. When Nanny had hugged him and given him a drink and biscuit, she sat down with Mother and Dad. There was lots of chatting. Billy swung his feet to and fro.

Grandad took Billy's hand. 'Come on. We'll go out to the shed.' It was a cosy place and smelled of old grass and sawn wood.

All the tools had their own special hooks. It was nice to take each one off, make a line of tools and hang them up again. 'See, Grandad, I know where they all go.'

Grandad was just finding a little hammer for Billy to bang a nail into a piece of wood, when there was a loud whistle outside.

'Uncle Ted!' Billy ran out to see his favourite person. Uncle Ted always laughed a lot and winked at Billy. He worked at an office in the West End. He didn't have a wife. Sometimes he had humbugs or a toy car, and he kicked a ball just right so that Billy could kick it back.

Today, Uncle was wearing his uniform. It was like soldiers wore, but Uncle wasn't one yet.

Billy jumped up and down. 'Uncle, Uncle, will you do that thing?' Uncle Ted could stand on his hands. 'Please, do that upside-down thing again.'

'Just a mo, then.' Uncle Ted took some things out of his pockets, then flipped his hands down and his legs into the air. It was very funny to see his face upside down and his trouser bottoms flapping down to reveal such white ankles.

'Oh Ted!' Nanny laughed, leaning out of the lounge window. 'Come and see Bert and Marcia.'

Uncle Ted stood up again, 'Coming. Billy, you look at this.' He flicked a pack of cards between his fingers and shuffled them so fast you couldn't quite see them. 'See the King? Now. King's gone. Oh, look! King's at the front of the pack.'

'It's magic! Do that m-magic again. Please, Uncle.'

'Okey dokey, but inside. Time to see what's up in the kitchen.' He went ahead.

It would be jolly good to be a grown-up like Uncle Ted.

Billy walked behind him, trying to make his strides the same size. Uncle turned sharply, 'Bo! Caught you out.'

Billy couldn't help squealing.

Mother came out, 'For pity's sake, Ted, do you have to encourage his noise?'

Nanny bustled from the kitchen as Billy put his shoes alongside Uncle's huge boots. 'Just enjoying themselves, aren't you, my love? Your Uncle Ted was always a bundle of laughs.'

Mother's face looked hard as a plate. 'Always an excuse for the favourite child. He had a lot to laugh about, didn't you, Ted?'

Dad came to Uncle's rescue. 'Let's everyone move to the dining room.' He led the way. Inside, he took his pipe from his mouth. 'Enjoying territorials then, Ted?'

Uncle nodded. 'Doing my bit, Bert.'

'As long as it's only territorials,' Grandad muttered, following with a tray of glasses.

Dad sat down on the far end of the table and nodded slowly. 'Better to steer Ted into a career where he'll be exempt, just in case.'

That word again. 'What's X M-ed?'

Uncle slid into a chair and pulled Billy into the one beside him. He grinned at Dad. 'Exempt, Billy. Means you don't have to go, don't have to do something. Like you could be exempt from dinner.'

Billy knew he was joking. Such a meaty smell steamed out of the kitchen that he felt hungrier than he ever did at home. Nanny had laid the table with the snowy cloth that had shiny leaves on it. Now the big dishes came in with the joint and vegetables, steam rising off them.

When everyone was served out he ate everything Nanny put on his plate, especially the roast potatoes. He was so busy eating that he didn't listen to any of the grown-ups talk. It was only as he dipped the last potato into his pool of gravy that he looked around.

Mother was telling Nanny about Kenneth's lovely knitted jumpers. 'I'm hoping Doreen'll knit Billy one.'

Nanny said, 'Why don't you go to the Women's Institute meetings? Then you can learn to knit and sew like Doreen.'

'Good idea, Marcia,' Dad joined in. 'Instead of your dances.'

Mother frowned down at the table.

Billy didn't like it when she wasn't happy. He said 'Mother likes d-dancing. She doesn't like knitting.'

Mother smiled. 'True. Knitting's a very poor swap.'

'Well, Sis, you'll be needing to sew and knit soon,' said Uncle Ted. 'You can't leave it at one nipper forever.'

'What do you know? You're fancy free as always, and probably will be for a decade more.'

'But he's right, Marcia dear,' said Nanny. 'We'd all like to see more young ones here.'

Billy squeezed his thumbs into the palms of his hands until it hurt. Was Nanny going to have another boy here? Did she mean Kenneth? He looked at Mother's face. It went tight and she opened her mouth to say something to Nanny, but then shut it again.

He waited until the spotted dick and custard was all finished and everyone went into the lounge, except for Nanny. He followed her into the kitchen. 'Can I help, Nanny?'

'You are a good little boy. Wait till I've stacked up these dishes.'

When she was washing up, Billy wiped up the cutlery and the small things that couldn't break.

'It's best just having one child in your house, Nanny, isn't it?'

'Oh I think you've been listening to your Mummy niggling about having a brother. It was just that she was quite a big girl when your Uncle came along. She doesn't mean half she says, Billy.'

Billy shook his head. He hadn't been thinking about Mother and Uncle Ted at all. Now that he and Nanny were on their own he could tell her about Kenneth.

Water splashed and china chinked as Nanny worked. It was easier not to have anyone looking at him while he talked about all the horrible times with Kenneth. There was a lot to say about it. He ended up, 'I d-don't really like playing with K-Kenneth. You'd h- hate having a b-boy like him here and s-so would Grandad.'

Nanny turned round, 'Dearie me.' She patted his head with damp hands. A trickle of water ran down his forehead.

'You're starting a bit of a stutter, Billy. You'll have to speak slower. Now listen. All children quarrel when they play. I expect Kenneth's good for you. You always used to ask for someone to play with at home. Now you've got someone.'

'I p-play with boys at school. They're my f-friends. That's b-better. I've told M-Mother but she s-says *we have no ch- choice*.'

'Speak properly, love, and then perhaps your mother will listen to you. Come along to the lounge and let's hear Uncle Ted tell us all about his training camp.'

She pulled the back door to and shut out the sunlight.

CHAPTER FOUR
September 21st 1938

Nazis smash, loot and burn Jewish shops and temples until Goebbels calls halt

Dad disappeared with his wig box and suitcase taking the last of the summer with him.

'Is D-dad going to be away long?'

'The leaves might turn brown before he gets back,' Mother said with her lips tight. 'He'll be in Lincoln Crown Court for some weeks.'

When Billy came away from waving to Dad through the window he heard her at the telephone arranging about dances with her lady friends. He always had to stay in his bedroom when those ladies came. Mother did a special tea for them in the front room and afterwards he came down to say *Hello*. They'd all pat his face and call him sweet, but never give him one. Then he'd go to bed while they whisked away in their frilly dresses, even Mother full of smiles. The lady next door popped in to check on him every hour, not that he heard her.

Mother was still on the telephone, giggling. He ran into the kitchen to make a whizzer. He used two cardboard milk bottle tops, and a piece of string off Dad's roll that hung outside the cellar door. When Mother came in, she let him borrow the sewing scissors with zig-zag edges. He used four different colours from his poster paints. It took ever so long but at the end it looked smashing. He cleared up and ran upstairs with his whizzer.

He'd just got it to whizz round so fast that all the coloured stripes went into a dark orange colour and

the strings had that stretchy feel when he heard
Uncle Frank rattle the letter box. 'Coo-ee!'

Billy jumped back against the wall.

Mother opened the door and let him in. 'Frank?
Everything all right, now Doreen's had the—?'

'Doreen's resting. She's not too bad, considering.
Kenneth is drawing as usual so I came to give you
a hand, Marcia. With Bert away, your boy needs
toughening up. I thought I'd exercise him.'

'Exercises? Well, I shall certainly be glad of some
time to myself if you're offering to take him off for a
bit?'

'I'll do it here. Keep you company at the same time,
eh?'

Billy stayed very quiet, hoping they wouldn't call
up for him, but they soon did. He dropped the
whizzer and went slowly downstairs.

'Billy. I came over specially for you, boy, give you
no time for that stuttering nonsense. I'll make a man
of you. Toughen you up. Take off your shirt and vest.'

He put them on the banisters as Uncle waited.

'Ready? Outside with you.' He put a hand behind
Billy's back and pushed him into the garden. He
found a smooth patch on the lawn.

'Twenty knees bend, twenty stretch ups, then
running on the spot till I say *Stop*. Right?'

The lady next door was hanging out her washing,
but stopped to watch. It was very very embarrassing.

'Running, I said. Faster, faster.'

Afterwards there were arm wrestles, fisticuffs and
heavy holds that Billy was supposed to escape from.
Uncle taught him press-ups, roaring with laughter
every time Billy collapsed onto the floor.

'Oh, Frank! You are a caution,' said Mother,
coming out at that point. 'Come and have a cup of tea.
Billy can stay in the garden with his ball now.'

Billy caught his breath, 'I d-do like football, Uncle.' It would be much better if he could exercise at that. At school, he was one of the best at football. He and Jim, Reg, Danny and Andrew played every day. Kenneth couldn't play football much because he was delicate.

Mother said, 'Yes, he's mad about football. At least, it drives me mad.' She giggled.

Uncle Frank folded his arms. 'Football? I'll show him football. You wait till I get you on the football field, boy. You'll see football there. I'll give you football.'

'Goodness, Frank. You make it sound as if you'll kick football out of him,' said Mother.

'Hasn't Bert told you? I was the star player as a youngster. If only I could give the time to it now. Responsibilities come first. But,' he looked at Billy, 'I suppose I should give this lad a bit of a kick around sometime. Don't suppose Bert will, even when he's home. His head'll be stuck in a book, no doubt. It was always that way when he was a boy –reading or drawing.'

'He has to study his documents.'

'As I do the tax returns. But not after work! Not at the weekends!'

Billy stayed outside while they went to have their cups of tea, just in case Uncle felt like kicking him around. He pushed a ball around the back of the shed and pretended he was playing with Jim and Reg.

When Uncle had gone, Mother called Billy indoors. 'Put your shirt back on, do.'

'I don't want to do any more exercises, Mother.'

'Uncle Frank says it's good for boys.'

'Kenneth doesn't do them.'

'Kenneth's frail. Now then. Uncle has been here to help me with you. We must help him. We'll visit Aunty on Friday. She hasn't been well. She's in bed.'

'Ill?' He didn't want Aunty ill.

Mother nodded. 'Aunty's been in hospital for a few days.'

He felt a gulp in his throat. People died in hospital sometimes. 'Is Aunty dying?'

'Of course not. The doctors have —done things to make her better. Now she's resting. She needs time before she gets back on her feet.'

At Friday home time, Billy stood under the *Infant Boys* arch until he saw Mother's grey coat and silky headscarf between the umbrellas. It was pouring with rain.

'Ready to go, Billy? Pull those socks up, they're rumpled.' Although she let Billy walk close enough to be under her umbrella, its points dripped onto his hands because of 'no hands in pockets.' His raincoat didn't cover the bottoms of his legs.

It was difficult to keep up with Mother's swishing walk all the way down Nightingale Lane and several turnings afterwards. Now the houses were closer together and smaller and uglier. Kenneth's was one, and it only took three steps to get from the pavement to the front door. In the back garden, the square of concrete with a clothes-line doubled to make two rows was far too near to next door's to risk playing with even a little ball.

Mother let herself in with the key Uncle Frank had given her and propped her umbrella inside the entrance. She called out, 'Doreen, we're here.'

Kenneth came out with his hair not properly brushed.

Mother stroked it, then hung up her coat. 'Hello, Kenneth, dear. Billy, put your wet coat on the boiler rail in the kitchen. Play quietly with Kenneth in there while I sit with Aunty.'

He could just see Aunty in a pale nightgown with her feet on a stool before the front room door shut. Billy heard the word 'operation' again but he knew it was rude to listen. Mother's voice started gently, and there was the sound of coughing or hiccupping or could it be crying?

Kenneth was frowning, so probably he could hear it but Billy thought it was best not to ask.

Aunty had to use her front room for sitting in every day. Otherwise there was only the dining room. That was as dark as the school cupboard. The window looked out onto the fence of next door. The table took nearly all the space and the thick, furry cloth smelled like a rainy day. The chairs were hard with no squashy bits to sit on.

Billy shivered. The bottoms of his shorts dripped onto the hall mat. He was so wet that he needed a towel.

'Ha-ha, wet dog, you are. Come on,' Kenneth led the way to the kitchen.

Billy put his coat on the boiler rail. The washing smells leaked from the scullery where he found a towel to dry his legs and hands. He used it until it was really damp all over, and he still felt wet.

Kenneth's head was bent over a picture of Blackpool Tower. 'We're doing a jigsaw, right?'

The oilcloth on the kitchen table was all one colour, like old blood. The jigsaw pieces slid around on it and wouldn't clip together easily but he sat down to help Kenneth.

'You do the sky and the pavement,' said Kenneth.

'I think j-jigsaws are really boring.'

'Boring like you. So there.'

'You're sickly.'

'I'm not. I'm frail.'

It felt like ages while they were doing the jigsaw. Kenneth was humming a song about a blackbird. It was annoying, but Kenneth's voice was rather nice. Billy did nine pieces of sky and he'd just seen a bit of tower when Kenneth slid the jigsaw to one side and put the lid on the box. 'We'll draw now.'

'I'm no good at it.'

'I know. You can just colour in.' He passed over a book. 'Don't go over the edge or I'll tell. You'll have to use the brown, I need all the others.' He worked away at a picture of a bird on its nest.

'Let's see.' It was ever so good.

The brown needed sharpening but Billy didn't bother. He coloured as slowly as he could. The rain had stopped. If only they could play outside.

He was really pleased to see Mother when she came in to make the tea. 'Can I t-take the football outside while Kenneth draws inside, please?'

'In the *road!* Certainly not.'

He made a pleading face towards her but she didn't notice.

'Aunty, he's coloured over the edges *on purpose.*' Kenneth looked at Mother with a sad face.

Under the table Billy's hands grasped the precious sabre. He closed his eyes and summoned up magic. Nothing came. He really needed to learn some special words.

'Billy! Can't you even play nicely when we visit?' He jerked forward as Mother buffed him on the back of the head five times. 'Naugh-ty litt-le boy.'

Kenneth turned his sad face down to his drawings, 'Oh dear.'

At that moment, the front door opened and Uncle Frank loomed into the dark corridor. The rain had started again. He peered into where Aunty sat. 'How are we, precious one?'

Aunty sighed and Mother stepped forward. 'We're here, keeping her company, Frank. I'm just in the kitchen with the boys, putting on the kettle.'

'That's good, Marcia. Just what Doreen needs. Good companionship. I'm sure Bert would have a saying for that.'

'Indeed he would,' said Mother, with almost a smile.

Uncle put his hat on a hall peg and his umbrella beside Mother's. He put his head back into the front room. 'You wouldn't want to be out in this today, my love.'

Aunty's weak voice came back. 'I don't suppose I shall *ever* feel like it.'

Mother clapped her hands. 'Nonsense, Doreen. You'll soon be on your feet. It's all over now.'

'Too right.' Aunty sniffed in the distance.

Mother stepped back into to the stove. 'Now, I'm making us all a warming cup of tea.' She put a hand on Kenneth's curls. 'After all, Frank, you've got this one. Much better to leave it at that, you know.'

'True,' said Uncle. 'No other kiddy could match Kenneth Wilson. No other boy can.'

Kenneth smiled up at him, and then over at Billy.

It was almost as if Uncle Frank had heard about Billy's colouring. He turned around fiercely and looked Billy up and down. He didn't seem to like what he saw. 'You, young man, need more training. I shall be coming round tomorrow to run you to the common.'

Mother's hand, which had been lifting the tea-pot, stopped mid-air. 'Oh would you, Frank? I shall have peace and quiet while you do. How wonderful.'

She finished pouring the stream of brown into the chunky cup with a monk's face on the handle. She passed it over the table with her little finger in the air. 'Here's your tea. I remembered your special cup.'

CHAPTER FIVE
29th September 1938

*Britain and France ratify proposals to keep
Hitler from war*

After P.T. they were all changing out of their plimsolls when teacher handed out an important note for each of them to take home. 'And don't lose it or forget it.'

Now he was very nearly six, Billy was big enough to go to and from school on his own. He skipped along until he reached his gate. He was like a postman. 'I've got a note, Mother.'

Mother was leaning back on the garden room settee with a damp handkerchief on her forehead. Dad was already home, very early, with a pile of documents in his briefcase. He read the school note and muttered to himself. 'The time has come.' Then he put Billy's cap on and said they had to get a gas mask.

'What's a gas mask?'

'You'll see.'

'As I did, Herbert,' said Mother. 'I went this morning, despite my condition. Most of the neighbours were there. It made me realize how imminent it all is. I feel quite sick. I don't know whether they disinfect the masks after fitting you. In the queue, I noticed a lot of Jews.'

Dad cleared his throat. He told her to sit quietly and keep calm. Then he prodded Billy forward, shut the front door and they walked down several streets to a brick building where Billy stood with other children and was fitted for his gas mask. It was a bit smelly in the room and it was nasty having something stuck over your mouth and nose, but you could still breathe. No-one made a fuss.

When he looked round, he wanted to laugh. The others' faces looked so queer squashed into the mask, their eyes all big and goggling against the see-through stuff. Afterwards, going home several children he knew grinned and waved, holding up their square boxes. They shouted to each other across the street.

'Got mine.'

'Got mine too. My sister's having a Mickey Mouse.'

'Mine'll never wear that. Bet they won't get her to.'

'She'll get gassed, then.'

Billy was going to ask Dad what 'gassed' meant.

'I'm very glad you're not shouting across the road, Billy,' said Dad.

So Billy didn't ask.

Later, they had gas mask practices at school. Jim said that you had to wear a gas mask if the air got bad, full of gas. Enemies could do it to you. Two children got very frightened and had to sit in another classroom. All the rest of them opened their boxes and pulled out the masks.

Teacher told them to spit on the glass thing so it wouldn't steam up, then fit the rubber bit round their head. It was quite exciting and there was lots of noise in the classroom and no work. Then it was playtime.

'What was it really like?' asked the frightened children who were still waiting to have the practice.

Billy told them, 'If you wear it too long, it gives you a headache. When you take it off you're ever so glad. You can feel how nice the air is.'

It was lots of fun in the playground, pretending to be gassed. Some of the girls played rescuers, running up and putting their hands over the boys' mouths saying they were putting their gas masks on. All the teachers had a day off the following week for something important. Billy had to go to Kenneth's while Mother went to a meeting at the town hall. Aunty said it wouldn't apply to her.

41

In the back yard, Kenneth did a display of the Swedish Drill they did at his school. There was a lot of marching and turning sharply, hands up, down, bending, stretching.

'And all of us do this in time, smartly,' said Kenneth. 'Don't you do drill?'

'Not that sort. We had gas mask drill.'

Kenneth's eyebrows twitched. 'Course. So did we.' He looked around.

Uncle Frank had just gone back to work after his dinner hour and Aunty was lying down. Kenneth beckoned Billy as he crept out of the door and up to the landing cupboard. He stood on a chair and reached down his box.

'Now', he said, 'we'll have a drill.'

He got out his mask and put it on Billy's face, then flicked the rubber strap very tightly around his head. Billy couldn't breathe and started kicking. Kenneth moved sideways and pressed down on the mask so that no sound came out when Billy tried to shout. Billy flailed his legs wildly. Just as he thought he'd suffocate, Kenneth slid the mask upwards.

'Drill's over. I've saved your life. You didn't breathe any gas, did you?'

Billy lay on the bed taking great breaths while Kenneth neatly packed his mask away. 'Wait there,' he said, and Billy heard him slipping the box back on the cupboard shelf.

When his heart stopped thumping, Billy said, 'That was d-dangerous. I'm going d-downstairs. I'm not playing up h-here with you any m-more.' He ran out of the bedroom door before Kenneth could stop him.

Aunty was just getting up. 'What are those marks on your face, Billy?'

For once Billy thought he'd tell her, but Kenneth said quickly, 'How's your headache, Mummy? Can I get you a tablet and a glass of water?'

'My own little man. So thoughtful. Yes, if you could, dear. Run and get them from the kitchen. Billy, I'm going to lean on your shoulder while we go downstairs, is that all right?'

There were some semaphore cards on the sideboard. Billy picked them up quickly and asked to play with them so that he didn't get sent upstairs again. 'We can keep you company down here, Aunty.'

Kenneth glared, but he couldn't do anything about it with his hands around the glass of water.

Billy watched Dad cutting round some of the printed columns in several newspapers, and sticking them in an exercise book. 'This will be history.'

'What will, Dad?'

He puffed at his pipe and didn't answer. He bent to turn on the wireless and spent ages tuning it.

The wireless had curly shapes cut out of its front as well as a big square, and there was shiny, bobbly material behind. When Billy touched it, it sometimes shivered, and the music or voice or hissing came out from either side of his fingers. He couldn't stop the sounds. Only the knob could do that but he wasn't allowed to touch any knobs in case the tuning went. Sometimes, it took Dad ages to get the voice back again.

'It's still whistling.'

'Shh.'

'Is it Children's Hour soon?'

'Shh. You've missed that. Tell your mother it's time, and then stay quiet.'

Mother came into the room before he could call her. She sat on the arm of the leathery chair that was usually Dad's and he arched his hand wide on her leg.

The doom voice came on, 'Radio 2LO. London calling.' That voice always made Billy feel a bit afraid. It said something about Munich again. He shut the door and hid behind the settee to read his comic.

Something was happening, but they hadn't said what. It didn't feel good. He got to the last page of Tiger Tim before he heard a loud 'Thank the Lord!' from Mother. Then she went to the telephone.

He heard her dialling but then she seemed mostly to be listening. When she put the telephone down he sidled through the door as she said, 'Herbert, Father thinks it's a let-down and it will only delay matters.'

'And I say Chamberlain's right and we should be grateful for one peaceful politician in Europe.'

'Well I'm sure I don't know. I'm just so glad it's not war here.'

At bath-time, Mother was smiley and humming to herself so he asked her what a let-down was.

'Little jugs have big ears,' she said.

He stared at her. They didn't have any ears at all. 'I know it's not war *here*,' he tried.

'Well, it's good news.' Then she explained that the government thought Britain had to go to war to save another country. That's why everyone needed gas-masks, but now there wasn't going to be a war in Britain after all.

Mr Chamberlain had saved Britain from that. She was very, very glad because she didn't want to bring a child into a world of war.

'No.' He nodded. It was very good that she wasn't going to bring him into a world of war and gas masks. But it was rather sad for the country that wouldn't be saved.

CHAPTER SIX

November 21st 1938

Nazi forces occupy western Czechoslovakia and declare them German citizens

Kenneth didn't get taken to the zoo for his birthday like Billy. He went to his Nanny and Grandad's and had his cake and presents there. The birthday was all over when Billy was taken to say 'Happy Birthday' and hand over the present.

'You'd have thought Doreen would have brought Billy back a balloon or a piece of cake, even if Kenneth didn't think of it,' Mother said to Dad when they got home from Uncle Frank's. Billy went upstairs, but only as far as the landing. He hadn't thought about Kenneth bringing anything back until then. But he did now. He lay on the landing and waited for Dad to say what was right.

'Billy has a lot of everything. He doesn't need a share of Kenneth's few treats. Frank and Doreen struggle to do their best for their boy. I shouldn't think bringing cake for Billy crossed their minds.'

'No, indeed,' said Mother.

Billy lay still.

'Now, Marcia. We're not church-goers but I'll remind you of a certain catechism: *'Not to covet nor desire other men's goods, etcetera, etcetera.'*

Mother slammed the parlour door then, so Billy didn't hear if she said anything back, but he did like the sound of 'Etcetera'. Perhaps it was one of Kenneth's goods— a board game. He could play Etcetera with him. He stopped lying at the top of the stairs, his favourite place, and wandered into his bedroom. Suddenly he wanted a piece of cake. But not Kenneth's.

Mr Durban had said that Hitler wasn't satisfied with the whole cake, but wanted a piece of everyone else's. No-one wanted to be like Hitler.

That 'being glad' Mother had talked about didn't last. Dad brought Mr Durban round for supper after work and they didn't look glad at all. Billy had to have his supper in the kitchen, not with the grown-ups.

'We need to talk in peace,' Dad said.

Billy pushed the kitchen door open once they were all in the dining room. He could hear a bit of the talk, and it wasn't about peace at all.

Jim rang the doorbell just then, asking if Billy could come round to play, and the grown-ups seemed very happy for him to go. They ran down the road, but didn't go to Jim's house.

'Guess what, Billy? There's men digging shelters right near the common. Come on. Reg is waiting for us.'

They ran on hard until they saw Reg jumping up and down and waving. There was a large, dark oblong hole nearby, men with large spades hard at work. It was very exciting watching the hole get deeper and longer. They stood at the side of the common as the entrance was bricked round and a doorway fitted. It was just like a secret passage.

Billy imagined its dreadful darkness. 'I can't wait till we're allowed to sit inside.'

Reg put his hands on his hips. 'It'll be scary.'

'We'll have to take torches.'

'And biscuits,' said Jim.

'Have you got blackout at home? We won't need it down that shelter, it's all black as black.'

Reg was bending so close to peer inside that they were all shooed off by the diggers. They ran off like aeroplanes, whizzing all the way home.

Next day, Mrs.Donnington made extra curtains with black material. Black curtains! They were to use as well as the ones they already had. Dad said they must close the blackouts carefully before ever putting a light on.

He stuck brown paper criss-cross over all the windows. It looked awful, like fearful kisses, but everyone else's windows had them too.

Mr Durban came round to talk about Safety at Home. He had a helmet, which looked funny with his suit. He did read Rupert the Bear Annual with Billy for a short while, but he soon wanted to talk about shelters and fire watch. Billy watched him hard the whole time.

'Good lad, you're listening well.'

Billy's face went hot because really he'd been trying to imagine Mr Durban as a young man, holding that sabre and fighting off Hitler and the enemy, not the today Mr Durban talking about keeping things safe at home. He so wanted to ask what a Cossack was, but that would have given the secret away, and Mr Durban had just been saying about Keeping Mum.

Dad took Mr Durban into the garden room, Billy and Mother followed. Both the men bent over to help Mother onto the reclining chair and she sank in with a sigh.

Then the grown-ups started talking about Billy having a brother or sister. He didn't listen to that much because everyone knew Mother wouldn't want two children.

'Just at the worst time!' she said. He'd heard her say ages ago that one was too much. 'And I feel so tired.'

'You should get away for a while, Marcia. Have some country air. Could you manage, Herbert, without her?'

Dad stroked his chin. 'There's our home help, Mrs Donnington. She could manage some extra hours, I'm sure.' He turned to Billy. 'You like her, don't you?'

Billy nodded. He remembered the time when Mother and Dad were so angry with each other that he'd been sent to the kitchen to sit with Mrs Donnington while they rowed. She was blacking the stove. She'd let him polish the little brass fire tools on their stand, each with a ship on the top of the handle. Behind him, the shouty voices spattered like coal dust from the hall into the parlour. He could tell that Mrs Donnington could hear it too because she stopped brushing away at the stove.

He said, 'They're really, really cross, aren't they?'

She shook her head until her hairpins fell out onto the hearth and put a black finger to her mouth. 'Shhh.' She gave him a barley sugar from the jar on the high shelf.

It was all right to eat it because it was wrapped. It was really sticky but he didn't lick the paper after he'd put it into his mouth because of the black on it. He took a long time sucking it and by then, the quarrelling had stopped.

Yes, it would be nice to be left with Mrs Donnington for a few days.

Dad shook his shoulder. 'Are you listening, Billy?'

He nodded, but he hadn't been.

'Billy?' Mother said. 'So, you don't mind if I have a little holiday, dear?'

Mr Durban bent down to him. 'I think your mother would benefit from some extra rest, young man. Perhaps you'll come and visit us a couple of times while she's away. Angela will like that.'

Billy could feel his mouth stretching into a grin. That would be super-duper, but should he say that in front of Mother? 'I'm glad you're going to have some rest, Mother,' felt much safer.

After Mother had packed and gone away, Billy waited for his visits. Annoyingly, it was Kenneth's that Dad took him round to first.

'Why, Dad?'

'Kenneth needs some company.'

'I need to see the shashka,' Billy muttered to himself as they marched through the smog. If they hadn't known the way, they'd have got lost as only the gates showed, the houses distant or disappeared, hiding behind the grey misty stuff.

'Have fun, you boys,' Dad said as he left Billy inside Kenneth's house.

'Of course, Uncle,' Kenneth smiled, smoothing down his latest knitted jumper, the colour of sick.

Dad waved and left for his club, becoming more and more mysterious as his shape became swallowed by smog.

Billy put one foot in front of the other to see how long he could be getting into the living room.

'Hello ducky. Kenneth's been longing for you to come.' Aunty was knitting as usual.

Kenneth would be mean as usual. The smile came. 'We two'll go to the kitchen to use the table, Mummy.' He pushed Billy into the passage.

Billy looked hopefully at the welsh dresser for signs of Kenneth's birthday presents. 'Have you g-got a new game, Etcetera?'

Kenneth laughed in a silly, high voice as if he was being tickled.

Billy put his hands on his hips. 'Well? H-have you?'

'No, stupid. "Etcetera" means "and so on." How could I have a game called that?' He went on giggling until Billy felt like kicking him.

Luckily, Dad had brought Billy's dominoes and Ludo over with them. Billy plonked them down on the table, hard.

'Oh, L-L-Ludo! I'll be r-r-red.' Kenneth set them out on the table.

Aunty brought her knitting in and sat by the boiler. 'Don't make fun of Billy's stutter, dear. We can't all have beautiful voices like you.'

Kenneth sighed sadly, his head on one side and his hands twiddling the red counters.

It would be so nice to stick out his tongue at Kenneth and as far as it could possibly go, but Kenneth would only get him into trouble. Billy took the green counters and willed them to win.

They played two games, and he did win both. Kenneth said 'Ludo's a game of chance. Anyway, I wasn't trying.'

Billy put the pieces back in the box slowly. 'Why weren't you?'

'Perhaps I had my mind on something else.' He nudged Billy and pointed at Aunty Doreen's knitting.

Billy stared at it. It looked all right, no stitches fallen off the needles. It was white, not grey or ditch green, that's all he could see. Kenneth stretched his eyes wide at Billy as if to say *you're stupid,* and pulled him out and up the stairs.

Billy stared at Kenneth's goggling eyes, 'So?' What was it to do with, his stutter or the Ludo? White knitting, so was it something rude, like a vest?

'What, Kenneth? What?'

'Not telling,' said Kenneth. He was giggling and jumping from one foot to another, up a stair, down a stair. It looked really silly.

'Tell me. I don't know.'

'Shan't. If you don't know, Billy, you're loony. And when she comes back home to you, Aunty Marcia is going to be FAT.'

Mother wasn't at all fat. Kenneth was really rude and if Mother could hear him, she wouldn't like him any more.

Mr Durban didn't even ask Mrs Donnington if he'd been good when he came to collect him. At his house, Mrs Durban met them with a smile. 'Come along in, Billy. I've made those cakes you like so much.' She had a smashing tea all ready.

Afterwards. Angela was allowed to 'sit' for him while Mr and Mrs Durban went to the Town Hall to discuss the new National Service Handbook. They put on their coats and told Angela they trusted her to look after Billy well.

He watched them disappear up the road together. 'What is that Handbook, Angela?'

'It's to tell people if they're qualified to be soldiers or sailors, sort of thing.'

'My Uncle Ted is. He's got a uniform and black soldier boots and I've seen him practising his marching.

She didn't answer. He waited for her to choose something to do. She knew better than to get out her dolls but she did get him to play a board game with countries on it for a while. Billy couldn't really answer the questions, so they didn't get far. He looked longingly at Mr Durban's study door.

'All right. Come on. You can look at the sabre. We'll play knights and princesses.'

Angela put the sabre on the desk, then pretended to be frightened, and to need rescuing.

It was ever such fun. Billy stood on Mr Durban's desk chair to be a knight, holding a cushion in front as a shield, fighting off enemy.

'It'd be more fun holding the sabre,' he said.

Angela bit her lip but held the sabre out. 'Just be very careful, mind.'

She wouldn't let him take it out of the scabbard, but she let him wave it and shout fierce words like 'Ahoy!' and 'Zounds!'

There was no-one to hear, so they practised shouting like people at war and then laughed as loudly as they could. It felt really dangerous.

Angela got worried. 'We'd better put the sabre away now.'

They went back into the lounge to bounce on the sofa.

'Do you mind your mother being away?' Angela asked.

'Not really. I like coming here. I'd like to come every *day.*'

Angela was going to be a real princess one day, and he'd be a real knight and protect her with the sabre.

If only he could have it for himself, just once. After all, there might be a war and he might be a hero by then.

CHAPTER SEVEN
January 14th 1939

Hitler and Mussolini hand in hand.
Dictators map out New Europe

It was a shame Christmas holidays were all over because there was snow, and Billy had seen people tobogganing on the common when his cub pack had been taken there for games. Tobogganing was the sort of thing Uncle Ted would do, but not Dad or Mother.

She'd had her little holiday, that was quite long, and come back in time to decorate the tree that he and Dad had dragged all the way back from the market. She was more smiley and she'd got so much weller she really *was* quite fat now, which she'd never been before. Kenneth was right. He always was. That was very annoying.

When Mother opened the front door and found Billy waiting by the Christmas tree, she threw up her hands and said, 'A tree. Marvellous.' Then, 'Were you a good boy, Billy? No trouble at Kenneth's?'

He shook his head. He hadn't got into any trouble at all, anywhere. Mother should be pleased with him. He said, 'Mrs Donnington came in almost every day to get the house ready.'

He thought of that now. She'd cleaned it out as though it was Spring, and he'd told her, 'You won't have to do it when it is Spring now, Mrs Donnington. We shall have a very clean Christmas instead.'

She laughed her hair untidy. It was because laughing made her shake her head. He bent down to pick up her hairpins and she patted his bottom. 'You're a one, you are, Billy boy. You're quite cheeky with your mother away.'

It was true he could do forbidden things like slide down the banisters and wave to the children opposite from the front gate. Mrs Donnington didn't tell him off at all.

'If you were my child, you could go right over and play with them, but I know my place and it's not allowed.'

Billy screwed his eyes up at her, trying to imagine what it would be like to be her child. She had to clean other people's houses so she must be poor, and poor people didn't have books and wirelesses and new clothes and chocolate biscuits.

There was one thing she wouldn't let him do, and that was to follow her into the end bedroom.

'Now, now. I've got my work to do and soon there'll be a little person in there. You've got your very own room, lucky boy. Lots of children have to share. So in you go and play for a bit and I'll tell you when I'm done.'

Dad had talked about a little person too. Billy smiled at this fairy story thing they said, like Father Christmas. Perhaps there was going to be gnome leaving a present under the tree instead of a Santa. Probably all the presents were hidden in that bedroom. He wouldn't go in there and spoil the surprise.

Altogether, he hadn't been too sad while Mother was away. Mrs Donnington's dinners were quite tasty. He got taken to Nanny and Grandad's twice, Mr Durban came for him three super times and he'd only had to go to Kenneth's that once. Dad said he was sick of seeing Billy's long face every time Uncle Frank or Kenneth was mentioned.

And now Mother was home and she *was* fat, at least round her middle. She also started talking about the little person 'in there' patting her tummy, which always made him giggle. The idea of Mother swallowing a little person like the old lady with the fly was ever so funny.

February was very cold. Mother said she couldn't possibly risk going out. There was quite a bit of snow. He wore his wellies every day and played snowballs every playtime. Mrs Donnington brought in the shopping and the greengrocer delivered.

One afternoon, Billy came home from school and a nurse lady in a hard white apron opened the door. Before he had time to feel hospital-frightened, she said, 'Be very quiet, there's a good boy. You've got a baby sister upstairs but your mother needs to rest in bed.' She hurried back upstairs as soon as he was in the door.

Billy stayed in the hall, trying to think what to do. Mother hadn't told him that she would be in bed when he got home, or that there would be a baby. She said she couldn't go out, so it must have been brought to her with the shopping.

He hadn't believed the talk about a brother or sister, or about a little person, but it wasn't a fairy story, it had been true! Mother must be very fed up that a baby had come and she would have to look after it. He'd better keep out of the way in case she wasn't smiley any more.

He sat down hard on the stairs. This was a shock. He was going to use the phone and tell Aunty. First, though, he wanted to know what the lady and Mother were saying. He peered upwards to her bedroom but couldn't hear much, just footsteps and water running, and a bit of puffing and blowing. It was difficult to work out what was going on.

There was no answer when he telephoned Aunty, putting his finger in the right hole for each number and pulling it round as far as it would go. Number nine needed a pull almost a whole circle round. He was fairly sure he'd remembered her number right.

Perhaps she already knew about this baby. He certainly didn't want Kenneth telling him. *He* wanted to be the one who told the news, and to make Kenneth be the surprised one.

He would try again later. Meanwhile, he went in the kitchen and learned his spellings. He wrote them out so the grown-ups would know how good he'd been. Even when he'd finished them all, still no-one came, so he took a custard tart and a fairy cake from the larder without asking.

Dad arrived home before he got to telephone Aunty again. Billy ran to the door. 'Mother's in bed, Dad. A nurse has come to look after her baby, a girl one. Now Mother'll have to look after two children, after all.'

'A baby girl!' Dad was grinning. It made his face look very different, lumps on his cheeks and dimples showing through his beard. 'I must go up and see her for myself. Stay there, be good.' He didn't say anything about not touching the cakes. Perhaps it didn't matter today, so Billy took another. He was going to tell Mrs Donnington they were lovely, because she was the one who'd been cooking lately.

After Dad had been upstairs a long time, he brought down a white bundle to show Billy. He pulled back an edge of lacy shawl and there was a tiny face and weeny hand, very pink and squashy-looking. Billy looked hard in case it was some kind of doll, but then it turned up its nose and moved its fingers. It was the first baby Billy had seen up close. It was a funny feeling, not all that nice. 'It doesn't l- look as if it will be an-nother child.'

'You'll never have seen one this new,' said Dad.

'No. It's very s-small.' He nearly said 'smell' by mistake. It did have a funny smell, one he hadn't smelled before. He stood back and away.

Dad was still looking at the bundle. 'They soon grow.'

The baby mewed loudly and Dad hurried it back upstairs. He hadn't said what Billy should be doing, but it probably wasn't telephoning Aunty, so he went into the garden room and looked at books. He practised his reading. They'd be pleased when he showed them later. But no-one came for ages.

At last he heard Dad making a pot of tea, then calling out that there were sandwiches and milk on the table.

Much later, he came down to tell Billy to get himself ready for bed and to do it very quietly.

It was all very strange and he felt somehow different. Things that people said wouldn't happen, did happen. Even when they didn't want them to happen, they happened. Would war? Everyone said they didn't want war to happen. For once there was no wireless on, no news to make Dad sigh. There was the newspaper Dad had left on the hallstand. He peeped at it, folded back to its third page. There was something about children. Jews coming on ships and an ever such long word beginning with 'kinder...'

'Are you getting ready for bed, Billy?' Dad called out.

Billy slipped upstairs quickly and quietly so that he could call from his bedroom, 'Yes, Dad.' He washed and slid into a freezing bed. He went right down deep below the blankets to get warm. It would be nice to have a soft one tucked round him, all cosily, like Baby's.

There was mewing from Mother's room, and his feet were very cold, so he took ages to get to sleep.

The next day was Saturday but Aunty Doreen came alone. No Kenneth.

'Dear little baby sister for you, Billy. Lucky boy,' and she crept upstairs where Billy heard her whispering and cooing. When she came down, Billy asked, 'W-will Mother ever be able to get up again?'

Aunty Doreen put an arm round him and said Mother would start getting up next week, but Billy could go upstairs to see her now if he wanted. He thought about it, but decided not to. He hadn't seen her in bed before and it didn't seem quite right.

It was a funny week with Dad putting out Sunny Jim cornflakes for him in the morning before he went to work and then Billy getting himself off to school. Mrs Donnington couldn't get in for long now that her husband was working nights. She came to do the cleaning and shopping, but she was gone by the time Billy got home. He felt like a man, going to work and coming back with no-one in charge of him. He wore the same socks all week and Dad didn't notice.

When Mother did get up again, she didn't seem quite the same person or perhaps Billy had forgotten her, or perhaps he hadn't looked hard at her before. Now, he noticed her dark hair hanging messily and her pink feet with lines like rivers and valleys. Her body wasn't so so fat, but thick and padded out, and she was more often in her dressing gown than in a dress.

'You'll have to be a quiet boy, now that we have a baby girl.'

'I'll be very quiet if I'm on my own, Mother.'

One lucky thing was that the girl baby took all Mother's time, so she didn't want Kenneth over. She didn't want any noise when Baby was sleeping, either, which was most of the time.

Dad took Billy over to see Uncle Frank (really, to see Kenneth, but when they got upstairs they both put their fingers in their ears and didn't talk to each other).

Afterwards, Dad took him shopping. He'd never done that before, but Mrs Donnington had given him a list. They bought tinned peaches from the grocer and gripe water for the baby from the chemist and tobacco from a musty little shop he'd hardly noticed before, a man's shop, with pipes in the window and wooden tubs with different tobaccos in them. Each had its own smell, rich and fruity, dank and dusky. Dad knew exactly which one he wanted but there was a queue to be served. He lit his pipe while he waited. Everyone in the queue was smoking, with little trails of smoke coming up from each mouth, and a big one floating out of the shop.

It would be nice to be a smoker like Dad. Billy was crouching over one tub, sniffing deeply when a man came up behind him and said, 'My word, is that tobacco-fancier Mr Billy Wilson?'

Billy nodded, grinning to see Mr Durban. 'Got a voice?'

'Yes, sir. Dad's got a b-baby now.'

'Has he indeed!' Mr Durban leaned over, all the folds in his face falling forward. 'And is that a boy baby?'

'N-no, sir, a girl one.'

'Nice for you to have a sister.'

Billy didn't know what to say. The baby was just a mewing thing in a bassinet.

'Well, now, you'll have to occupy yourself while your mother is busy with her. So you can keep yourself amused with these.' He passed over a bunch of little furry sticks that you could bend in all directions, pink, green, red, blue and brown.

'Thank you very m-much, Mr Durban.'

'Just a little something for a fine lad.' He clapped his hand on Dad's shoulder, who'd just been served. 'What a lucky chap you are, Herbert, a new little girl and this extra special son.'

Dad looked at Billy, his eyebrows like up-and-down arrows, and put his new tobacco inside his pouch. He started talking about ministers and policies, so Billy turned back to the barrels, rescuing one or two fronds of tobacco that were lying on the edges. He wanted to eat them, but probably it wasn't allowed.

When Mr Durban had finished chatting and gone on his way, Billy showed Dad the fuzzy things Mr Durban had given him. Dad said they were pipe cleaners and demonstrated how you could twist them together to make little men, bend their legs and arms and even make feet and hands. Billy put them in his pocket and kept his hand on them, all small and furry and ready to play with.

It was funny, really. Mr Durban had given him these soft little sticks, when what he really wanted was the hard as hard big one that was the shashka.

CHAPTER EIGHT
15th March 1939

Promises broken.
Hitler seizes the rest of Czechoslovakia

Most of the baby things happened in Mother's bedroom, so Billy didn't see much of Baby. Aunty Doreen looked after her sometimes when Mother had to go out. Billy liked that because then Kenneth stayed behind with Uncle, and Aunty was quite chatty when Mother wasn't around.

She'd just arrived, and was taking off her squashy hat. 'Do you like babies, Aunty? I don't think I do.' He swung to and fro on the hall chair, his legs going high in the air. He quickly stopped as Mother came downstairs, smartly dressed. Her hair was smooth and flicked over her shoulders. Her jacket was made of the same stuff as her skirt and her heels went clip-clop on the lino.

She said, 'Baby's just been fed and changed, Doreen. Sleeping peacefully. You shouldn't have to do a thing.' She looked at Billy sternly. 'Be a good boy for Aunty Doreen, I'm going out.'

'He's actually a very good boy for me, Marcia.'

'Boys!' Mother said.

He stepped behind Aunty, looking at the floor. He knew he was a nuisance. He'd been kicking the ball against the shed door, keeping out of the way. Mother had just told him that her body had felt every thwack of the ball when she was trying to rest. The whisk of her skirt now, as she went through the front door, showed how glad she was to be getting out and away from noisy boys. As the door shut, a blast of fresh air shot into the hall. Billy spun around, pretending to be a top.

Aunty beckoned him into the kitchen. She made herself a cup of tea and poured Billy some milk. She brought some biscuits out of her bag. They had jam in the middle. And she gave him three.

Then they went in the garden room and sat together on the settee. Aunty's face looked pink and powdery and kind. She asked him what games he liked to play when he was with other children. He knew she meant when he was with Kenneth, but he told her about playing horses in the playground at school. It wasn't Aunty's fault she had such a mean boy.

When Baby started crying. Aunty went upstairs and brought her down, walking up and down, patting her back. It seemed a funny thing to do, but Baby stopped crying and Aunty sat down again, the baby beside her on the settee.

He moved away from it. 'I d-didn't know I was going to have a girl baby in my house.'

'You're a very lucky boy, dear. Kenneth can't have a baby sister.'

He tried to imagine Kenneth leaning over a cot, looking pleased.

Aunty was rocking the baby in her arms, staring into its face. He thought there were tears in her eyes. He stayed very quiet, twisting his pipe cleaners. He made a tank instead of a person.

Aunty said, 'Babies need a lot of looking after.'

'How d-do you know what to d-do?' Supposing Mother went out and left him in charge!

'You have to know all their different cries. One is hunger, one's when they're uncomfortable and need their nappy changing, and this one, well, she just wants some company and comfort. She needs to be held and to know someone loves her.'

The baby just looked like a baby. How could she know what she wanted and things like love? 'Oh,' he said.

Aunty drew out a pack of cards from her bag and they played *Beggar My Neighbour* for ages. He might be lucky to have a baby sister, but Kenneth was lucky to have a grown- up to play cards with.

When the baby started its cry again, she put it on his lap while he sat far back on the settee. It was a funny, nice but dangerous feeling he'd never had before, especially when Aunty put his hands either side of the soft, woolly shape. It was smaller than his Donald Duck ball. The baby moaned a bit and he tried patting like Aunty had done and the moaning stopped.

'I s-stopped her from crying!' he said.

'That's it. You did. You're going to be a fine, loving brother and—'Aunty broke off suddenly and whipped the baby up smartly. Mother's footsteps were at the door.

Aunty jerked her head towards the garden, widening her eyes at Billy, so he scuttled outside.

Dad helped Mother with the breakfast, which was funny. Mrs Donnington was away, seeing her son off to the army.

'Will Colin Donnington be a soldier like Uncle Ted?'

Mother swept her head from one side to the other although there were no flies around. 'Just hurry off, Billy. Come on. Off to school.' She didn't look pleased.

Outside other people had long faces too, although a cheery new poster was up by the greengrocer's. Instead of *California Syrup of Figs*, this one said *AD 1939 will be brighter thanks to Sunlight Soap, Now only 4d.*' So everyone should've been smiling.

At school, Mr Finlay said there was going to be another drill today, not just for gas masks but for air raids too. That would be fun. Everyone nudged each other and got into trouble for whispering.

The class hadn't done more than copy the date off the board, before a horrible noise sounded all around. It was scary and some people screamed.

Mr Finlay and the biggest boys walked up and down the corridors saying 'It's only a practice, don't panic.'

They had to line up quickly with no talking, then go to an underground place with long, fat pipes. They were squashed up close together and it was damp and dark. They had to stay there until another squealy sound came, then line up and be counted before marching back into school. Everyone missed mental arithmetic and the twins sniggered because they hadn't done their homework anyway.

Miss Spender, a thin teacher with a grey straggly bun and brown lace-up shoes with double bows, took everyone in the hall. She could play the piano. She practised *There'll always be an England* with all of the infants and a row of the oldest juniors to lead them. It was difficult learning the words and some of Billy's class couldn't get the tune. The littlest children were too fidgety, and in the end Miss Spender said they could play quietly in their classroom with the door open so that they could listen. She said everyone must sing to show what a wonderful country they had; a wonderful country to be saved *from* War and *by* War.

Sonia, the cleverstick, whispered that you couldn't be saved by both.

The juniors told the infants what War meant: guns and fighting.

They played at War all the time in the playground and after school dinner they played again, the sound of the air raid warning still in their ears. If no-one liked a boy, he had to be the enemy and crouch behind the lavs and run away with everyone after them.

A few boys who were very new and couldn't speak properly because they were foreign, were just right to use as enemy. When they ran away, they really looked frightened. That was especially good. Billy, Jim, Reg and Andrew ran screaming after them, waving their arms, pretending they were holding rifles. Mr Hendrick, the top class teacher, was on duty. He came over and stopped them.

'But why, Sir? It was super fun,' Jim said. He was always the one who spoke first.

'Fun for you. Look at these boys you're using as enemies. It's very frightening for them.' He lifted a finger so that all of them looked up at him. 'Perhaps you need to know something.' He put his arms on the shoulders of two of the enemy boys. 'These lads had to run away from the German guns that were threatening their whole village. The Germans killed lots of their people and took their lands and homes.'

Several children gasped.

'That was wicked, sir. I don't like the Germans,' Andrew spoke up. Billy nudged Jim. Andrew liked things to be right.

'We hate Germans,' everyone chanted.

'Yes, Jones. Czechoslovakians have come to England to be safe. You must be kind to them.'

Czechoslovakians! They all tried, but no-one could say 'Czechoslovakian'. Billy laughed so hard, he had to double over and lean on people. Now everyone was a stutterer.

After Mr Hendrick had gone to the shelter where the monitor had put his cup of tea, the boys crowded round the foreigners. It was very exciting.

'Did you really have to run in front of the guns?' Reg began. Two of the enemy boys nodded, the others didn't speak enough English yet. The bell went before they could be asked any more, but now Billy understood that the foreign boys were heroes and knew all about war.

At home time, Aunty Doreen collected him, bringing Kenneth. 'We thought we'd pick you up on the way, Billy. I want to see your Mummy about something.'

Billy walked behind in step with Kenneth. For once he had something to tell that Kenneth didn't know already.

It was jolly annoying that Kenneth could say 'Czechoslovakia' the very first time he tried, but Billy could tell that he hadn't heard about the land stolen from them. Kenneth didn't have any foreigners in his school. Billy told him about the boys running from the guns.

Kenneth listened and was quiet for a bit. Then he said 'Now if there's war, Billy, there'll be fighting all the time, everywhere. All the fathers will be soldiers and you'll have to fight the enemy in your house because Uncle Bert will be away at Assizes.'

Billy hopped forward to ask Aunty. Kenneth pulled him back. 'Stop! We don't frighten the women, stupid.'

When they got home, the two mothers went into the parlour to talk, but Aunty didn't stay very long. Kenneth had only had time to line up all the planes before he was called down to go.

'Think about it, Marcia', she said as the door closed behind them.

It was a cold day and Mother had lit the parlour fire. Billy hunched by it imagining all of Wandsworth running away from enemy guns. Where would they hide? They'd have to run all the way to Grandad's Anderson shelter or to the one on the common, which might be crowded.

He knew he shouldn't tell Mother but he needed to know what was happening, and he'd be in bed by the time Dad got home. When she came into the parlour, Billy just said quietly, 'There might be war and guns in England.'

She passed him the tongs. 'Put another couple of coals on the fire. Let's warm ourselves up. I don't want you to worry, Billy— the war's likely to stay overseas. Even if things happen in England, the government plan to look after all the children, mothers and babies, so that none of us will be near any fighting.'

He nodded. Governments were big, important people who could do all sorts of things. It was good they were going to look after mothers and children and make sure no fighting came near them. But governments didn't care so much about men. They made them turn into soldiers.

'What about Dad? Will they send him to be a soldier after all?'

'No. Your father's work is important. And he'll be out of London mostly. That's why we're not bothering with an Anderson. If the war comes, we just won't be here.'

She took up a book with trees on its cover. *How Green is my Valley*. She was smiling as she read.

The fire was fading. Mother took up the poker and dug it hard into the back coals. Flames licked up, orange and scarlet. Billy leant forward.

Mother said, 'Sit back. That's dangerous.'

CHAPTER NINE

May 22nd 1939

Italy and Germany sign friendship pact

The telephone rang and it was Billy who lifted the receiver. 'Southview 1281?'

'That must be Billy. How's that baby of yours?'

'Hallo, Grandad. Baby's got bigger and bigger. She fills up her cradle from top to bottom.'

'Does she now?'

'Yes, she spends much more time downstairs nowadays and her crying's got louder.'

'Well, I'm sure. Now I need to talk to your mother and father, so put me on, there's a good lad.'

He left the receiver on the telephone table for Dad and galloped to the kitchen to finish his milk and biscuits.

After a bit, he heard the receiver ting as it went on its rest, and Dad's voice talking to Mother, ' — bad as each other. Grim news for us.'

He went into the hall to rock the pram. That usually stopped the crying. Mother seemed a bit grumpy. Billy hadn't done anything wrong so perhaps it was because Baby kept yelling. It was called *Teething*. He put a finger on Baby's cheek where a red spot showed.

'Leave her, Billy. Just take yourself off somewhere, will you.'

Dad put a hand on top of hers, 'Come along, Billy. Put on your blazer. You and I will take a walk.' That was nice, and it didn't often happen.

He walked along with a lilting walk to keep up with Dad's long strides. He practised whistling and nearly had the hang of it when Dad said to stop because it was common.

That was funny, because just then they stopped at the common. He couldn't remember Dad ever taking him there before. He was hot in his blazer. Would Dad buy him a bottle of pop? He didn't like to ask.

Overhead, a plane droned. Billy squinted upwards to see the propeller with two blades and the stumpy body sitting on its wings, the sun glinting on them.

'Cor, Dad. A smashing plane.'

Dad said, 'Not a nice sight really. Those wings have four Browning machine guns in them.'

Billy peered again to see if guns were pointing down at them, but it flew too fast.

The slides and roundabout were filled with children enjoying the sunny weather. It would be nice to have a turn, but he wasn't sure if he was allowed.

The park-keeper was doing his rounds in his brown uniform.

Dad said, 'He won't be doing that much longer.' Another low-flying plane nearly drowned his words. While Dad stopped at a news-stand to read and tut, Billy looked over at some boys kicking a ball. There were a few fathers too, joining in with their sons.

'Dad?'

'Mm.' He turned a page.

'Dad, did you play football when you were young?'

'I left that to my brother. He was the sporty one. Muscly, strong, full of energy, like you.' He turned back to his paper. 'Off you run and have a turn on the roundabout.'

Billy ran off and whizzed round fast leaving the thought of Uncle's muscles behind with Dad, who sat smoking his pipe and reading. Soon, Dad would be working away somewhere, taking his pipe with him as well as his wig in its special box. Mother wouldn't have his help. The baby would trouble her and

Uncle Frank might come to do more toughening up. That would be rotten.

On the way home they passed Wandsworth prison. It looked wide, grand and frightening with brick walls all around it. The men in there must be very toughened up.

'D-do you have to be very, very bad to be in there, Dad?'

'Mostly. But not all. Men who won't fight in the war may end up there.'

'You d-don't want to fight. Will you have to g-go to prison?'

'No, no. I will probably be needed here in the job I do.

But I'm afraid there'll be a lot of people who will have to fight although they don't want to, because prison seems worse.'

Billy shuddered as they walked right close to it. 'Prison is the worsest, isn't it?'

'*Worst*. No. War's the worst. Best avoided. Small chance,' he took a big puff of his pipe. The smoke rose dangerously near to the barred windows of the prison.

There were so many, and such long walls. There was room for hundreds and hundreds of men. A whole army could get in there. But inside they would be safe, and soldiers wouldn't be, because Hitler would be waiting for them.

'Come along, stop staring. We must get home to your baby sister.'

Perhaps Mother would be in a better mood by the time they got through the front door.

Billy had just hung his blazer up and had a long drink when he heard Uncle arrive with Kenneth.

Probably the whole street heard his bellow, 'Ah, Marcia, I've brought Kenneth to keep that son of yours out of trouble for five minutes. We thought we'd see how things are going on with the nipper.'

The front door closed behind them and soon enough, Billy was called into the hall. 'Play upstairs, boys.'

For once, Uncle didn't start on Billy's exercises or make him say sentences without stuttering, but took Baby from Mother and lifted her high into the air. 'Look at this little darling,' he said, and tickled her under her chin.

Billy and Kenneth stood side by side watching as he made a great fuss of her. Had Uncle magicked into another man? Mother was smiling and nodding.

Kenneth yanked at Billy's arm and pulled him upstairs.

Billy opened his bedroom door. 'What do you want to play, then?'

Kenneth didn't answer but climbed onto Billy's chair. He flipped the aeroplane hanging from the ceiling, to and fro, to and fro. 'I'm glad *we* haven't got a smelly baby.'

'She's not smelly. They have to have nappies when they're little.'

'Ugh. And they cry. And when she gets bigger she'll be a girl. Mummy and Daddy were saying that will make Aunty Marcia happy because she didn't want a boy.'

Billy felt his eyes fill, so he quickly picked up the King Arthur book that was open on his bed. He held the picture away from Kenneth and just stared at the sword in the stone until he almost felt his hand on the hilt.

In real life it wouldn't be King Arthur's sword in his hand, it would be the sabre and he, Billy the Cossack, would be the brave-as-brave warrior who no-one dared challenge.

CHAPTER TEN
August 25th 1939

*Can Hitler's demands be met? His "horror" at idea
of Germany and Britain at war*

Billy spread himself out on the carpet by the open
French windows with his book. It was so hot, and it
had been hot for ages. All summer holidays
aeroplanes had been droning overhead, like now. Dad
said they were pilots, practising.

He had *The Tales of King Arthur, illustrated*,
from Boots library again. The man in the blue tunic
had his hand on the hilt of a sword. It was exciting,
but not nearly as good as a Cossack sabre. He turned
a page. There was no picture on it but some long
words, so he went to ask help.

Mother and Dad were sitting in the parlour
with the wireless droning in the background. They
always seemed to be listening to the wireless these
days. The BBC man droned on something about Mr
Chamberlain.

'What's this w-word, Mother?'

'Excalibur. Shh a minute...'

They were leaning forward, towards the wireless.
Dad had sent Billy out for accumulators that
morning. 'Best to have some spares,' he'd said to
Mother, and then put them on the high shelf in a box
wrapped in brown paper.

'And what's *this* word?'

Mother waved him away. 'Not now, Billy. We're
listening to the news, so go in the garden or stay
upstairs, but don't wake Baby with loud footsteps
please.'

King Arthur was much more interesting than the
wireless because he had Excalibur. With Excalibur

anything was possible. Enemies could be *vanquished*. Squish, like treading on a snail.

He shut the door behind him and just caught Mother's murmur about armies.

When Baby woke, Dad said, 'Get ready to go shopping, Billy.'

'We're always shopping these days.'

'It's necessary, Billy.'

Mother had already brought back large parcels, which she put in the loft 'in case' as well as lots of tinned food until the larder was so full Mrs Donnington said she couldn't clean it out properly. Mother put a lock on the larder and said she needn't bother as it was Stores.

Now they were going to buy more stores. It felt funny, because Dad was coming too. Fathers didn't shop. Not unless they had a really new baby.

Baby sat up in her pram that was like a great carriage. Its wheels came up to Billy's thighs, and when he pressed on the handle, the whole thing bounced on its springs. Mother walked briskly talking to Dad about Preparations.

At the common, all the railings had been taken away for making ships and a whole chunk had been dug up and changed into allotments.

'What's allotments, Dad?'

'For growing vegetables, so everyone has enough food.

Your Uncle Frank has one of these,' said Dad.

'He's welcome to it,' said Mother. 'Spoils the look of the park. But Battersea's much worse off, allotments all the way round, I heard.'

Billy slowed down to stare. It would nice to dig at the allotments instead of queuing outside the grocer's, the baker's, the butcher's and then the draper's. He was big enough to stay home on his own, these days. He sighed.

'Don't sigh,' Mother said. 'After shopping we're going to Nanny and Grandad's.'

'While we can,' Dad muttered.

The shopping took ages, and then there was the long walk up Lavender Hill.

They found Grandad planting vegetables at one side of his garden. The Anderson shelter was on the other. It had a funny door with a curved top. Inside there were two bunks as well as two camp chairs. It was a wonderful new place to play. He scrambled in and felt safe and secret. Outside, Grandad was saying, 'I wish you'd get on with yours, Bert.'

Billy put his head round the shelter door.

'There's an old French proverb,' Dad looked to the sky where perhaps he could see the words. '*One meets his destiny often in the road he takes to avoid it*. It would be just my luck to slip a disc digging the foundations.'

'Cheerful soul, you are. Never mind about proverbs and we're not French anyway. What about protecting your family?'

Dad waved a hand towards Billy and Mother, heaving his shoulders and acting as if he was carrying a large weighty bag.

Grandad stared. 'What? Now?'

'Very soon, I think.'

Grandad looked down and nodded grimly.

He took Billy into the kitchen and gave him half a crown. That was so much money and he hadn't done anything good! He promised to put in his money box, but Grandad said, 'You can take it with you, in case.' Nanny nudged Grandad to be quiet and Mother also mouthed something silently.

Of course Billy would take the half-crown home with him, so he didn't understand what their secret was.

Suddenly he heard an aeroplane and took Baby outside to look up at it. 'Hurricane!' he shouted. All the boys at school knew a Hurricane and a Spitfire, but the girls didn't.

Nanny followed Billy and Baby into the garden looking worried, as if children weren't safe there. She always wore a little apron when she cooked and she kept twisting this in her hands.

'You're such a good little boy, Billy. We look forward to your visits so much. You won't forget that, will you?'

Why would he forget it? They'd always visited Nanny. He looked at all the grown-ups' faces; worried faces, but they didn't say anything about worry.

Then Uncle Ted came up the garden path wearing a soldier's uniform with huge black boots. 'Uncle! I want to tread on your boots. Walk me on your boots!'

Uncle Ted let Billy put one foot on top of each of his hard boots and they walked down the garden together. Billy couldn't stop giggling.

'Have you f-finished for today?'

He knew Uncle Ted had joined the Territorial Army ages ago and had to learn all about fighting. Billy pulled him further down the garden, while Nanny and Mother went inside to make tea.

'Can you show me all your fighting things? Have you got a gun, a sword or—?'

'Billy, I'm off to a training camp somewhere secret.'

'Ooh, su-*per*. Will you have tents? Are you c-coming back?'

'Of course, afterwards. Don't know how soon. If there's a war, I'll be called for, but I'll be with chums I know. That'll be topper, won't it?'

Billy looked at the hard earth where he and Uncle had played kick ball. The war was *Abroad*. He didn't want Uncle Ted to go to it. It wouldn't be topper if he went away for a long time. 'I don't want you to go to the war. Can't you stay here and just practice war?'

Uncle Ted ruffled his hair. 'I've practised all I can. Come on, let's see what cakes Nanny's got for us. I can see she's bringing them out here.'

Dad was putting two wooden tables on the concrete part of the garden. Mother carried the tray of tea and Nanny followed with the plates and cake.

'Isn't it nice to be outside in the sunshine?' Mother said pouring the tea.

Grandad got everyone a deckchair and they admired the blue sky and warm weather.

'Has to come to an end sometime,' said Dad, as more planes passed overhead. *"Dost thou love life? Then do not squander time, for that's the stuff life is made of."* Benjamin Franklin.'

Grandad frowned and passed round the cakes. 'American, wasn't he?'

'Thought we were thinking of war, not love,' said Uncle Ted.

Then everyone turned to talking about his trip. It was a long time to wait while Uncle answered all their questions, but as soon as he could, Billy asked him to show him his marching, which he did, up and down the garden very smartly.

Mother giggled and Dad said, 'Ted, you'll soon be very sick of that! Come and eat your cake.'

Uncle Ted grinned. 'I'm nearly a professional, y'know, Sis.' He looked proud of himself, but Nanny turned to Mother with a sad, worried face. 'I don't know what I'll do if he has to go abroad.'

Grandad put his arm round Nanny and said, 'Perhaps it'll all be settled and over before Ted's finished his training. Storm in a teacup. The Hun won't want a go at us again, not really. Too busy where he is, the devil.'

'Chamberlain's got it in hand,' said Dad.

'We hope. Meanwhile we're off to proper camp,' said Uncle Ted, coming back for another cake. 'It won't be for long and makes a change from work.'

Dad nodded grimly, pulling Billy away from Uncle Ted's arm. 'Let your uncle eat his cake in peace.'

Uncle Ted laughed. 'Won't get this at camp, mother's cooking, eh? Or the taking it easy.' He looked at Mother and Dad on their deckchairs. 'I'm glad you were here for me to say Cheerio, just in case we get sent straight off after camp to collar Hitler for you.'

Billy said, 'I've heard of H-Hitler. He's the war. He's got a horrid n-name, a hitting name.'

Dad put a hand over Billy's mouth and carried on talking to Ted. 'I'm not in favour of war but if it does come to it, I have to wish you all the best. *It's a great life if we don't weaken,* John Buchan.'

'You're a case, Herbert. Did John Buchan, whoever he was, face the Nazis? All your sayings! I'll try to remember some when I'm on the march, ha-ha. Now— time for the off.' Uncle Ted stood up and dusted down his smart uniform trousers.

'Good luck with camp, Ted,' said Mother. 'Rather you than me.'

'Hope the grub's good, that's all.' Uncle Ted went into the kitchen, where Nanny packed him up a fruit cake to go in his kitbag.

Billy followed. 'Do you want to take my half-crown in case you don't have enough food or guns?'

Nanny gave him a hug. 'The army will feed him well, Billy.' she said. 'That's the least they can do after your Uncle doing his drill three times a week all this time. No, your half-crown is to buy yourself something nice, if you— Well, for later.'

Uncle Ted said, 'You know what? That half-crown needs a shilling to go with it. But mind you don't spend it yet, Billy boy. Save it for some special time, good or bad,' and he pushed both coins into Billy's pocket.

He took him by the shoulders. 'Listen, Billy. Whatever happens to you, make it fun, right? Keep your chin up,' and he winked twice. Billy tipped up his chin and tried to copy the wink but Uncle didn't smile.

By then, the grown-ups were all standing in the hall. Billy stood where he was. He had a lot of money, for nothing. He hadn't done any jobs. Things felt important but not nice, not safe.

Grandad followed Uncle Ted out of the front door and pushed it behind him so no-one heard what he was saying.

Billy saw Nanny make a face at Dad. 'He takes it hard, seeing Ted go off at this point. Took him such a time to get over his own service in the Great War. You were lucky you just missed it, Bert.'

'I had the contemplation. And remember my father copped it.'

Billy hadn't seen Dad's contemplation. Where was it kept? It might be bigger than Mr Durban's sabre. He'd ask Dad when he could.

Nanny and Mother went out to Uncle Ted, and Billy waved from the window as he marched down the road with his haversack. It was ever so big.

After that, Mother spent a long time upstairs with Nanny. Grandad shook his head at Dad. He gave Billy some dinky cars to play with, while he and Dad listened to the wireless in the other room.

When Mother came downstairs again, Dad got up to go. Nanny and Grandad gave Billy a specially hard hug, and Nanny said again, 'Don't forget us, will you?'

He shook his head. Nanny was a puzzle. Why would he forget them? It was only a week till next Sunday.

Then Dad wanted to go on to Uncle Frank's. They didn't normally do this on a Sunday. He had a heavy bag he was taking with them. Mother put her felt hat on and sighed. Dad said, 'Look, Marcia. It's going to be the last time for one of us.'

'Indeed,' said Mother, pressing the long cruel pin through her hat brim.

Billy tried to look as if he hadn't heard. Who was going there for the last time?

He pretended there was hop-scotch on the pavement as Mother and Dad walked along in front of him with the pram. He heard Dad say, 'You mustn't worry, Marcia. Even apart from exemption, I reckon they won't call our age group up. They're taking all the youngsters first. And if they start on civil servants, Frank should still be all right. He's thirty-nine.'

Billy looked at his feet with a secret smile. Grown-ups didn't usually let you hear how old they were. And now he knew.

When they got to Uncle Frank's, to be safe from Kenneth's jabs, Billy pretended Baby wanted to sit outside because usually Kenneth stayed inside, drawing. It was best to be careful when the grown-ups would all be talking and not notice boys.

He stayed by the front door, 'I'll watch over the pram while you're indoors, Mother.'

Aunty said 'Aaaah' and Mother looked pleased with him, but Uncle Frank muttered to Dad that Billy wasn't normal.

Kenneth moved his mouth down like an old man, nodded hard and wiggled a finger into his head. He followed Billy into the yard, arms folded.

Billy turned on him, 'Your D-dad is thirty nine.'
'He's not.'

'He is. I heard D-dad tell Mother.'

Kenneth tried to give him a Chinese burn, but Billy ran to pick Baby up and held her in front of him. Mother looked out of the window to check on her, so Kenneth smiled at Baby and stepped away. 'You wait,' he muttered.

Billy said, 'This w-will be the l-last time here, for one of us.'

Kenneth looked at him, frowning. Billy knew he was cross not to be the first to know something. He opened his mouth, but they were called into tea just then. Billy let Kenneth take the best biscuits without saying anything. It didn't matter if today was the last time.

After tea, Dad collected the heavy carrier bag from the hall. It was full of stores. 'I'm just going to fill a shelf in your Anderson, Frank.'

'Obliged, I'm sure.' Uncle sniffed, but looked pleased.

'Kind of you, Bert,' said Aunty, 'but let's hope we won't need any of it.'

The side door swung to behind Dad and Uncle clapped his hands. 'Let's have a concert to brighten our spirits.

Good practice for us. They'll be no singers on the wireless, you know, if we have a war. Those stage people'll have to go and fight like the rest. Then we'll have to do our own entertaining; no wireless programmes. There'll just be war announcements to listen to, I bet.'

Mother shuddered. 'There's not going to be a war. Stop it, Frank.'

Aunty said, 'We won't think about it now. I thought this was to cheer us up, Frank? I have to bear up over my own tragedies, without worrying over war. Come on, I'll go first.' She stood up and sang 'Roses of Picardy' all the way to the end, until they felt better.

Then Mother did a lovely dance, the frills on her skirt flapping along with her sleeves.

'Ooh, hoo,' said Uncle, clapping his beefy hands, 'What a mover! Think what Bert is missing!' As he stood up the table wobbled.

'Perhaps we should have waited for him,' said Aunty.

'He'll come in a minute. Now it's my turn.' He stood beside the glass-fronted cabinet, one hand on its side and started talking in a wireless voice. 'I will recite. I shall entertain you with *The Lion and*

Albert, a cautionary tale for certain young people who go to the zoo.'

Billy sat still. That was him. He'd gone there last year. Kenneth hadn't ever been to the zoo.

Uncle started off in a very strange voice, so the mothers giggled behind their hankies, although it was a very sad tale and the boy got eaten at the end.

'Clever, clever,'said Kenneth. 'It all rhymed, Daddy. I liked it ever so. It was the boy's fault he got eaten, wasn't it?'

'It was, Kenneth. Quite right, sonny.'

'Your turn, sweetheart,' said Aunty straightening the points of his shirt collar. Take your slippers off and stand on the little table where we can see you best.

Kenneth stood in his socks with folded hands He closed his eyes and began. He could sing lots of songs. He sang the first part of *Oh for the wings, the wings of a dove*. Some of the notes went up terribly high.

Aunty and Mother sighed with their heads on one side. 'Ohhh, Kenneth,' they breathed. 'Perfect. Such feeling.'

He sang again. Kenneth was a horrible boy, but his singing was ever so good. Everyone clapped hard.

'Billy next,' said Aunty.

He backed to the far wall. 'I c-can't.'

'What do you mean, boy?' said Uncle. 'We're all doing something. Right?'

'I haven't g-got anything.'

Mother said, 'I don't think Billy's good at that sort of thing. I've never heard him do anything '

'Then he'd better recite, and answer questions. Make him aware of his own voice. Or v-v-voice, ha ha ha.'

Kenneth tittered. Mother tutted.

Billy managed a verse of The Grand Old Duke of York, but couldn't answer the questions, and all his *Don't Knows* were d-d-don't kn-knows. Kenneth turned his eyes up to the ceiling.

'Never mind, Billy.' Aunty looked at him kindly. 'Why do you stutter, dear?'

Billy shrugged because *Don't Know* was a very stuttering thing to say.

Mother said, 'Ignore the stutter, I do.'

Aunty looked at his shrug. 'He doesn't really know why he does it, Marcia.' She sounded kind but looked across at Kenneth, smiling fondly at the boy who never stuttered.

Mother sighed. 'You're seven, Billy, not a baby. You can't talk like one.'

Uncle said, 'I've tried to toughen him up. Marcia. You want to take him in hand, you and Bert, with that stutter.

Or he'll be hammered when he gets to—' Billy wandered into the hall before they said any more about him.

Kenneth followed. 'Stutterer!'

'Don't even know what it means.'

'Stuttering, Billy, is when you say K-K-Kenneth instead of speaking properly.'

'I d-don't.'

'You do. You're doing it now. And you've got to stop it. Daddy says so. You mustn't stutter. It sounds soppy and you might get thrashed.'

Billy stared at Kenneth's neat lips. He nearly told him he had a sabre, but that wasn't true. *Yet*. He had to get one, it was the magic he needed. 'I'm g-going in the g-garden,' he called to the grown-ups.

Before he could go anywhere, the side door opened and Dad joined them.

'We've just done a concert, Uncle,' Kenneth chirped.

Uncle Frank stretched out his long legs. 'Yes. 'fraid you've missed your chance to perform, Bert. But you need to take note. This boy,' and he leant forward to pat Kenneth on the head, 'sings like an angel,' but this one,' he poked Billy in the chest, 'can hardly get a word of a rhyme out without stuttering. Show him, boy.'

Billy looked over his shoulder at Mother in his most pleading way, but she shrugged.

Dad said, 'Don't you want to show me your rhyme, Billy?'

He shook his head.

'Seriously, Bert, listen.' Uncle Frank leant forward. 'Billy! Recite it again.'

Billy stared hard at Mother.

She tipped her head on one side and spread her hands on her lap. 'You'd better try, Billy.'

He looked at Dad, who gave him one brisk nod.

Kenneth was leaning against the cabinet, one foot crossed over the other. He put the tip of his tongue out.

Billy stared hard at the green zig-zags on the carpet. 'The g-g-grand ol' D-duke of York, he h-had t-ten thou-.'

Before he got very far, Dad said loudly, 'Stop that rubbish! Just slow down and speak properly.' He turned to Mother. 'You've got to see to this stutter before— the other.'

Another? Was there a stutter somewhere else?

Mother leaned back in her chair and stretched an open hand towards Dad. 'What am I supposed to do? Aren't there more pressing things,' and she pointed to something in the newspaper.

CHAPTER ELEVEN
August 28th 1939

Plea to country towns. Accommodation for
thousands needed, should war not be averted

They were just finishing breakfast when the door-bell rang. Mother went out to answer it. Billy heard Mr Durban's voice.

'Good morning, Marcia. Sorry to come early. I wanted to catch Billy before he—'

Mother held up a flat hand. 'Thank you, Peter. That will be good if you have Billy for a bit. You can imagine how much I've got to do now. Billy, you'd love to go to Mr Durban's house for a bit, wouldn't you.'

Billy nodded hard. Soon he was skipping down the road with Mr Durban, counting the windows where the blackout looked torn.

'Hmm. I shall have to make a few evening calls, I see.'

When they got to his house, Mr Durban called Angela. Then they all sat round with fizzy lemon and Mrs Durban's nicest cakes. It was almost like a birthday.

Afterwards Mr Durban took Billy into the living room on his own. He pulled out a book with a green cover and gave it to him. It was about heroes. There was a strong-looking boy on the front cover pulling a boat ashore.

'You keep this. I read it a lot when I was a boy. A lot. It's all about people who have done brave things. Those stories made me try to be brave. Now you can read about them. I'd like you to have it, if you go away.'

Go away? Perhaps he would be a soldier one day and then he'd need the book. It was a super one. 'Th-

thank you, sir.' He held the book carefully. 'I'd like to b-be a hero.'

Mr Durban put an arm on Billy's shoulder and said, 'You will be, in your own way. But not just yet, God willing.' He pulled him nearer. 'I'll tell you something. You know, Billy, I'd have liked a son. A boy just like you.'

'Really, t-truly, sir?'

'Indeed. Just like you. And if I had a son I'd share this secret.' He bent down with his face near Billy's. 'Our King has to speak really carefully because he has a stutter.'

Billy looked at him hard. 'The *King* has?'

'Yes. You see, you're not the only one. The king has to practise, you know. He has to think before each word he speaks. The trick is, you have to watch out for the words that make you stutter, and avoid them. Choose words which start with a different letter.'

That was such a good idea. But what words could be instead of 'Yes' or 'No'? Those were the words he seemed to say most. Bother. It was a nuisance. But the stutter didn't seem to come so badly when he was with Mr Durban.

Angela put her head round the door. 'Shall I play with Billy, Daddy?'

'Yes, off you go, you two. Have some fun.'

Angela shut the door behind them and took Billy upstairs. She leaned on the banisters, looking at him.

'I know what you want to see. The sabre.'

He could hardly breathe. 'Yes please.'

'You have to kiss me first.'

She was like the girls in the big playground.

'Ugh.'

'Go on, you have to, or I won't let you see it,' Angela leant forward.

He couldn't miss seeing the sabre again. He breathed in and kissed Angela on one soft cheek.

Actually, it wasn't awful. It made him think of marshmallows and that's how she smelled.

'Right. I've done it. Can I see the sabre now?'

'We have to wait until they go into the kitchen. Daddy's going to put wood shutters on the windows.'

Once they heard the voices move, they crept downstairs and into Mr Durban's study. The curtains were closed against the bright sun, so the small room felt dark and mysterious. There was a musty smell from the velvety chair, which Billy crouched beside in case someone came in. Angela put one hand inside the cupboard doors and brought out the sabre. She pushed one curtain a little to the side. A shaft of golden light hit the blade as she drew it out and laid it carefully on the desk.

'Can I touch?'

'No, just look. I'll be for it if you cut yourself.'

'I want to hold it. Please. I'll be ever so careful.'

He turned and lifted the sabre by its knobbly handle, catching the light on its dangerous tip. A snaky shudder went through him and he put it down again.

He was going to tell her that Mr Durban wanted a son, but stopped himself. Angela might be cross. She couldn't help being a girl. He stayed staring at the wonderful thing.

'Did you tell your father he c-could leave it to me when he gets old and dies?'

'No! Why should I? I don't want him to die. Here, give it to me, that's enough.'

She slid the sabre back and closed the cupboard doors.

They went back up into her bedroom and talked about secret things. He kept his finger on his lips. Then she said, 'Now you can tell me boy things.'

Angela was nice, so surely she wouldn't tell on him. He told her all about Kenneth, the beastly things, the gas mask, the Chinese burns and the tale-telling.

She listened all through without fidgeting. 'He sounds a meanie. Never mind, Billy. You might not have to see him for some time. Come and see what's happening in our garden.'

They ran downstairs. The drone of voices filtered through the lounge door as they went out to the one square of grass. All the rest was turfed up into a heap ready for the Anderson shelter, which lay in pieces.

Billy put a foot on the sheet of corrugated iron. 'My G-Grandad's built one of those, but we haven't g-got one. What are they t-talking about anyway?'

'Evacuation.'

'What's that?'

'Haven't they told you?' She put an arm round him. 'Why do you think I let you see the sabre again? Why did I need a kiss? *Evacuation* means going away. Children have got to go. The government are sending us to the country, to be safe.'

Mr Durban took him home and it was still warm, still nice and light. He talked about the heroes book, which made Billy long to read it. He didn't say anything about evacuation.

Was Angela telling him stories, like Kenneth always did? But perhaps she believed it. Girls might not always get things right.

CHAPTER TWELVE
August 29th 1939

Hitler "only desires Danzig and a small section of the Polish Corridor"

A thin brown envelope came in the post. Mother showed it to Dad. Then Dad told Billy to get his gas mask out. It sat on a dusty shelf in the parlour. Everyone had stopped carrying them since spring.

'You'll need to carry this everywhere from now on.' Dad put an arm on Mother's shoulder. 'The time has come, Marcia.'

Billy looked at the cardboard box. No-one had been bothering to take them around lately. It would be a nuisance always having to carry it. School holidays were very nearly over. Would he have to take the box into the playground? How could they play football?

Dad walked him into the garden where they blew the dust off the gas mask box. 'You haven't forgotten how to put this on, Billy, have you?'

Billy shook his head. He waited while Dad filled his pipe. A train whistled in the distance. Dad struck one match after the other before his pipe got going. He didn't say anything. Perhaps he was choosing a saying.

Billy looked up at the sky. It had clouded over, but he could still feel the sun.

Then Dad told Billy about evacuation and it was just like Angela had said. There was going to be danger and children had to be kept safe by going away. Dad nodded at him, sucking at his pipe.

'Go away? On my own?'

'You'll go with the school. We've put your name down.' 'But what about you and Mother? And Baby?'

'Mother will be evacuated too, with Baby. They'll go together, not with your school. That's just for school children. The teachers will look after you.'

'But Dad, what about you? If Hitler comes, you'll have to fight, or you'll be sent to Wandsworth prison.' In his mind's eye he could see all the little windows with their criss-cross bars and imagined Dad's face, peering from one of them.

'No, no, Billy. Other men are needed as soldiers, younger ones, like your Uncle Ted. I'm needed for my work, various places just as usual. I'll hardly be in London at all.'

He remembered that Mother had said they just wouldn't be here if there was war. They still didn't have an Anderson shelter.

They walked around to the side path, some way apart. Dad lit his pipe and leant on the front wall. A lorry trundled past the top of the road. It was full of soldiers looking out of the back, shaded by the canvas. There were rucksacks beside them stuffed full.

'Is Uncle Ted in a lorry like that? He hasn't come back from camp.'

'No, he's joined his regiment. He's more trained than other young men, so he'll be needed.'

'Nanny gave him fruit cake for his kit-bag.'

'I expect he had to pack all sorts of things. Like you will when you're evacuated. Quite soon now.'

Billy stood looking at the house, his bedroom window. So that's why they'd given him money. He was going away, just like Uncle Ted.

'What's *quite soon*?'

'Two days.'

'That's the day after tomorrow!'

Dad gave a nod and puffed at his pipe.

Billy's arms ached although he hadn't been carrying anything. He rubbed them, his arms crossed in front of him. 'I'll take my heroes book. Can I take my toys?'

'One small toy.'

The smallest toy he had was his whizzer, but it would be better if he could have one of his aeroplanes to go with him. He waited for Dad to tell him more but the only sound was the drone of aeroplanes.

Dad puffed on his pipe again. A little wind blew the smoke upwards. Billy watched it go away to the heavens.

Dad zipped his green ribbed cardigan right to the collars, although it was still warm. He sighed, then knocked the black bits out of his pipe onto the grass. H e gestured to Billy to go on indoors.

Mother had made a Shepherd's Pie. They sat round the table and Billy passed the salt. There were tinned peaches afterwards with evaporated milk. It was ever so nice, but no-one was saying much except Baby, who was doing all the grizzling for them.

Dad had to say Goodbye the following night. His holiday was over and the Courts would be sitting in Kent. He said he wasn't sure when he'd be able to see them next. Mother was in her prettiest dress. It went in at her middle and out lower down. It was the one she used to wear to her dances. Dad stroked his hand down her back. Mother put Baby in his arms, then her head on his shoulder.

Billy heard him say quietly, 'You're not one of these women who make a fuss. You're used to me being away, so this is not that different. Think, some time in the country will be good for the children's health.'

He hugged them, put Baby down to crawl around, then placed a hand on Billy's shoulder. 'You'll need to be brave and sensible, Billy. Remember that. Do as your teachers tell you and things will be all right. I'll see you Christmas-time, probably.'

'Christmas! Am I staying away right up until Christmas?'

Baby was hugging Dad's legs, but he didn't seem to mind.

'Nobody knows much of what's ahead, Billy. Evacuation is safest, better for you.'

Billy tucked his chin down, waiting for Dad to change his mind, but the large hand just came down on his shoulder twice more. Pat, pat. 'Goodbye, Billy. Be good.'

Mother stood beside him at the door, Baby holding her skirt. Dad had a suitcase and his briefcase. It was like he was going to war, but he was going away to work as usual. It was Billy who was really going away, Mother too.

Dad walked up the road, turning to wave once. The sky was red behind him. Planes passing in the distance looked like teacher's crosses when he got his sums wrong.

CHAPTER THIRTEEN
Sept 1st 1939

Germany Attacks Poland.
Many cities bombed, including Warsaw

The next morning it was difficult to eat breakfast. Baby was quiet in her high chair. He whispered, 'Baby, I'm going away. Then you are too, but don't worry, you'll be with Mother.' He put her rattle in one sticky hand.

He knew it was time for school, but hesitated on the front doorstep, in case the going away wasn't true. Mother handed him his gas mask and his case. 'When you get to— wherever they put you— there's a clean change of clothes inside for the day after tomorrow. Don't forget. There's a packed lunch in there, too. Now, don't worry about anything. The teachers will make sure you're all right, and you'll have some friends with you, I'm sure.'

He looked up and down the road. Surely Dad would come and stop this. Billy had never been away from home. Surely Aunty would never let Kenneth go.

'Is Kenneth being evacuated, Mother?'

'No. Not all children are going. It depends what their parents have decided.'

He scanned her face. So she had decided, and Dad had.

Several children passed his gate carrying their gas masks. 'Watcher Billy! Come on.'

He went towards the front gate. Mother suddenly got hold of him and kissed him.

That was startling. 'Goodbye, Mother.' His feet started moving after the other children. He felt the damp place on his cheek all the way up the road.

Jim caught him up. 'Billy. You got sweets in your bag?'

'Dunno.'

Jim's bag wasn't big. 'I'm staying,' he said.

When he got to the school wall, Billy looked in his bag and saw his heroes book and a bag of barley sugars under the clothes. He was wearing a cap and a mackintosh and he was too hot.

Inside school, everyone crowded into the corridor and there was an awful lot of noise. The tall teacher with long skirts, Miss Johnson, pushed forward to the middle. She clapped her hands. 'Now some of you are excited and others are jittery, but if you keep chattering, you'll miss the instructions when they come. Calm down everyone.'

'Where are we going, Miss?' said Mick.

'No-one knows where they're going, Miss,' said Dick.

Miss Johnson held her hand out wide. She told them that not even the teachers knew.

Mr Hendrick was staying behind. It was because had a stick and was very old. He had a moustache too and it quivered when he shouted at the class. Everyone was noisy until he banged the stick on the floor. The next door classroom quietened too.

In the pause, Mick called out, 'Sir? Sir? Are we going yet?'

'When are we going, Sir?' said Dick.

Just then, Mr Finlay came in and gave Mr Hendrick a big nod.

'Line up, those on the list for evacuation! Quick sharp! No talking!'

'Put your label on,' muttered Jim, 'or they won't know your name.' He stayed sitting down.

Mick had his wicked grin on. 'We're going to swap ours when we get there. No-one will know which of us is which.'

'That's stupid.' Sonia was always sensible. 'Both of you are going to need a home, whatever your name is. They're going to find us all homes.'

Homes! Billy hadn't thought of that, only about the going away. He scrabbled in his case and found his label. It had his name, school and address. Silly! He could have told anyone all that anyway.

When the register was taken and everyone checked again, they marched down to the local railway station. The ones with brothers or sisters were allowed to walk with them. Although Mr Hendrick and his stick had stayed behind with the non-evacuees, Mr Finlay from the top class was coming. He taught P.T. in a green vest with words on it, and black shorts so you could see his great muscles move like steam engines, but he told the class he had asthma so he couldn't be a soldier even if he wanted. Jim said he was forty-four, anyway. Forty-four! Too old, so it was good he wouldn't have to go to Wandsworth prison.

A few mothers had run down the road to wave, and some were crying. Some followed them all the way to the station and onto the platform. He knew Mother had to stay home with Baby. He looked around at everyone else. Jim had stayed behind, so had Reg and Andrew. Mother was wrong. His friends weren't with him.

After a while, the train chuffed in. A plume of thick smoke buffeted down the platform towards them. Some older boys cheered.

A guard opened a train door and held it open wide. Billy was going to say Goodbye to the mothers he knew, but they were busy hugging their children and telling them last minute things. A gust of wind blew some smut in his face. The label round his neck flapped up and then back.

He clambered on board alone. There was a great press of knees and suitcases, elbows and excited voices, the chestnutty smell of train smoke. The guard slammed the door shut. Billy was pressed against the carriage wall as heads poked out of the window shouting and waving Goodbye. He saw the hats and waving hands slowly and then more quickly left behind then found himself sitting in a carriage with Sonia and the twins, John, who was in a higher class, and four girls.

'I'm the oldest,' said John. 'So toe the line, you lot.'

'We won't be gone long, will we?' one of the girls asked. No-one answered.

At first they all looked out of the windows and shouted every time they saw an army truck, some cows, and their first haystack ever.

It was the first time the twins had been on a train. They wanted to climb up to the luggage rack, then they wanted to see what everyone had in their greaseproof paper packages. Their mother didn't seem to have packed them up much. Bill shared his barley sugars with them and John gave them some lemon squash to quieten them down. But soon they were rolling and tussling on the carriage floor.

'It's a good job there's no corridors, twins,' Sonia said. 'Miss would be ever so cross with you and Sir might give you the cane.'

'So what!' said Mick.

'They can't see, so there,' said Dick.

The girls started playing cats' cradle and John buried his head in his comic. Billy waited for a little while in case John finished it and passed it on, but he didn't.

If only Mother had put a comic in his bag. The train was too jolty to read the fine print in the heroes book. The twins were too noisy to think about difficult words anyway and he was glad when John said, 'Let's have our lunch now.

It must be time. Anyway I'm hungry.'

'Rath-*er*' said Mick.

95

'Grub. You bet.' said Dick.

They all opened their packages and peeped inside each other's. One girl had chocolate biscuits that had melted onto her paste sandwiches.

Sonia turned her nose up. 'Ugh, look at yours!'

'I can't eat them now.'

The twins looked at her, hopefully. They were always hungry.

'I will.'

'Let's have 'em.'

Sonia said, 'You'll have to eat them, Elsie. We're not having anything else for ages and ages.'

Perhaps he ought to give the girl a Bovril sandwich, but he didn't have many. John had lots in his paper bag, so Elsie had a share. Then everyone had to put their paper bags into one big screwed-up bundle, not to leave a mess.

One girl had a paper book and crayons so the girls took it in turns to colour in. The boys said it was cissy and started kicking the girls' seats so that the pencil jogged. The boys had nothing to do. They played paper, stone, knife but John kept winning and the twins said it was a rubbish game.

Some singing sounded from another carriage, *Ten Green Bottles* and *Fire Down Below* so they joined in for a while. Their singing petered out.

Mick said, 'I've finished my drink. Can I have some of yours?'

Dick wasn't having any. 'No-o. You didn't share, why should I?' Then there was more fighting.

'Shut up you twins,' Sonia buffed the nearest one. 'Just our bad luck to get you in our carriage.'

It seemed like a whole day had passed before there was a hoot and the train stopped. Mr Finlay came along the platform, telling them to get off. Billy swung his gas mask from his wrist and looked around. He'd expected fields for miles and miles but there were houses all close together, right by the

96

station. 'Are we at the country, then?' he asked no-one in particular.

No-one answered. Everyone seemed dazed, and for once there was hardly any noise.

A coach stood outside the station. It took them to an empty church hall. It was made of pink brick with a slate roof like a Chinaman's hat. They filed slowly into the hall after Mr Finlay. Even the twins had gone quiet. Inside there were loads of ladies sitting waiting for them and one or two men with big brown boots and rolled-up sleeves. They were looking round the children, some of them with screwed up eyes.

A few ladies gave out milk and some rather dry biscuits.

Mr Finlay arranged the school on benches in groups. He told Billy to sit with the oldest children because he was tall. John squeezed up to make room for him.

A large lady with a blue flowery frock sat with an old whiskery man. They had a list that they showed to the teachers. Miss Johnson was pointing to the smallest children.

'Why are they first, John?' Billy asked.

'That's so that any crying can be dealt with by someone else.'

The older sisters and brothers were allowed to sit and comfort the smaller ones. Everyone else kept still on the benches drinking their milk, while the village people walked around. Billy kept his eyes on them while they chose which child they wanted. He saw them point out little girls with pretty ribbons and small boys who were sitting cross-legged, quietly.

Billy was sitting quietly but he wasn't little. The older children beside him exchanged ideas between each other.

97

'She's chosen. See, you've got to look small and sweet.'

'But *he* isn't. I know him!'

'Let's pretend we're brothers and we've got to go together.'

But it didn't work. One of the ladies came past and John got chosen.

'Its 'cos he looks grown up,' said a large boy with messy hair and unlaced boots sitting next to him.

Billy sat up very straight and folded his arms, trying to look grown up but then a fierce-looking man beckoned to the large boy, 'Reckon you'll put in a good day's work,' so Billy slumped down again to look as small as possible. Mother and Dad wouldn't like it if he went to work instead of to school.

When the village people had the children they wanted they took them off to their homes. It was mostly boys left, apart from two girls holding hands, one very tall and thin and a smaller one with lots of spots. Sonia had gone. He couldn't see anyone he knew, except for the twins. Billy looked at the dry biscuit in his hand. He might as well eat it.

Mr Finlay stood up and said in a loud voice, 'All remaining children line up.' He led the older children, younger ones copied, the twins doing a silly walk behind them. Miss Johnson walked nearby to keep them in order. Billy was left at the back.

They all marched out of the hall and alongside the church where the gravel on the path crunched under their feet. Pieces of pink and blue confetti were trapped between the stones. So funny that a wedding had been there earlier!

As their crocodile walked around the town, both teachers started knocking on doors to see how many children each house could take.

The first houses were strange, made of grey lumpy stones stuck together to make walls, not like brick at all. They were good houses with gardens round them, the soil around the flowers a gingery brown. One garden even had a swing. The door to that one was closed and no-one answered the teacher's knock, but at most of the others the ladies were standing by open front doors and some called out that they'd take one child.

Surely he'd soon be chosen because he was the smartest and had kept himself clean on the journey. The twins kept messing around and they already looked filthy because of rolling around on the platform and under the train seats. It would be ages before anyone chose them. But a farmer passing in his hay cart called over to the teacher, 'They two, Miss, they twins —they look as if a bit of rough won't hurt 'em. I'll take 'em off your hands.' And off Dick and Mick went, laughing as they scrambled up onto the hay cart.

'Yippee!' The cart moved off and they threw bits of hay back at the others.

The crocodile turned up the next road. There were some big houses here, followed by lots of small ones close together. The following road was the same. One after the other, children were taken. Billy watched the grey socks of the boy in front of him sinking lower and lower down his legs.

Then a lady nudged the teacher. 'I'll tak 'im. That ginger one. He reminds me of my son.'

The girl with spotty skin and her thin big sister, were taken up to the next gate. One of the women standing there said 'I suppose I *have* to take a child, Miss? All right then, but only one.'

The spotty sister started crying so Miss Johnson held her hand until some people at the house at the end of the road took her in.

'There, Mavis, you're not far from your sister,' Miss Johnson comforted her.

Billy thought how far he was from his sister.

When Mr Finlay led them into the fourth road there were very few children left, and soon there was only one.

Billy gripped his gas mask handle until his fingers hurt. Mother wouldn't like it at all if she knew he was the last to be chosen.

Mr Finlay took his own case into a fairly big house where he was going to stay.

'You go on,' Miss Johnson said. 'I'll see to this last boy.'

'Thanks, Miss Johnson. Don't you worry, young fellow. It won't be long before you're settled in somewhere.'

The long road petered out into the country. They turned uphill to a line of brick houses. They'd already been there.

Miss Johnson sighed. 'We'll have to make the rounds of the streets all over again. I'm sorry. What's your name? Billy? Well, you need to look a bit more cheerful, I think, so that one of these ladies takes you.'

Billy's suitcase banged against his legs. If only he could dump that and the wretched gas mask.

At the bottom end of the town, several rows of very little houses were stacked so close to the pavement that they had no front garden. Front doors opened straight onto the street, but now they were nearly all closed.

'Someone will just have to take a second child,' Miss Johnson said.

And that someone was a girl in a flowered apron that tied all the way round her middle and back again, with a bow at the front. She was only standing at her door because she was minding two little children playing with sticks on the pavement. She didn't look up until Miss Johnson asked her, 'Excuse me, is your mother in?'

Then she blushed and twiddled the hair over her ear, 'I am the mother, Mam. Mrs Youldon, me.'

Billy was very surprised she was a mother because he was nearly as big as her and her hair was traily and curly like some of the girls in his class.

Miss Johnson said, 'Oh, I'm sorry. Of course.' Then, for the umpteenth time, she said, 'Good evening. I wonder if you can take this nice lad?'

'I've got a lad already, Ma'am.'

In the gloom of the house, a closely freckled boy stood behind her door, his hands hanging by his sides, his eyes bulging.

'But you can manage another?' She put down her bags and took out her purse.

'I suppose,' said Mrs Youldon, holding out her hand.

Miss Johnson placed some money in it.

Mrs Youldon looked at it. 'Oh.'

'It's only eight and six for the second child.'

'It's not a lot if they're going to need clothes too.'

'The mothers should be sending on any extra clothes the children need. This child has a mackintosh as you see.'

'More than my own'll ever have,' Mrs Youldon said.

Miss Johnson picked up her bags again. 'There now, Billy, so you're all right. Take your case indoors. I'll be off back for my tea, then.' Billy heard her sigh with relief as she turned away.

Mrs Youldon looked at Billy and then at Miss Johnson's back. It was a worried look but she said, 'Come in, then. I'm sure you're a nice boy. There's another here to keep you company.'

She must surely have the smallest home in the village. The front door opened straight into the living room where there was only a cupboard door with wooden slats, a bench and a battered easy chair, a hearth with a stove and a pot on it. A door at the back led into a scullery, and then out into a thin yard.

Behind the easy chair was a twisty staircase. There were no mats on the slate floor, no carpets.

The other boy had gone to sit on the bench, his suitcase and gas mask beside him. He sat with round shoulders, doing nothing. Billy hovered just inside the door.

'Come on in, dear. What's your name? This is Alan, do you know each other?'

The boy didn't look up. Billy shook his head miserably. The two very little children scampered back in, then stood and stared at the newcomers. He remembered the Mary Mouse books at home, and all the tiny mouse children with their matching shorts and skirts and the stick legs beneath. He managed a wavery smile. They hung together and looked at their mother.

She put her arms round them and pointed. 'This is Billy and here's Alan. They're both going to live with us for a bit.'

The little children stared with big eyes. Billy fidgeted. He and Alan looked suddenly very big. The ceiling wasn't far off.

Mrs Youldon smiled. 'Billy, these are my little ones, Tim and Sally. They'll get used to you.' She set about folding some rags that were on the end of the bench. Billy saw that one of them was a sort of shirt. She went to the scullery and brought out a plate of bread.

'I'll have to get their tea now. I hope you've been fed at the centre, because I haven't got that much tea for you. We were told you'd have had your meal.'

Alan took out a tin of corned beef from his case and handed it over. Billy remembered his and got it out. He was starving. She beamed and put the tins on a shelf above the stove. She took a damp rag and wiped her children's hands, then perched them on the bench with a hunk of bread.

'You boys go up and put your cases away.'

They looked at each other carefully. Alan led the way up the narrow stairs. The room at the top had a double mattress on the floor and a large chest with Mrs Youldon's skirt on it. Next door there was a cupboard with a camp bed squeezed in it. Billy stared at it.

Alan plumped down on the bed. It made a creaky, metally noise and wobbled. He sat with his feet firmly on the floor.

'You shouldn't be here. This was meant for just me.'

'Mm,' said Billy, wondering where to put his case. Alan was lucky he hadn't been the last child to be chosen.

They sat still for a bit, feeling their way into the silence. The room was so very small, there was nothing to look around at.

'Where's the bathroom?' Billy said after a bit.

'Don't know. Let's go and ask.'

Mrs Youldon was watching her children eat. She took the boys into the scullery where they passed a broom, a mop and a hip bath hanging on a peg, an airer swinging over their heads. She pointed down to the bottom of the thin yard. 'That's the privy,' she said, pointing to a little hut with a roof, 'and you can wash here.' A half bar of carbolic soap waited on the corner of the large sink. 'We'll need another towel out here. I don't suppose you've brought one?'

They both shook their heads. Billy realized there wouldn't be an airing cupboard full of them, like at home.

He hesitated, then went down the yard. There was a bit of grass on both side and a picket fence to divide them from the neighbours. Then there was a very little rickety shed thing. He looked back at Mrs Youldon.

'It's all right, dear. We don't have to share the privy with anyone.'

He swallowed. He hadn't even thought about that. He went in. It was nearly black inside. A large wooden seat had a bucket beneath it and a tin potty. That must be for the little ones. The floor was earthy, and damp. Strips of newspaper were looped on a string.

He came back, making a face at Alan, and washed his hands in the scullery sink.

A large tin bucket stood beside him filled with clothes. Mrs Youldon came to the doorway with her children's dirty plates.

'What ab-bout in the dark, Mrs Youldon?' He hadn't seen any light bulb in the privy. He looked up, and there weren't any light bulbs in the room either.

'I keep a torch by the back door, don't worry. Candles just blow out.'

'Candles!' said Alan.

'Candles for indoors. And I'll put a potty under the bed so you don't need to go outside at night.'

Billy kept his eyes on the floor. There was no way he was going to use a potty like a baby.

'Now then, cheer yourselves up. You both got long faces. Fancy some tea?'

'Yes please!'

She busied herself at a cupboard and enamel table top.

When her back was turned, Billy muttered to Alan, 'I haven't eaten anything since those biscuits at that hall place, have you?'

'No, and I didn't have much packed lunch. Teacher said we were having our main meal at tea-time.'

It seemed like days ago since Billy had opened the greaseproof paper for his cheese sandwiches on the train. Since then he'd made the long walk round the town twice.

He held his stomach and doubled over, looking at Alan, who began to grin. Now they were friends.

Mrs Youldon called out, 'Here you are boys. Come and eat up.' But she just put the tail end of a loaf on the bench with a small tomato each. Billy nudged Alan and frowned. Alan frowned back.

After they'd eaten everything, Alan was the braver and asked if there was anything else. Mrs Youldon made a face and said she hadn't known she'd be having two extra and it was time to play outside.

They wandered out together and looked at the ginger hills far beyond the houses. There wasn't a wall anywhere to sit on, so they just stood. Billy twiddled his fingers. Mrs Youldon was very poor. She hadn't enough food. Her clothes didn't fit properly, there weren't any cupboards and the little children hadn't got socks on. Dirt poor, Dad would have called it. He remembered Angela's voice, 'Evacuation.' At first, he hadn't known what that meant, that he'd be in a dirt poor house, no garden, no table, no bedroom, no toys, not enough to eat and not even a bathroom. They hadn't said.

But late that night, squashed up against each other, it was Alan who was crying and wanting to go back home.

CHAPTER FOURTEEN
September 2nd 1939

Outcry over Poland.
German invasion forces penetrate further

The breakfast porridge was grey but they both ate every speck. Mrs Youldon cleared their plates and told them to play out.

'Out?' Billy started. She hadn't even told them where they were. How far could they go, and how would they find their way back?

'Is the park and swings near here?' said Alan.

'Park? There isn't that sort of thing. Not here.'

They both stared at her.

She laughed, 'Londoners! There's a field by the school. Up the big road and turn round right. And much further on there's some nice woods with a stream. If you're good, I'll take you up there one day. Timmy and Sally like that place, don't you?' She turned to the little faces, with their pink noses and bright eyes. 'You boys run about and enjoy yourselves. There'll probably be school Monday.'

'School!' Alan nudged Billy. 'Do you think we'll go together?'

Billy felt his tummy lurch. He looked at Mrs Youldon. 'Well, I don't know, dear. We'll be told by the billeting officer, I expect,' she said as she took the dishes to the scullery. 'The school's not far. If you want, take the ball.' It was a sad-looking rubber thing with nicks and scratches all over it.

Billy saw the little mouse faces looking at him and he smiled. Timmy smiled back, while Sally hung her head. She had wisps of pale hair that hung round her ears. Timmy pushed a little wooden car along the bench just a few inches. It only had three wheels. Billy wondered who would mend it. He might have a go himself.

'Come on,' said Alan. They nodded and made for the door.

'Just a minute, boys. Take Timmy and Sally with you. They'll want to play. There's some other boys and girls in this road, so you can make some new friends.'

Did she really mean the little ones could play outside without their mother? Shouldn't Sally be in a playpen? But Billy could see there wasn't anything like one here.

Mrs Youldon moved to the scullery and poured water and washing soda into the sink.

'Let's explore,' Alan said.

Billy frowned, but Mrs Youldon said, 'Yes, perhaps that's best this first time. Find your way round the village. You can play with the little ones later. She took Sally's hand as they went outside.

They wandered from lane, to road, then another road where one or two houses were bigger, some with nice gardens. One had a thatched roof, very strange, so they stopped to stare at it. A cat came down the path, then a small, nearly bald person.

Alan nudged Billy and whispered. 'Gosh, it's a girl with hardly any hair.'

She was waving. 'Billy!' she shouted out, almost joyfully.

He couldn't work out for a moment how this awful thing knew his name. But as she got near he saw it was Sonia. Sonia, with no curls or ribbon, just tiny stubs of hair like a convict in Desperate Dan. He gawped at her and she began to cry.

'They cut my hair off in case I had nits,' she said. 'I can't go to school like this.'

The boys both said, 'No.'

Billy said, 'G-go in, go indoors. St-stay in bed when it's school day and say you've got a headache.'

Alan didn't know Sonia but he added helpfully, 'Ask to go to bed early, so they'll believe you in the morning.'

She started to say something, but a large lady with her hair in a bun came to the door and called, 'Sonia! Are you talking to rough boys?'

They moved off, just in case the woman searched their hair. Billy risked a small wave to Sonia.

'Gosh!' he said to Alan when they were at a safe distance. 'S-Sonia looks awful. She's got curls really, you know.'

'She hasn't now!'

'We sh-should rescue her.'

'Not likely— we don't want to be caught! That woman might be a witch. Let's go back.'

They ran faster and round a corner back to their lane. The little ones were hovering at the door. It looked as if they'd been waiting for Billy and Alan all that time. Billy ran forward and took their hands.

'Swinging?' Timmy said.

Billy followed Timmy's glance and at the end of the lane, children of various sizes were swinging round a tree at the end of a short rope.

Billy and Alan stood watching, wondering if this was allowed. 'C'm on,' Timmy pulled at his hand.

'Coming?' Billy asked Alan. They wandered down towards the game. Timmy stood behind the line of boys and Sally sat down on the side of the lane on the hard mud. No-one stopped her. 'She'll get grubby,' Billy muttered.

'S'pose Mrs Youldon doesn't mind.'

'Vaccies, vaccies,' two of the bigger girls called over to the boys while the other children stared without smiling.

Alan rubbed one sandal against another. 'Not keen on doing this, Billy.'

'You joining in, or what?' asked a large boy in tattered plimsolls.

They moved forward slowly.

One girl with her thumb against her lips, opened her eyes wide at them, especially at Alan. It was a rude look. She giggled. 'You, Freckles. D'you talk different? Say something.'

'Let's hear you,' said the large boy. 'Go on.'

'All right then. I'm Alan. He's Billy.'

There were shouts and laughter. 'Listen to 'um. Say some more. More.'

'It's you that talks funny,' said Alan.

'*Tohks funne e.* Yaw!' they all shouted as one, laughing and pointing. 'Vaccies!'

Billy bit his lips. They did sound different from these children. How could they change the way they talked? Suppose they got bullied at their school?

He looked back into Mrs Youldon's door. Did they *have* to play outside? Fancy allowing her little ones to! Dad would call swinging on the rope 'misbehaving'. You never saw such a thing as rope swinging in Primley Road. Probably a policeman would stop you. He hadn't seen any policemen here, none at all.

The set of four older children minced towards him and Alan, pretending to be them. 'Po-osh, po-osh. Look at youse, then, in youse London clothes.' They were laughing but not in a nice way. One of them had his fists clenched at the ready.

Billy couldn't run back to Mrs Youldon's because the little ones were ahead of him. He glanced at Alan as the four came nearer.

Alan took a step back. Before they could attack, Billy grabbed the rope and swung himself round as fast as he could. Whi-i-zz. It took the breath out of him. He could smell the grass, onions cooking, smoke as he swept past different doors and hedges. All he could see was a mash of children's heads, muddy road, and green banks with the twine of the rope in front of him. He staggered to a stop. The

109

threatening boys had been watching him, but were making right for Alan so he shouted, 'Come on, Alan. It's good fun.'

Alan shook his head.

'Yaw. Freckles can't do it. He's too namby pamby.'

'Alan, you do it,' Billy yelled urgently, throwing the rope towards him.

Alan grabbed it and swung round faster than Billy had.

'Ha! I'm faster'n that,' said the boy who'd spoken first, pushing the threatening four out of the way. 'I'm Big Ronnie, I'm ten. I live next door of yours. See how fast *I* go.' He swirled round, then pointed to Alan. 'Come on, Freckles, let's see you again then.'

Timmy ran towards the rope, Sally close behind him. She was too little but Timmy wanted to swing. Billy got ready to lift him up to the rope's end, Alan holding it.

This was quite a lot of fun, but it felt very wrong and he could see Alan felt bad about it. 'Playing out' wasn't the sort of play Mother and Dad would like at all. Did it matter, if it was all right with Mrs Youldon? Home seemed very far away.

'Look', said Alan, taking his hands off the rope. A neatly dressed lady rounded the corner and came towards them, holding her gloves. The other children ran off in a group, leaving the little ones squatting on the mud.

Billy stopped swinging the rope. 'Miss Johnson!'

'Billy, I've come to see whether you're all right. Yesterday was a hard time for you, walking all around the village. I'm sorry you were left till the very last.'

The awfulness of it rushed back like a swish of dirty rainwater. His eyes filled.

'But now you've got a new friend here. Is it Alan?'
He nodded.

'How is everything, Alan?'

'All right, Miss. Mrs Youldon is nice. But there isn't much to eat and we have to share a bed.'

'And there's n-no b-bathroom,' Billy choked back his tears.

Miss Johnson bent down to them. 'I'm afraid that's something you'll have to get used to. Not many of us have proper bathrooms down here. We're all somewhere very different from home. We have to make the best of things, boys. I know you'll try your very best. Now, I'll just go inside and speak to your foster mother. You can wait for me here.'

Billy kicked a ball lying in the mud, and ran after it so that Alan wouldn't notice his tears.

Miss Johnson came out again after a few minutes, a smile on her face. 'Good boys, you've made the right impression. I'm sure there'll be more to eat soon. Just be polite and fit in. We don't want this village to think badly of Londoners, do we? Now there may be church tomorrow, so make your way there when you hear the bells, all right?'

They went back to Mrs Youldon's just as a big girl stepped inside. She had a laughing voice, and a laughing face and a dress that only just covered her knees. 'H'llo, Joan. How is it? I heard you'd got vaccies. H'llo boys. Londoners, eh?'

It turned out that she was Mary, Mrs Youldon's older sister, but she had no children. The two girl-women chatted in front of the broken bit of mirror propped on the shelf, doing each other's hair and giggling. Mary had a handbag with a lipstick and powder. They took it in turns putting it on. Timmy and Sally hung onto their skirts.

Alan felt in his pocket for his fivestones. He and Billy went through to the back yard and played three contests with their backs to the privy, waiting for the sister to go so they could have their meal.

Alan groaned. 'I'm awfully hungry, are you?'

Billy nodded. He felt empty and miserable inside, deep down. 'Miss said there'd be more food soon. Are you going to tell her?'

'I don't know. Mrs Youldon doesn't seem to have much. If she hasn't got it, she can't give it to us.'

'And it's rude to ask.'

'I'm never hungry at home, are you?'

Billy shook his head. Suddenly he longed for Mother's soggy potatoes and mince with gravy. There was always enough to eat and often he left some on his plate. He didn't tell Alan this because his throat was all achy.

They hovered at the back door and neared the bench when Mary went on her way. Mrs Youldon said, 'Ready for your dinner?'

They nodded hard. 'Yes, please.'

She went into the scullery and found a wet cloth, wiping her hands with it and then the hands of Timmy and Sally.

'Up on the bench, you two.'

'Shall we go in the back and wash our hands, Mrs Youldon?'

She looked a bit surprised, then nodded. They squeezed by the clothes horse which had damp washing on it, and ran the scullery tap. There wasn't any soap now. Alan looked at Billy and shrugged. The bit of towel on the peg was torn and damp. They shook their hands hard, keeping the water drops away from the washing, and squeezed back into the main room, turning hopeful eyes on Mrs Youldon.

She had cooked sausages and some potatoes and cabbage. There was one sausage each and two over. Billy tried not to look at them, but he did, even though his mouth was full of potato, and he saw Alan doing the same.

Soon, their plates were probably the cleanest they'd ever been. Billy put his hands by his sides, politely. He couldn't put his hands on his lap without sitting on a chair and there still wasn't one.

Mrs Youldon had stopped to cut up the little children's food. Sally didn't look as if she was going to finish hers. Such a waste! Mrs Youldon finished her own, so slowly. Then she looked at the boys and said, 'My, you've finished already? I don't suppose either of you would like a little bit more?'

She started at their quick 'Yes pleases', but Billy was almost past caring. She gave them half a sausage each and shared the last small potato between them. It seemed only fair that she had the last sausage herself. 'Keep my strength up, for looking after all you,' she said.

When it was bedtime, they didn't feel at all tired but without electric light it seemed later than perhaps it was.

The candle was too low a light to read by although they both pored over Alan's comic.

'This is going to have to last a long time so you're not to touch it when I'm not here.'

Billy nodded. 'I wish I had some of my *Wizards*. We could've swapped.'

When Mrs Youldon called up to tell them to sleep they wriggled down sideways, one facing each way.

Alan was cross. 'Shove over, I haven't got room.' 'Neither have I.' He'd fall out if he moved any further. He put one hand on the crumbly wall.

Alan settled down after they'd given each other a few kicks.

Billy's knees pressed against the wall. If only he could stretch out in his own bed and look up at his aeroplane hanging from the ceiling. He thought of it all by itself in the empty room. And he'd never found out where Dad kept his contemplation, or what it looked like, or whether he'd even kept it after the Great War.

CHAPTER FIFTEEN
3rd September 1939

"War is declared, but win we will"

They were playing out, but keeping clean because of going to church later.

Suddenly, Mrs Youldon called out, waving wildly at them. She was with the lady next door who shouted, 'Come here, you boys. It's important.'

Big Ronnie pulled Billy and they all ran forward. She pulled them inside her open front door. She had a wireless that was crackling on a sideboard. Faint church bells came from it. Ronnie bent down to tune it better and the bells pealed louder. When he stood up, his round face looked bigger than Mrs Youldon's white one, although he was only ten.

'It's the Announcements, boys,' said Ronnie's mother. 'The eleven o'clock news said we had to listen at eleven fifteen. I told Joan you'd better all come in to hear.'

Mrs Youldon's eyes were wide and her fingers fumbled at the dishcloth in her hand.

They stood looked at the wireless, waiting. Billy held his stomach. It sounded deathly, the church bells ringing like that. Then the announcer's voice began, sounding like the pounding of a bell itself. Something about an 'ultimatum'. Then he said the country was at war.

A gasp. It was Billy's. It was everyone's.

The announcer was giving out lots of Don'ts. No sounding a hooter or whistle, because they were going to be used for air raid warnings. They'd hear rattles if gas was coming and then they must quickly put on their gas mask. They must always carry them.

Alan clutched Billy's shirt. 'Ours are under the camp bed!'

If they heard those noises, they had to go to the shelter straight away. And schools would be closed all week.

Ronnie let his breath out with a whistle. 'All ruddy week!'

'Shh! You heard the man,' said his mother.

When the announcements ended, the boys stayed standing exactly as they were. Timmy and Sally made no sound. Mrs Youldon put a hand on Alan's and Billy's shoulders. 'That's why you've come here, boys, to be safe from Hitler, see.'

Billy didn't answer. The voice had been so grim, nobody anywhere could feel safe, even in the country.

Ronnie was grinning and nudging Alan. 'No school for a week!'

Mrs Youldon moved to the front door, the little ones moving as one with her. Alan pushed Billy forward. 'Come on.'

Other mothers came out into the lane, saying it was awful. One of them was crying. 'Don't fret. It's not us down here that'll get bombed or gassed,' said another. 'It's them in London'll cop it. That's why we're lumbered with this lot,' and she jerked her head towards Alan and Billy. The women's eyes swivelled towards them.

Alan nudged him and they walked off down the road together. 'We didn't ask to come,' he muttered. 'I wish I was back home,' he turned around to squint at the groups of women sympathising and worrying with each other, 'and not with those lot.' He pulled out two barley sugars from his pocket. Here.'

'Thanks.'

They both sucked hard on the sweets. 'Have you got a brother?'

Billy shook his head. 'Have you?'

'No. We'll have to be like brothers then. Stick together.' He put his arm round Billy's shoulder.

It felt friendly. He said, 'I have got a c-cousin, he's comes round my home a lot. But he's really m-mean. And he hasn't been evacuated because Aunty can't do without him. He's always t-taking my toys or giving me Chinese burns, and he b-blames me for everything.'

'Rotten luck.' Alan was on his side. 'But why don't you do something about it? It won't change if you just put up with it.'

The church organ began distantly. It was quite a nice sound, like God trying to cheer everyone up.

'We've got to go to church,' said Alan. 'Remember, Miss said.'

Billy had forgotten. The barley sugar was all sucked away and he swallowed the last sugary drops. He stroked his throat. It was hurting. Everything was very scary. Surely, everything did have to be put up with?

They turned the corner. Some way down the road, there was Miss Johnson with several children hanging on to her hands or clothing.

'C-come on, Alan. We're all right.'

They ran up to her.

'You listened to the announcements, boys? Good.' She stood in the middle of the group. The faces of everyone turned to her. 'I know it's bad news, children. But, listen. We got you here to safety in time, didn't we? Now we all have to be brave and do our best. There won't be school for a bit because we teachers have to sort out how to fit everyone in.'

'When's air raid drill, Miss?'

'Oh, you'll be told exactly what to do and where to go if we have an air raid. But that's just in case. We're not likely to have one down here. That's why we've all come to the country.' She laughed in a long trill like a person on the wireless. 'Come along, we're going to church now.'

They walked on in an untidy group as the church came into sight bit by bit between the trees. The bells finished chiming. Mr Finlay stood sternly at the church door. 'No talking.' He stayed watching until they were all inside.

The twins weren't there. John slid into a bench beside Billy and Alan. He'd been billeted in a cottage right by the twins' farm.

'Dick and Mick are milking cows, lucky beggars. They're going to get out of going to church and all sorts of things, I bet.'

Alan nudged him. 'Shh. Vicar's coming.'

The service began and although Alan helped by picking up the right book, Billy couldn't possibly keep up with the words of the hymns –great long words that no-one had ever heard of.

After the Vicar talked of War Being Declared and Being Brave, he talked of Evacuees and welcomed the newcomers, so then everyone began listening. He told them that Life would be difficult for them and for their foster families but that everyone had to get used to different people and different ways.

'We have to shake down,' he said, 'shake down and do our best. We're living in turbulent times. This terrible news that we are at War means we don't know what's coming, but we fear it. It's a time when we all have to make changes and stand together firmly against the foe. Remember, God looks after his own.'

He did go on and on, but he didn't use too many long words. Soon he was saying that he was sure the Evacuees would be good and do their best, and that the locals would be very kind and do theirs, before touching the bible and blessing everyone.

The vicar stood at the door, shaking hands with the grown-ups. Billy filed out with the other children, looking as holy as he could.

Outside the church gates, the local children thumbed their noses and made rude noises. 'We didn't want youse here, anyways.'

CHAPTER SIXTEEN
October 18th 1939

Nazis require all Jews to wear Star of David

Billy could hardly remember his old life. On this golden October day he was lying on his bed struggling to remember something, anything about home. He got as far as remembering his father's beard but not his face. He saw a green dress for his mother and the tip-tap shoes she wore for going out. There was a line going down the back of each leg. She'd say, 'Are my seams right, Billy?' and he'd have to put his finger on the line and trace it down to her ankle so that she'd be sure. Where was Mother now? And Baby; he could just about hear her crying and picture her curly hair and dummy.

Billy had written his postcard giving the address after the very first night he'd slept there, but he still hadn't had a reply. Mother must've forgotten him already. She would be busy with Baby and Dad wouldn't have seen any letter if he was away at work.

Other boys had letters. At school, the 'vaccies' boasted about what they got from home, like clothes and paper books. Worst of all, they had food parcels and so did Alan. When Alan passed food over, Billy had nothing to offer Mrs Youldon. Mrs Youldon didn't hold it against him for not having food treats for her. 'It's not your fault, Billy.'

But having no comics or treats to share didn't help him at school. He'd already got thumped 'for speaking dotty.'

'An'when you *don't* go "d-d-d-", you got a posh voice,' the locals jeered.

But school wasn't really bad. Miss Johnson and Mr Finlay took the vaccies for nature walks when the locals had the classrooms for lessons. That was ever such fun, and afterwards they usually had a story.

It wasn't *horrible* in the billet. Mrs Youldon was kind. Tim and Annie did everything he said and always wanted to hold his hand and play with him. They made him feel important. Alan wasn't all that good at sharing, but otherwise he was all right. He wasn't mean like Kenneth so they didn't quarrel much at all, and Mrs Youldon didn't do any tellings-off or sendings-to-rooms. She seemed pleased to have big useful boys. They'd collect the wood for the fire, take the wet washing to the washing line, tear the newspaper into strips for toilet paper, empty the washing tub, wipe the little children's hands and keep them amused.

The main trouble was that he was always hungry. Alan was too. But Mrs Youldon was fair. They got the same as her own children and as she did herself. But the food wasn't enough and it wasn't particularly nice except when she opened a tin of corned beef. That came from Alan's mother.

All of this had taken his mind off home and family so far. But now he lay on the camp bed, back from school because of a sick headache, alone until Mrs Youldon got back from her ironing day at The Grange. Timmy and Annie would be playing in that lovely garden while they waited for her. They weren't much bigger than Baby, but she couldn't possibly be left to play on her own. She'd shriek the place down, or touch something dangerous. But perhaps Baby was bigger after all this time. Perhaps she didn't have tantrums any more.

Billy tried hard to remember what he could about 'Before'. He stretched out and waited for his headache to go away. It was a luxury to have the bed to himself. At home, he'd never dreamed of it ever being different.

He thought about his toys and his bedroom, not just a whole bed but a whole room to himself. His row of books, comics and annuals stood on a bookcase. If only he had them here! They were no use on their own in an empty bedroom. Were his planes still safe in the boxes under his bed? Suppose Kenneth sneaked up there! But no-one was at home now.

If he was at home he wouldn't even mind bedtimes! He remembered Mother saying, 'Into the bath, Billy. Time for bed.' A bath! A bathroom! Here it was a 'sit down wash' on Sundays in the hip bath which hung on a peg in the scullery. He wasn't always the first to use the water, so he hated that too. He missed the bathroom and the lavatory. He'd never get used to the privy at the end of the back yard. And dinners! Home ones now seemed wonderful and he never remembered being hungry there. His stomach was rumbling right now.

He heard Mrs Youldon come through the door. He padded downstairs in his socks. 'I was sent home. Had a headache.'

She pulled raw-looking hands from her pockets to feel his head. 'Been lying down?'

'Yes. But please can I have something to eat? I missed school dinner.'

She turned her mouth down and said, 'That's a bother. I've got broth for tea but only just enough bread.' She felt his head again. 'You're hot. Lie down again. I'll find a bit of porridge, all right? It might make you feel better.' She put a saucepan on the stove and started stirring. 'I can't have you being ill. It's hard enough as it is. When did your headache start, love?'

He thought. It wasn't there when he got up. It must've started at school. 'Miss was putting the date on the board for us to copy and my head hurt then. October 18th, my birthday. I'm eight today.'

'Oh my! Eight! We'll all have to sing the birthday song then, when it's tea.'

His last birthday he'd had presents from everyone. He wouldn't think about that. He'd think about the sabre. He gazed into space and summoned it up. He saw it lying across Angela's open hands, ready for the rightful owner to seize it just as it had been for King Arthur. He could thrust the sabre into the nearest enemy when he was old enough to go to war. He would go instead of Dad.

Mrs Youldon spooned him out some porridge and gave him a spoonful of brown sugar from the bag Alan's mother had sent. 'There, that'll make it taste really nice.' She licked her lips at Billy, and he knew she was enjoying the treat at second hand. He did that sort of thing sometimes too, like when a mother walked home with her boy from school, her arm around him. He spooned the porridge all up and his tummy stopped rumbling.

Mrs Youldon patted his shoulder. 'Can't have you hungry on your birthday. There. I reckon your headache'll go now.'

It was a good drying day. Alan was helping Mrs Youldon hang out the clothes. Most of the children were playing hop-scotch. Billy and Ronnie found a good rut in the lane for rolling marbles along.

They were busy racing them when a slight rumbling noise made them stop. A car was rolling down their lane. They often saw the milk cart and the bread van, occasionally the coal lorry, but not cars. So when this one slowed down right next to him, Billy looked wonderingly at its shiny black wheel hubs.

Ronnie stood up to peer in the window. The driver rolled it down a few inches. 'Young man, do you know William Wilson?'

Billy looked up. 'That's me, sir. I'm William Wilson.'

The man looked down at him disapprovingly and turned to his passenger in the back. 'He's right here.'

She put her head out of the window and gasped, 'Billy!'

At the same moment that he recognized his mother, Billy realized how shocking it was that he was playing in the road, in the earth. He looked at his knees and sure enough they were dirty. His socks were wrinkled around his ankles, like every-one else's. He'd lost his garters long ago.

His mother got out of the car and he stood beside her. He didn't quite like to look up. His face was probably a bit grubby. It was a moment or two before she spoke, 'Well, Billy, here I am. I hope you've been all right. It's been a long time but now I know where you are.'

She'd come to collect him at last! 'Yes, Mother. Am I going back with you today?' He turned to run inside and gather up his things right away.

She stepped forward, 'No, wait ' She tapped on Mrs Youldon's door. Together, they went indoors.

Mother took just one step, then stayed still at the door. Billy remembered Angela's Dutch doll. Its wooden arms and legs swung forward and back but not sideways, and didn't bend.

She spoke to the back of the room. 'Good afternoon. I'm Mrs Wilson, Billy's mother.'

Mrs Youldon had her hands to her apron, then her mouth. 'My goodness, Ma'am, we didn't expect you.' She brushed the easy chair for Mother to sit down then scuttled over to pull down the washing from over the stove, looking small as a mouse.

'Please don't trouble yourself,' said Mother, looking around, her eyebrows lifted high. 'And you are—?'

'Mrs Youldon, Ma'am.'

'*Mrs*?' Mother sounded surprised. 'The foster mother?'

'Yes, Ma'am.' She fiddled with a pillowcase, its corners tucked in. Her cheeks had gone pink. 'And these are my little ones, Sally and Timmy.' The two little faces peeped round the scullery door.

'You have children too! My goodness, where do they all fit?' Mother turned her head slightly to one side and then the other, her eyes wide and shocked.

'Yes, Ma'am. But Billy and A - ' she blinked a couple of times - 'Billy is such a helpful boy. He's been wondering why he hasn't had a letter from you. I said it was probably lost.'

Billy stood at the door half out of sight, licking his handkerchief and trying to clean his hands while Mother explained to Mrs Youldon that sadly Billy's postcard had arrived after she had been evacuated herself with her baby girl. His father found it when he returned home from working away.

'He sent Billy's card on to me and I've come straight away. Such a thing! Baby and I have been living with a vicar's family not even five miles away,' Mother said with a slight laugh. 'Fancy, and all the time Billy was right here.'

Mrs Youldon gaped. 'I must offer you tea, Ma'am but I haven't enough milk. I could run to my neighbour's. It'll only take a minute.'

'Please don't worry. The vicar who kindly brought me is waiting outside.'

She opened her velour bag and brought out some jumpers and underclothes.

'I expect you could do with a few more clothes for Billy,' she said.

'Ooh, they're lovely,' Mrs Youldon held them up. 'Shop clothes. They can go under his bed for best.'

'No,' said Mother, looking Billy up and down. He felt very awkward. The shirt was tattered and the shorts were Ronnie's cast-offs.

'Worn-outs more like', Alan had muttered privately when they'd first been given them.

'These can be worn now. It's getting colder. He'll need them.' She eyed the shirt and baggy shorts. 'Erm— thank you for lending him clothes, but he can give them back now and wear his own. This green jumper is suitable for school and— '

124

Billy leaned forward, 'But aren't I going with you, Mother? Now you've found me. I can have a wash...'

Mother looked at Mrs Youldon. 'It'll be a while yet, I think.'

Mrs Youldon stood nodding and nodding, still fiddling with her pillow-case.

After giving him a jumper to cover up the shirt, Mother took Billy outside. 'I can't take you with me, Billy, I'm sorry. Safest for you to stay here; although not in this billet if I can help it. Outrageous!'

'I could stay at your billet.'

'But there isn't any more room where I am, there really isn't. The vicarage is overcrowded as it is. They have two teachers and an older child, as well as us. And Baby still has tantrums, so we walk a lot, to keep the noise out of the way. I don't know how I'd manage if I had to get you to a school as well.'

Her voice rose higher and she twisted her gloves between her fingers. 'It's very difficult, being away from home. Very difficult. I've just come to visit you, check that you're well. Now I know where you are, I can come again.'

She put a hand on his front to push the shirt collars under the jumper. 'Dear me, what a mess you look. I'm so embarrassed, but you'd better come over to the vicar and say How do you do.'

She looked all flying hair and worry lines as she went over to the car where the vicar, looking fairly patient, sat behind the wheel.

'This is my son. Forgive his appearance. You would have thought he would have been placed in a home like his own, not a hovel.'

Billy followed her. 'How do you do, sir.'

The vicar shook Billy's hand doubtfully and then looked at his own as if working out how long it would be before he could reach a washbasin. 'Mrs Wilson, let me visit my counterpart in the vicarage here while you and Billy go for a little walk together.' The car

125

purred off, several of the children in the lane running after it.

Mother's eyes went wide and hard. 'I hope you wouldn't do such a thing, Billy. Now, where can we walk?'

'The Grange? It's the nicest place. Mrs Youldon does ironing there.'

'I see.'

'And we had a party there once, with balloons. A man played the piano, we sang songs and they gave us two sherbet dips when it was over.'

'Lucky boy! No such luck for us.'

'You could bring Baby next time you come, Mother?'

'No, dear. It's too difficult with her fidgeting and crying. I can't expect the vicar to bring us by car again. I shall have to come by bus and find someone who'll have Baby for the afternoon. As it is, the vicar's wife is very kindly looking after her this once, while I visit you.'

She looked down at his face. Then she said in a comfortable, strange-but-kind-lady voice, 'I've got an orange for you and some sweets.'

He went to take them, 'Oh thank you.' He hadn't seen an orange since his seventh birthday party. He began to tear off the peel.

'Not here!' Mother said. 'In the street? Eat them when you get back to the hou— to your billet.'

'But then I'll have to share them.' He stopped. 'Perhaps I should. I bet Sally's never seen an orange.'

She didn't answer.

They walked on. He saw his mother looking down at his legs and feet. It was no good pulling up his socks, they only fell straight back down. He could tell she was about to say something.

It was Mother's visit being so sudden that stopped his news from rushing out of him. Words seemed choked in his throat. He didn't even manage to say she'd missed his birthday, or that he was always hungry. He could tell she didn't like the way he looked, or his new home. He swallowed. He was guilty of getting to be a worse boy. He must find something that would please Mother.

'I came top in mental arithmetic,' he tried.

It was no good. Now that they were well away from any other people, he could sense that Mother was going to tell him off.

'Billy! It was such a shock when we drove up and saw you. What were you doing playing in the road like that?

Why don't you play in a friend's garden? Where are your garters and where are your proper clothes?'

'Under Mrs Youldon's bed in a parcel. I wear them for best. I go to Sunday school in them. But I play in these.' He looked down at the plimsolls and tattered shorts.

She tutted. 'No more. And I can't have you playing in the gutter. I don't know what you were thinking of.'

'Mrs Youldon likes us to play out after we've had our food.'

'Out? She *lets* you play in the street, do you mean? Doesn't anyone around here have a garden?' She looked despairingly at the tightly terraced homes with their thin muddy strip at the back. Billy didn't dare mention the privy or the hip bath. It was all his fault for being chosen last. It would be awful if she found that out. And he didn't want her to be mean to Mrs Youldon. It wasn't her fault. Wasn't there really any room for him at the Vicarage?

'Do you have to share beds where you are, Mother?'

'No of course not! Do you?'

'I share with Alan. He's eight, like me.' Surely she'd remember she'd missed his birthday now.

'Alan? There's actually another evacuee in your billet?'

'Mm. He's nice. You'd like him.'

There was a pause as they marched on at a smart pace.

'I shall ask for you to be moved to another billet. It's totally unsatisfactory. And I'll send you some garters.'

They neared the school. Billy felt her looking at him.

She said, 'You look a bit peaky.'

'I get a bit hungry.'

Her face softened. He rushed to take his opportunity.

'Mrs Youldon doesn't always have enough.'

'Oh dear. I'd see about a food parcel for her if I was at home.' She patted his hand, the one with the orange and sweetie bag in it. 'You can eat your sweets now if you like, but don't throw the papers down, please. As I say, I shall have to get you a different billet.' She looked down, frowning, and stopped talking.

Now he'd found his voice again, Billy chatted about his new life while they walked past The Grange for her to admire the drive and the gardens, then around to the church and back down the narrow road to the lane where he now lived.

'The vicar will be back. I must go. Look out for his car. Now, keep yourself clean, Billy, or no-one will want to take you in.'

So that's why Mother wasn't taking him with her! But he *had* been clean when his school arrived in the village and no-one had wanted him anyway.

'I promise I'll keep myself clean, Mother.' He could find a rag to hang in the scullery ready for cleaning himself up when she visited.

They walked back, a fierce wind blowing from behind. Mother looked at her watch. 'We're nearly back to your lane, aren't we? Time for me to go, Billy.'

He felt around in his jacket pocket. 'I drew some aeroplanes, Mother. They can be for Baby but I don't suppose she'll like them.'

'Oh, she will. She's kept all the ones Kenneth has sent her. He's a wonderful drawer, isn't he?'

'He's written to you, to Baby?'

'Auntie writes and puts his little drawings into the envelopes.'

He kicked at a stone. 'Is the war nearly over?'

'Not yet, dear, I'm afraid.'

'But there haven't been any bombs, have there?'

'Well not yet - but there might be.'

He breathed in and looked right up at Mother. 'Why's Kenneth not having bombs in London *and* he's not evacuated.'

She shrugged her shoulders. 'It's no good asking me, Billy. He's not my son. And perhaps Doreen was right to keep him back. What do I know about war? I'm kept away from my home the same as you.'

The vicar's car reappeared in the lane ahead. Mother waved. Several children were running alongside it. Big Ronnie was standing outside his house, hands on his hips, waiting.

'Have you *got* to go, Mother?'

She bent and tidied his shirt collar. 'Now, keep yourself clean and tidy. I'll see you soon, Billy.'

'Will it be next Saturday?'

'No, but I will come when I can. Now, say Goodbye to the vicar, properly.' She looked meaningfully at him.

He went round to the driver's side, his hair blowing into his eyes. 'Goodbye, sir. Thank you for bringing Mother to visit.'

The vicar nodded. 'Remember your prayers, young man.'

Billy moved away quickly. He blinked his eyes hard. Apart from school prayers, he hadn't remembered them at all.

'Oof. Glad to be out of this wind!' Mother slid into the back seat where a magazine lay open.

'Goodbye Mother.'

She leant out of the window. 'Goodbye. Be good, and get your hair cut, do.'

129

Big Ronnie was sitting on his doorstep watching. He thumbed his nose at Billy and shouted '*Be good. Get your hair cut*'. His face divided into an evil grin.

Mother didn't hear. She'd wound the window up. The car moved off. Billy kept waving until he saw her open her magazine to look at hairstyles and skirts.

He shivered. The wind was so strong that if she'd brought him a comic it would probably have blown right away.

Billy turned his head away from Ronnie and ran indoors. He slipped upstairs to sit by himself to think about his family.

He shut his eyes and 'saw' Baby, Nanny and Grandad, Angela, the Cossack sabre. If the war went on long enough he'd be old enough to be a soldier, Mr Durban would be very old and die. Although that would be sad as sad, Angela would give Billy the sabre because he'd be going to war while she'd just be staying at home, a girl, a woman, being kept safe.

CHAPTER SEVENTEEN
November 29th 1939

*Many evacuees return to London against advice
to leave children safe in the country*

Billy kicked a stone to and fro outside the front door. Some of the Vaccies had already been collected and others had been put on trains back to London. Even Alan's next letter from his mother said she was coming to take him home.

Alan danced around outside. 'Yippee!' Then he stopped and put his arm round Billy. 'You'll be next, don't worry.'

Billy shrugged. Mother hadn't visited for a while, so it didn't seem likely that she'd collect him even though Dad had said 'Christmas' when they told him about evacuation.

It would mean more room without Alan, especially in bed, but it was miserable, him going. He and Alan did everything together. 'It won't be nearly as good here without you.'

'Cheer up! If Mummy brings me chocolate biscuits, I'll give you one.'

When the day came, Mrs Youldon had all Alan's clothes clean and ready packed. Alan stood on the doorstep for ages before his mother arrived, and then he gave her such a huge hug. His mother had lots of smiles on her face but wet eyes. She thanked Mrs Youldon many times and gave her a tin of biscuits. She was really kind because she gave Billy a bag of bull's-eyes before she took Alan away.

'I'll see you when war's over,' he called to Billy, and marched smartly down the road with one hand in his mother's and the other holding his suitcase.

Billy held a heavy hand up to wave back. When would that be?

At bedtime, having the bed to himself felt colder and sadder. Mrs Youldon found a second blanket but it was only thin. Winter was deepening and it was very cold at night. It was dark soon after tea, now, so he played inside with Tim and Sally, making up games for them with all sorts of scraps.

Mrs Youldon was chopping onions again to make soup. It wasn't a horrible smell but it stayed around all the time.

She wiped her eyes. 'Only onion tears, me. You're not sad, now, are you, Billy? Not fed up because you haven't got Alan to help with the jobs?'

He shook his head. It felt very comfy in other ways, being Mrs Youldon's big important boy. No-one nagged him about his stammer. Actually, he hadn't noticed whether he had stammered for some time.

'It's going to be Christmas ever so soon, Mrs Youldon. My father said I was here until Christmas.'

'Then your Ma will come for you, I'm sure. Perhaps things aren't quite ready at home yet. She'll come soon.'

He didn't believe it. Mother was probably very happy at the vicarage.

Mrs Youldon didn't have a wireless, but what Ronnie told him about the news was horrible, all about ships being sunk and planes being shot down. The only good thing was that Uncle Ted was a soldier and not a sailor or an airman.

Miss Johnson had the younger vaccies and village children together all day. Now the school wasn't so crowded they could all fit into the classroom, not have it for just half the day. That was good, because it was jolly cold for nature walks. She led sing-song classes, because it was important to *Keep Your Sunny Side Up*. They learned new songs, ones they could almost shout in, like *It's a Long Way*

132

to Tipperary. Singing was quite jolly and soon more singing went on in the playground than fighting.

They made Christmas decorations the last week of term. They couldn't get red and dark green, only pale green and pink. Billy managed to save some of the strips to bring home for Timmy and Sally, but Mrs Youldon hadn't any glue to make the chains. He was going to ask Miss Johnson if he could have the left-over glue when it got to the last day of school.

He was building a tower of his playing cards with Timmy when there was a bang on the door. Mrs Youldon stopped her sewing and went to lift the latch.

A deep voice said, 'Good evening. Mrs Youldon?'

She took a step back and let the man in. He had a beard. The man reminded him of Dad. He looked at the face blankly until it said,

'Billy? Aren't you going to come and say *Hello* after all this time?'

Billy's hand was halfway in the air, ready to put another playing card on the tower he was building for Tim. He couldn't think, suddenly. Tim took it from him and the tower fell, flip flop flip off the bench onto the floor.

'Oh dear,' said Dad, stepping over the pile to put a hand on Billy's shoulder.

'Mr Wilson!' Mrs Youldon cleared the newspaper strips and offered him the chair.

'My apologies for the lack of notice,' he said as he sat down. 'I've been working just over the county border and I wanted to take the opportunity to collect Billy. It does seem safe enough in London, at least for the time being. And Christmas is nearly upon us. A colleague with a car is kindly giving us a lift home. We're very lucky.'

With Dad's legs almost touching the bench, the room felt very crowded. Billy stayed crouched very close to Timmy, staring at Dad's black shoes. They were the same. He remembered them.

'Have you lost your voice, Billy?'

133

He put a hand to his throat. 'Dad? Are you taking me home?'

Dad nodded. 'Indeed. No moss gathered here.'

Billy had left his at school on the Nature Table. That was a shame.

Mrs Youldon was still standing, pressing her hands together. 'I can offer you tea, sir - er Mr Wilson.'

Dad waved a no-thank-you hand. 'So. Billy. Are you going to get your things?'

'But what about Mother and Baby?'

'They've already gone. They went by train. Go and pack your suitcase. Bring everything.'

Sally sidled up to hug Mrs Youldon's knee, staring at Dad. 'Not go, Billy.' Her face puckered.

Timmy collected all the cards together in a pile, one by one. His hands hung loose on his lap.

Billy ran upstairs and packed very quickly, leaving all the play clothes on the bed.

When he came down, Dad was thanking Mrs Youldon for looking after him all this time. 'I'm sure you'll be glad of the peace with both boys gone. Here's what I think we owe you.' He handed over an envelope and a brown package.

She bowed her head. 'Really grateful.'

'Don't mention it. Now. Ready, Billy?'

Billy had changed into his school uniform with an extra jumper on top and then his mac and his cap. His socks were pulled right up. Mother had sent him garters after her first visit and he'd been careful not to lose them. He pulled his fingers through his hair. He felt fairly sure he looked all right. 'I'm ready, Dad.'

Dad looked him up and down. 'Where can he have a wash, please? I can't take him out to my colleague looking like this.'

'Oh dear.' She put the envelope and package on the bench. 'He looks all right to me, but I'll give him a rub. We weren't expecting you,' she said.

134

She took Billy into the scullery and found a towel. She wetted one end under the tap and scrubbed away at his face and knees.

'I shall miss you,' she whispered.

Feeling bold, he put his arms round her, and her shoulders were bony. If only he could bring her, all of them, back with him to share all the food locked up in the larder at home. 'You're the bestest billet,' he whispered back.

CHAPTER EIGHTEEN
December 21ˢᵗ 1939

Winter may be the worst for decades

That first night was lost in the long car journey. The man driving gave Billy a blanket to put over his lap and told him to stay quiet in the back so that he could concentrate on his finding the way. Dad soon seemed to be dozing.

The driver murmured to himself, 'Darn good job I know this route.' It was jolly hard to see the way ahead with no lights. Billy was used to it in the country, walking around with a torch like everyone else, but last time he was on the road at night there were lights from all the traffic. Now car headlights and traffic lights were shielded with sort of folders. They drove through dark villages and then into a town. Even now there were no lights. The buses had lights inside dimmed to a glow, so were almost on top of them before Billy saw them. Once, the car almost bumped into a person crossing the road, and he cursed.

More countryside and almost invisible villages before a really big town where all the shop windows were completely dark. Then they reached the black of hills and woods. It was easier to nod off than to wonder about enemy hiding in them.

When Dad said, 'We're home,' Billy opened bleary eyes onto a sea of black. They could have been anywhere. Dad shivered, 'Certainly a bad fog tonight.'

He thanked his friend and shut the car door quietly. The car slid away, becoming invisible within seconds. Billy could see white rings gleaming faintly. They seemed to be swimming mid-air.

'What's them?' he muttered sleepily.

'So that you won't bump into the trees. Look out now.'

He saw that the nearest white ring was painted round the tree trunk, and round all the trees up the road.

Billy stumbled forward to a ditch-dark doorway. When Dad tapped on it, Mother stood there in a blue dress he'd seen lots of times long ago, but now it seemed like a fairy tale. The long hall yawned behind her, the doors and stairs a wilderness. He could hardly believe this was his home. No light showed until the front door shut.

'Took forever,' said Dad, as he put the bags on the hall floor and kissed Mother's cheek. 'You settled in then? Did you manage to light the boiler?'

She nodded, then looked at Billy. 'Good to be home, dear? We came back yesterday. Phew what a journey, my goodness! Straight upstairs, now, Billy. You're half asleep. It's so late. And quiet footsteps. Don't wake Baby.'

Dad took him upstairs, which felt very odd. He put him to bed with a sheet over him as well as under, and long enough to tuck in. The blankets felt so thick and cosy. He lay in the soft bed, almost dreaming the voices in the room below him as sleep washed over him again.

When he woke, the bed felt wrong, too big and too bouncy, and the ceiling looked high and different. Then he saw his aeroplane dangling from the ceiling and sat up, excited. He'd really come home. He ducked his head underneath his bed and drew out his box of small aeroplanes. There was a film of dust on top. He smiled to himself. He'd play all morning with them.

He padded round his room reminding himself of all his things: planes, cars, puzzles, farm, bricks, shelf of books, even the wardrobe of clothes and the chest of drawers. He'd forgotten what loads of things he owned. The hobby horse leant sadly against the wall. He patted its head. 'Sorry, Horsey, too old for you now.' But he still liked looking at Horsey. He'd leave it standing there.

Behind his door was his checked dressing gown. Suddenly he had more than a pyjama jacket for facing a cold morning. He slipped it on and the sleeves still touched his hands. He hadn't grown.

Outside the door a little voice called out, 'Mummy.' Baby! He was curious to see her again. Did she still have tantrums? Would she still grab his toys? He peeped round his door. A small girl with a flushed face and a trailing nightie stood by Mother's bedroom. He tried to see Baby in her, but she was different. She stared at him with a wobbly lip, then Mother came out and took her hand. 'Look, it's your brother Billy.'

'Hello Baby,' Billy said.

'It's Jill,' said Dad's voice deep from the bedroom. 'She's not going to be a baby forever.'

Billy shut himself in his bedroom again. Jill. He'd almost forgotten her name. Bill and Jill. How silly of Dad and Mother. Hadn't they noticed? He fingered his biplane for quite a while, until he was told to wash and dress.

As soon as he'd done, he ran downstairs and found them all sitting at the dining table.

'My name rhymes with hers. Bill, Jill.'

'What a cross voice on your first morning back home. Jillian and William, not exactly the same.'

'S-sorry.' But they sounded the same to him, and he was glad Mother was still calling her 'Baby'.

'Sit down there and eat your bacon. We may not get much more of this from now on.'

Billy sat and ate his bacon and egg eagerly. A long time since he'd had this! Any cooked breakfast was a tremendous treat and he knew all about not getting much any more. He felt each mouthful deliciously tasty on his tongue before he chewed and slowly swallowed. Looking across to the larder door, he saw it wasn't locked. Would it still be full of food, like before he went away?

Mother was wearing a red jumper with white fuzzy blobs and a little red scarf round her hair. She had lots more clothes than Mrs Youldon, as well as having bacon. Baby crashed her spoon onto her plate saying 'La, la, la-la.'

He smiled at her as he put in another lovely mouthful. Mother was cross. 'You are not a country savage now, Billy. Put your fork down between mouthfuls. And stop that infernal noise, Baby.'

Dad's voice sounded deep. "*A house divided against itself cannot stand.*"– Abraham Lincoln.'

Billy looked up. It seemed very strange to have a man beside him. He'd forgotten all about Dad's sayings. What did this one mean? Bombed houses could not stand.

Mother placed a larger plate of breakfast in front of Dad and a cup of steaming tea. 'Wise words are all very well, Herbert. It's so difficult just being back. It took all my time yesterday getting the boiler going, doing the beds and queuing for food. I can hardly find anything clean in the house. It's so dusty after all this time. And no Mrs Donnington! The evacuation was all for nothing. I wish I'd never gone away.'

'Better safe than sorry. To me, it was worth it for peace of mind. But, by Jove, it feels nice to have you bring my breakfast again, Marcia.' He smiled up to her. 'I'm sure you'll adapt. We can't resent Mrs Donnington for doing her bit for the war. The buses need conductors.'

'I suppose I shall have to manage.' She was looking anxiously at Baby banging her spoon as if she'd never be able to manage her, or perhaps that Dad wouldn't put up with the noise.

'And wonderful for me to have the children here, of course,' he added, turning to say something to Billy, but Mother interrupted,

'You have egg on your chin, Billy. Where's your napkin?'

He'd forgotten about napkins, it had been so long since he'd seen one. He pulled his out of its silver ring and flicked it onto his lap. In Mrs Youldon's home this would probably be used as a towel except it was too smart. In the village right now she'd be sending Sally and Tim to play out after their grey porridge. They'd have to run up and down the street without him.

Billy hadn't said Goodbye properly. The little ones had been huddled by the playing cards and paper strips as Dad had taken him to the car, Timmy's arm around Sally. He'd come away without doing their Christmas presents or making their paper chain. He should have used some of his Uncle Ted's shilling to buy pipe cleaners at the village shop and shown them how to make cars and little people holding hands. Now they might not have anything for Christmas because Mrs Youldon wouldn't have his billeting money any more. Could he could post his shilling? Was it right to ask? Mother was frowning over the teapot. Dad, he could see, was very busy eating and thinking about work.

Dad said, without looking up, *'Silence more beautiful than any song* – Rossetti.'

Probably he was practising what he'd say at work. It must be a funny place, Court, with people doing these sayings. After Mrs Youldon's home, Dad's voice sounded strange. And Dad was like a stranger after all this time.

Mother muttered, 'Well, Herbert, I should think you've had enough of silence without us.'

Billy nibbled a piece of toast. Christmas was only a few days away but no-one had said anything. Were there presents wrapped up and hidden under his parents' bed? Where was the tree, the decorations? He wanted to ask Mother about Christmas, but she might get cross. He couldn't tell what made her cross now. He'd only seen her three times since being evacuated and she was wearing a skirt and jumper he'd never seen before. She was snappy even to Baby and her face was all sort of tied up.

His eyes strayed to Baby. To *Jill*, if he could get used to saying that silly name. Silly Jilly. No, it was "Silly Billy" people said when they made mistakes. Why did he have to be called Billy? It wasn't fair.

Jill's face was quite fat. He was used to Sally who was about the same height. Sally's face was thin and she had a shy little smile. Baby was cross and looked it. She didn't have a dummy any more but she did look as if she might still scream.

'You can play with Baby after breakfast,' said Mother. 'Jill,' said Dad, as he put his coat on. '*Jill*, dear. You must use her name. She's walking. She's a child now. If she goes to a nursery, she can't be called "Baby", can she?' He went to the door. 'I'm afraid I must be off to Chambers. *No peace unto the wicked* – Isiah. I have to report in and look at the next listings. Judge Wiggins presiding. Everything must be just so. I'll be back by tea, Marcia. Don't forget to pin up the blackout properly. It's sagging.' He clucked at Jill and said 'Be helpful' to Billy before disappearing to his important work.

Baby, *Jill*, stared after him, then turned her plate upside down.

Billy asked, 'What does she p-play?' as he rescued it.

Mother didn't seem to hear him. She was clearing the breakfast things and looking at suitcases which needed unpacking. 'There'll be a lot of sorting out to do,' she was muttering, lines in between her eyebrows.

Billy knew what was wrong. Mother didn't like having to do Mrs Donnington's work, now she was back home.

She lifted Baby down from her high chair and stood her in front of Billy. 'There you are, Billy. Now I have a lot to do, so you keep her amused, please. And keep the toys to one side so that I don't trip over them as I come to and fro.'

A pile of her toys sat on a box ready for her to play with. It should be easy to amuse her.

Baby stood on chubby legs. Her pink shoes had a shiny white button on the side of each strap. He couldn't imagine her playing out and spoiling them. He picked a toy up and showed her, and put it down again. She did nothing. After a lot of staring at Billy, she showed that she liked putting her doll in a blanket and taking it out again. She wasn't interested in building houses of cards. When Mother came back into the room she toddled over and clung to Mother's skirt, although Billy was trying to play with her.

'Oh well,' sighed Mother, taking Baby's hand. 'You might as well play upstairs then, Billy.'

He went upstairs gladly. His own room now, all and everything to himself.

He'd just pulled his box of aeroplanes out from under the bed and organised some bricks to be aircraft hangers when Mother trilled up the stairs in a new voice.

'Billy! Guess what?'

Billy's heart started thudding. Dad might have hidden the Christmas tree in the garden. He rushed to his door. 'Is it a tree? Or fairy lights?'

'No, dear,' Mother said in a calming down voice. 'It's your cousin. So long since you've seen him. Look out of your window.'

His tummy seemed to turn upside down. He looked out, and saw the back of a boy going round their path towards the side door and Aunty Doreen, further behind, still on the pavement. He heard the door open and his mother's voice, friendly and welcoming, then Aunty's, excited and chatty.

'Bi- lly,' sang a familiar voice up the stairs. 'Coming to ge-et you.' And it was followed by the clip-clop of feet in heavy shoes. Billy shoved all his toys quickly under the bed and came out onto the landing. He started down the stairs and met Kenneth who was bigger, his hair longer, his camel face the same. He pushed his face forward so that Billy backed up the stairs.

'Hello, Chicken. Had to run away to safety? Evacuee. I stayed at home. Mummy couldn't do without me. Where did you go? To the country. With all the pigs and cows, Mooo-ooo.'

'Not with pigs and cows. It was a village. With country round.'

'There weren't any bombs here anyway,'

'I know.'

'So it was a waste you going.' His hand came out from under his newly knitted jumper and pushed Billy backwards into his bedroom. 'I've been playing with all your friends.'

'You haven't! You're not even *at* my school.'

'I am now. My school closed because too many children went away. Our lot that stayed behind joined up with what was left of your lot and had your school. It's nice as pie. Reg and Andrew and Jim are all my friends now.'

'Bet they're not.'

'Bet they are. They've forgotten you, you've been away so long.'

Billy sat down on the stairs. This was awful. He could hear the chatty voices downstairs. Mother hadn't seen Aunty for ages and she was cooing about all the new things Baby could do.

'I'm going to say Hello to Aunty,' he said, pushing past Kenneth.

'She's busy. I want to play with your things. Come on.'

'Not now.'

'Yes. I want to see them all again.

'No.'

'I'll tell.'

Billy ran downstairs, as if he couldn't wait to see Aunty Doreen again, and perhaps he couldn't. He liked Aunty. He stood at the parlour door. She looked sort of fluffy, her hair very curled up and a frill on her skirt. Baby was clinging to Mother's knees and staring at Aunty whose hands were stretched out towards her.

'She'll get used to me soon enough, now you're back, bless her.'

'Hello Aunty—'

'Oh it's Billy! Hello dear. So grand to have you home.'

She smiled and patted his arm. 'Long time, no see. Excited to see our Kenneth again, I'll bet.'

Billy twiddled one of the tassels on Aunty's chair cushion. 'Is Kenneth really with all my f-friends at school?'

'I expect so. Now the stay-behinds are put together so there's enough teachers. And you'll have made some new friends out there in the country, won't you?'

He nodded, suddenly remembering how awful it was not to have Alan any more.

Aunt Doreen drew him towards her and looked him up and down. 'The country air hasn't fattened him up any, Marcia. Look. His arms are quite skinny.'

Aunty wouldn't understand. She'd never have been in a cottage like Mrs Youldon's. 'Mrs Youldon hasn't got a lot of food, Aunty. She does share it and Alan's mother sends food parcels sometimes.'

Mother put her hands to her face. 'Oh dear, I just brought things when I visited. I didn't really think.

Billy did say he got hungry, but then boys always say that. Baby and I were fed ever so well at the vicarage.'

'I must say, Marcia, both you and Jill look positively blooming.'

'Yes, we do enjoy the country food. I'd have thought Billy got the same. The billets do get an allowance for evacuees, after all.'

'She g-got eight and six for me,' Billy said.

'Do I cost eight and six, Mummy?' Kenneth pushed his way forward.

'And the rest! Whatever you cost, you're worth every penny, my little man,' said Aunty.

Worth every penny— Kenneth? Ugh! But he knew Aunty meant it. She poured herself another cup of tea from the second best teapot. There was no lump sugar on the tea tray for her. He used to take a lump, sometimes, when it was only Aunty around.

'You h-haven't got sugar, Aunty.'

'Learning to do without, Billy. Aren't we all?'

Mother said, 'The Simpkins, next door to you, Doreen, are they back from Wales?'

The mothers started to chat about all the people they knew and what they were doing. He needed desperately to tell Aunt Doreen lots of news so that they wouldn't be sent to play upstairs. The words wouldn't come out quickly enough. 'Aunty, w-when I was away we had n-nature w- walks and I –I've been m-making d-decorations at my n- new school. P-paper chains and— '

Aunt Doreen looked across to Mother with a sympathetic glance. 'He still has his little problem, then?' She turned to Billy.

'Yes, dear. Let's speak slowly. Paper chains? That's nice.'

'And I lived with a n-new friend called Alan.'

'Not A-A-Alan?' said Kenneth.

'Kenneth! That's not like you. Don't make fun of Billy's stutter,' Aunty Doreen said.

'I thought you'd lost that stutter, Billy,' Mother said in a disappointed voice.

'I had.'

'He can't help it,' said Kenneth lowering his lashes.

'That's right, dear,' said Aunty. 'He can't. You have to give him time to get the words out. Remember that when you're playing, Kenneth.'

'Of course, Mummy,' Kenneth lifted his lip at Billy and whispered in his ear, 'because he's so soppy.'

'Such a lovely smile, your Kenneth,' said Mother. 'Billy, I never see you smile like that. In fact, you don't smile much.'

Billy put his hands to his mouth to feel if it would stretch sideways like they wanted.

Aunt Doreen got out her knitting. It was long, a dirty sort of green. 'I've joined the WVS, Marcia. You'll have to. We can be ever so useful, turning our hands to whatever's needed. We don't have the formality of the services, you see.'

'Oh, I couldn't. I still can't knit.'

'It's not just knitting. There's the catering side.'

'Ugh. And I've got the little one.'

'Anyway you could knit while she plays. Of course you can learn. You could have learned at the Women's Institute before you were evacuated. I'd better teach you now.'

Mother looked doubtful. She glanced at her fingers with their long pink nails and then at Aunty's, which were flicking to and fro like machinery.

'These will be army socks,' Aunty said. 'The soldiers will be glad of them. If we're shivering in this bitter cold, think how it'll be in the trenches.'

'Is that where Uncle T-Ted is, in the trenches?'

'I'm sure he's fine,' said Mother. 'He would have said, if not. All his letters are very jolly.'

'And is Uncle F-Frank a soldier now?' Billy asked. It would be awfully good without him here, and the trenches might make him nicer when he got home afterwards.

146

'No dear. Tax Inspectors are exempt.'

Bother. He'd just had a tiny hope that the government had made Uncle go to war.

'Daddy's job is too important. He can't be spared to fight,' Kenneth said.

'Well, my D-dad's still here. So his is im-p-portant, too, isn't it Mother? He does Assizes.'

Mother raised her eyebrows at Aunty, who grimaced.

Kenneth said, 'And I'm still needed here, too, aren't I, Mummy? I *can't* be evacuated.'

'Oh yes, my little man. You're needed here.'

Billy squinted at Mother sideways. 'You had to take Baby away to keep her safe, didn't you Mother?'

She nodded.

'So there was no-one at home for me.'

Mother smiled with a little bit of her mouth. The lipstick was only on the front bits. She'd told him once it was a cupid's bow.

'That's right. We thought it was safest if you went away with the school.'

Kenneth put his head on one side and flicked his eyelashes at Mother. 'Are you and Jill staying home all the time now, Aunty Marcia? Then Billy can. We haven't had any bombs here. He can be back at school with me.'

'Oh, you missed your cousin, didn't you, Duckie? Such good fun you always have together,' said Aunty Doreen.

She turned to Mother, nodding her head. 'Work on Herbert, Marcia, so you can stay here. There's some lovely dances on. You know how you love dancing. Got to have some fun, war or no war. Nothing's really happened here after all. It's all happening at sea, or in France. You'd be better off here. And Billy will. He and Kenneth can go through the war together.'

Having the war AND Kenneth. That wouldn't be fair. Billy wanted Alan back and their country school,

147

the nature walks and the shared lessons. He wanted Mrs Youldon and the little ones. He didn't want the war and Hitler. 'I can't stay home, can I Mother? I have to be evacuated.'

'We'll see. We'll learn what your father thinks. He'll know best.' She turned to Aunty Doreen. 'To be honest, I can't think straight. I'm just home. Mrs Donnington's left us to do war work. Everything's covered in dust. I haven't fully unpacked. There was nothing much in the shops yesterday. Baby can't understand where she is or who she's with and she's a handful at the best of times. Plus I've got Billy to look after now, too.' Her voice rose to a high pitch. 'It's so difficult, you just don't know. Christmas is almost on us, Herbert's busy at the chambers and I've absolutely everything to do.'

Aunty Doreen put her knitting down and placed a hand on Mother's knee. 'Don't worry about Christmas. That's all sorted. You're coming to us.'

Billy froze. With Kenneth for Christmas! He bit his lip to stop himself shouting out NO!

'Frank's got a goose,' Aunt Doreen went on.

'A goose! Never!' Mother giggled and let her breath out at the same time.

'Yes, really.'

'How wonderful. *Goose!* How on earth?'

'A manager at the Coop depot has a brother who's a farmer in Kent. He got it for us. Something tells me he doesn't pay that much income tax. Don't ask me if he owes Frank a favour,' Aunty spluttered.

The mothers both threw their heads back and laughed in a screaming sort of way. Kenneth folded his arms across his front and smirked.

'Doreen, thanks so much. It's a huge relief to have Christmas taken care of.' Mother took Baby's hands off Aunty's ball of wool and put a stacking toy on the floor.

Billy bent and started the pile for her. She put on the smallest piece. There was coal dust on the floor where the mat ended. Baby put her finger in it. He moved her further onto the mat. 'Is it just for Christmas D-Dinner we're going f-for, Mother?'

Mother's brow puckered threateningly.

Baby put on a larger piece and the stacking toy collapsed.

Kenneth said, 'Aunty Marcia, do you think we can play with Billy's aeroplanes? We could play upstairs, quietly?' His lips curled above his wide white teeth and his cheeks rounded.

'Of course, dear,' Mother said, smiling at Kenneth as if he was the angel for the top of the tree. She passed Baby another piece of the stacking toy. 'And mind you share nicely, Billy.'

'He will, Aunty,' said Kenneth.

There was no escape from two pairs of motherly hands ushering them away. It wasn't fair. Billy slouched off to the stairs, Kenneth close beside him.

Upstairs, he quickly set to, searching out all Billy's toys and treasures. Billy shouted, 'Leave them! I only got home last night. I haven't seen my stuff myself yet.'

'So?' Kenneth darted at the boxes under the bed, where Billy had shoved them when Kenneth arrived. He knew exactly which were Billy's best things. Some were easy to break, especially those Billy had made himself.

Kenneth got started with a fighter plane straight away. 'Whee-eeee! He zooms down and crr-aa-shh. He bombs the cars, and the cows in the field and all the cottages.' He acted as if he was really in a raid. 'Get out some more of the farm while I'm doing this. Let's have some casualties. I know you've got more. I remember everything you've got.'

Billy looked at his farm animals, some of them made of matchsticks and wool and the little cardboard planes that last year had taken ages to stick together. He didn't want them bombed. He hadn't had any of these to play with at Mrs Youldon's.

149

Or anything else. He hadn't had Reg, Jim or any of his friends for company. He hadn't had his parents. Kenneth'd had it all.

Suddenly it was all too much. It was time to play out.

CHAPTER NINETEEN
December 23rd 1939

*Admiralty will lay mine barrage off East Coast
as reply to German action*

Billy pretended to go into the bathroom while Kenneth carried on whizzing and zooming planes into victims, then he slid out from behind the bathroom door and down the stairs. He crept out of the back door and was well down the road before anyone had time to notice. It was only like playing out.

There was one place that Kenneth didn't know, and one friend he'd never met, and one thing that was very powerful and was going to be Billy's and *only* Billy's one day.

He remembered the way to the Durban's very well. Angela hadn't been sent away after all and she'd be pleased to see him. Before evacuation she'd been very nice to him and she was the one who told him about things.

He ran on, being careful how he crossed the roads. It seemed funny to have carts and vans to worry about. He'd almost forgotten about the big red buses that looked so huge on the main roads.

There were new posters up outside the newsagents' and the metal fences all along the road had been removed. Otherwise, everything was the same as before the war.

Actually, it wasn't really Angela he was going to see, but what she might show him. He might have forgotten about buses but there'd never been a moment when he'd forgotten Mr Durban's treasure.

Billy started to run his hardest because he hadn't had time to pick up his coat and it was bitterly cold. When he got to the house he reached for the ding-dong bell with a freezing hand, then put his head against the door. Suppose they were all out? He'd have to run home again and Kenneth would still be there. He'd be telling on him right now. But if the Durbans were in, Billy would stay as long as they'd have him. Afterwards, when he got home he'd just say he was very sorry and they couldn't do that much, surely, because it was going to be Christmas. He could just go to bed after the punishment. Spending it with Kenneth was a real punishment anyway. He shivered and wished he'd brought his coat.

At last, the door opened. Mr Durban stood there wearing a maroon checked dressing gown. He stared for a moment, 'Wait a bit. Let me see, I know you, don't I?'

'Yes, sir. I'm Billy Wilson. I've come to see you all. I'm back from evacuation.'

Mr Durban smiled widely. 'Of course you are, I'm teasing you! Back for Christmas? That's very good. Well, you come on in. No coat! Better come near the fire.'

He led the way into their living room, where reddened coal flickered behind the criss-cross stove doors. Shabby paper lanterns dangled and tinsel glittered on a small tree.

'Sit you down, Billy.'

There was a Tommy helmet on the arm of the settee. Number *723 1939* was painted on the rim. It looked very heavy. Mr Durban sat by it. He moved a large pile of newspapers so that Billy could sit down beside him. 'I'm afraid Angela's at her friend's and Mrs Durban does war work most days. I've just got up. I'm on nights this week.'

He patted his tommy helmet. 'So with the women out, it'll be nice to have another man to chat to.'

Billy looked round for another man but then realized Mr Durban was making a little joke. He tried to think what another man might say back. 'Not much happening in London, after all, is there, sir?'

'Not much bombing, but a lot's happening all over London. Getting ready for the worst. Never fear, it'll all be sorted, one way or another, by the time you're of age.'

'Old aged?'

He laughed. 'You're good fun, young Billy. *Of age* is what I said. It means you're old enough to serve your country, go to war. Like I did in the last one.'

'Not now?'

'No. I'm an air raid warden after work. I don't go away with the judge like your father, I'm always in Chambers.

Easy for me to do the midnight to four shift, looking out for the safety of everyone here. I'm too old to fight, so I'm serving my country that way, you see.'

'Will I have to serve my country?'

'Perhaps. That's a long time away for you, so you just make sure you enjoy yourself, meanwhile. Why aren't you playing at home, now you're back?'

'I want to.' Billy's voice rose and quickened. 'I was looking f-forward to getting out all my toys. But my c-cousin's there and he's got all my things and they've l-let him. And if I d-don't he always gives me Chinese burns and g-gets me into trouble.'

His voice trailed away again.

'I see, I see. You have a bit of a problem there, have you? So you've come over to see Angela instead, and now she's out? Shame. But I'm up and fancy free for a little while. What sort of toys do you like? I should look out some of my keepsakes. As long as they're not in the attic.'

Mr Durban's cheeks were pinky-red, quite different from Dad's longer, waxy-white face with its beard. There were little lines at the sides of his eyes and he always looked friendly. Billy took his chance.

153

'I'm very interested in swords, sir, especially foreign ones. I've got a wooden one but I'm too old for it now.' He looked up at Mr Durban hopefully.

'Swords, eh? Then I might have something to interest you. The women are out, so we shan't bore them with men's things. Mind, you can only look. It's a dangerous weapon.'

Billy felt his face go hot. He was breathing fast. He mustn't give the truth away. He'd thought of Mr Durban's dangerous weapon so often at Mrs Youldon's, and when Kenneth sneered at him, he wanted to see it more than anything, more than going to the zoo or even getting a Christmas present. Mother probably wouldn't have time to shop for one anyway.

Mr Durban was standing up and telling Billy to wait there while he went to get his 'surprise'.

When he returned, he was holding the Cossack sabre the same way the village vicar held the chalice and his face looked the same, faraway and solemn. He laid it on the coffee table beside Billy. 'There. See this treasure? This is the scabbard. Isn't it fine? One day, I'll tell you a foreign tale about it.'

Billy stroked it, remembering every last detail of the decorations.

'Inside this scabbard, is something very dangerous, as I said. I expect you can guess what it is, can't you, young man?'

He wasn't supposed to know about it so he said it wrong. 'Sir, it's a sword.'

'It's a sabre from Russia. Its proper name is a shashka.'

'Sha-ska,' Billy breathed. Angela hadn't told him that. Perhaps she didn't know. 'Russia? That's a very far away country.'

'Indeed it is. Now stay sitting there and I'll show you.' Still standing, Mr Durban drew out the blade very slowly.

Billy gasped. It looked even more shocking than the very first time he'd seen it, partly because of the slow coming- out. The curved blade glinted in the winter sun that slanted through the window. Mr Durban held it up for some moments, moving it just a little from side to side.

'*Sir!* It's - spiffing!'

Mr Durban placed the scabbard on one side of the coffee table and the blade on the other, the furthest from Billy.

'Is it for something different than a sword?'

Mr Durban screwed his eyes up and stroked his face. Stubble showed. It would probably be scratchy. He looked as if he was thinking. 'I'm afraid they're both for killing. Let's talk about the technical side. The sabre's a very strong sword design and the shashka is a special type. The blade's hollowed out to make it light and stiff.' He slid it a little nearer to Billy. 'Put your hand over mine and you'll see it's not nearly as heavy as you'd guess.'

They lifted it up together. Billy's chest felt fluttery. It was as though he and Mr Durban were going to fight together against the enemy.

'It's still heavy enough to be used for work when it's not war-time.'

'Work?'

'In the fields, cutting crops. The design came from Persia or somewhere Eastern, but the Russian Cossacks found this shashka perfect for hacking, cutting and thrusting.'

'What's thrusting?'

'I'll show you. Sit back, right back.' He stood a little way from the settee and demonstrated with a wild empty arm: 'Hack, cut, thrust.' The air whistled. Although the shashka wasn't in Mr Durban's hand, hacking and thrusting, Billy couldn't help jerking away further.

Mr Durban sat down again and pointed to the hilt, with its closely patterned silver grip. 'You see the shashka has no guard? Sabres normally have them, but the Cossacks were such skilled fighters they reckoned they could fend off sword strikes with their bare hands.' He gave a grim laugh.

'Why don't they have a guard, Mr Durban?'

'Having no guard means better cutting. The cutting motion can begin closer to the hilt. You see how it's curved forward?' He pointed. 'This very small grip ends in the large pommel.'

'Pommel.' He whispered the new word. It was magnificent, much better than a sword, and surely the best sabre ever, a prince of sabres. Perhaps it had belonged to a prince in Russia. All those times he'd brooded over it, Billy hadn't thought of its real owner. He sat very still, his eyes hard and dry.

Then Mr Durban took several steps backwards into a space between the chairs and table. 'Can you keep very, very still?'

Billy nodded, holding onto the settee arm to make sure.

'Don't move then, not an inch, and I'll demonstrate.' His wide wrist grasped the shashka, flourishing it forward, left and right, twisting it beside, below and above him, swish, swish, swish. The cut air whistled against Billy's face bringing a faint smell of metal.

Billy flinched and curled back into the corner of the settee. His eyes hurt with stretching so wide. It was dreadfully scary to think of how terrifying it would be to face that curved blade! He hadn't remembered its awful sheen and cutting edge. The shaska would make such terrible wounds no-one would be able to bandage them. They'd probably never stop bleeding.

Mr Durban, tall and proud above him, looked a bit like a foreigner, his dressing gown a strange uniform with a shiny corded belt. Would he be a dangerous enemy?

Mr Durban lowered the shashka carefully. 'I can't do it as well as the Cossacks do, but that's more or less what it looks like in action. Except, that they often did it with two. One in each hand.'

'Two!' Billy gulped, trying to think of a double swishing and thrusting through the air. 'I'd like to see that. Sometime.'

Mr Durban smiled. 'Enough excitement. Let's put it away safely.' And he did, the fearful point sliding into the scabbard where it, and the silvery blade could do no harm.

Then he sat in the big leather chair at one side of the settee.

Billy let out a little sigh. 'How did you get it, Mr Durban? When did you meet Cossacks?'

'Ah, now, that is a tale. Do you like stories?'

'Sword stories. Yes, I do. I read about King Arthur lots of times before I was evacuated. I got a big book from Boots library. He pulled his sword from a big rock.'

'King Arthur is a famous myth, but this is a true story.'

'Like the heroes book you gave me, sir? They were true people. It would be really super to hear the Cossack story.'

'Now the shashka's safely back in its scabbard, you can hold it on your lap while you listen and imagine the man who once owned it.' He passed the scabbard across and laid it over Billy's bare knees. The leather was soft and hard at the same time, the thrilling weight of the sabre denting his skin. 'Did he kill anyone with it?'

'Probably many.'

'In front of you, sir?'

'No. If he'd used it then, I wouldn't be here to tell the tale. Shall I start?'

Billy nodded hard.

'Listen, then. This isn't girls' stuff. It's not to talk about with the women, mind.'

Billy shook his head. No way! And certainly not with Kenneth. He kept his hands lightly round the shaska, so he couldn't harm it. His eyes felt hot, but he kept his gaze on Mr Durban's face.

Mr Durban sat back in his big leather chair and closed his eyes for a moment. 'Nineteen fourteen. I was seventeen, enjoying the summer before starting at University in the October. One of my school friends, Otto, invited me out to spend the summer with his parents in the far north east of Germany, near the border with Russia. At least it was then. All the borders are different now, since the Great War.

'At first, we had a wonderful time, walking, riding – his family kept horses – and visiting his friends who were older and seemed very glamorous. The sea was not far off and the weather was beautiful. All the local men were in the fields getting in the harvest. There were lots of parties in the evenings and it was very cheerful.

'Everyone was shocked when we heard that the Archduke, Franz Ferdinand of Austria, had been killed by some wildcat Serb. Otto's father said there'd be an apology from the Serbian government.

'A lot of soldiers began parading smartly in full uniform in the streets. We saw armoury as well. I said to Otto, "It's like they're preparing for war." He made a face. "The German army's the strongest, the best in the world. They need to show everyone that."

'We carried on enjoying ourselves in the bright sunshine - world affairs no concern of ours! But there came a day soon enough, when Otto's parents seemed very panicky, speaking in German so that I wouldn't understand. Otto shrugged it off.

'That night Otto's friends came to warn me that now the harvest was in, the menfolk could be freed to be soldiers. Austria had declared war against Serbia. Russia was Serbia's ally so would fight with them. Germany backed Austria and soldiers had already started their damn raids before even declaring war. All the countries of Europe would be drawn in. An Englishman would be in great danger.

'Within an hour, Otto's friends helped me escape towards the Russian border which was about fifty miles away, first sewing English sovereigns into the waistband of my trousers.

'I had never travelled alone in the dark even in my own country. I spoke no Russian, but the sovereigns bought me food from farmhouses and inns in the next few days. I hid when soldiers were on the road. Twice I was nearly handed over, but my sovereigns saved my skin.'

Billy thought of his half- crown that Grandad had given him 'in case'. It had seemed safe enough in a purse, but perhaps he needed a better place. After all, it was wartime here too.

Mr Durban was deep into his story. 'I saw German soldiers, drunk, rolling out of inns. There were killings, young and old people, children kicked aside, houses ransacked. This made me hate the German army. I vowed I'd fight them when I was no longer alone and unarmed.

'Eventually, I saw Russian soldiers and let them capture me. Their commander sent for an interpreter. When they understood that I was an English student, accidentally caught up in Germany and ready to fight beside the Russians, there was a cheer. The commander then let the captain give me the first proper meal I'd eaten for very many days. He found me a uniform and a rifle and taught me how to fire it.

'The Russians were disciplined, having sworn no wine or women until the war was won. I was proud to march along beside them, although I couldn't understand their language. I had no knowledge of where we were, or of the progress of the war.

'For our first battle, I fed ammunition to my comrade at the rear as the riflemen forged ahead. Each wave was shot down, but we fought for hours.

The roar of the firing was deafening and the air thick and smutty. When the noise eventually died down, I climbed on a nearby truck to get a sense of what was happening.'

Mr Durban's eyes were dark. He swallowed. 'The fields were littered with bodies, dead or dying, all in our uniforms. I turned to the captain, dismayed, but he told me there were even more German bodies. I was appalled. This was my first experience of death and it was so massive.'

Billy screwed into the back of the settee, imagining it all. Mr Durban didn't seem to notice him. He sounded like a long-ago man, his eyes gazing far away.

'They were so brave, those Russian soldiers. The battles went on for weeks, until it was deep winter, thick snow on the ground. I was given a greatcoat and a cap with fur flaps. Just in time, for I thought my ears would drop off. Some men did lose fingers or toes.

'Every day was so terrible I stopped being shocked. In an icy trench without relief and under heavy fire, we couldn't move to right or left. Sometimes, there were several layers of bodies with a lowest layer of blood, shit and snow. Sometimes, uninjured men suffocated under the press of dead bodies above them, while below, the blood merged into one stench of filth.'

Billy stuffed one knuckle into his mouth to press away the very bad 'shi-' word as well as the truly awful scenes but Mr Durban spoke on.

'It was almost better to be under fire in the open, deep snow slowing every step. We kept on firing and being fired at, the waves of our riflemen mown down by the greater German force. Then, our Cossacks came speeding in, brandishing their sabres. Their faces were so fierce, I thought they would terrify all the Germans away. Our cannons gave the best cover they could, but the German machines had a better

160

range. One after the other, the brave Cossacks fell, their horses writhing beneath them. As the sky darkened, it all became horribly silent. We had run out of ammunition and needed to retreat. The enemy had stopped firing too. We were told to rest as best we could where we were. I shinned up a tree to take stock.'

Billy opened his eyes a bit, he'd had them screwed shut. He saw Mr Durban's eyes were far, far away.

'The ground ahead was flat and in the bitter blue sky, I could see for miles. The sight was far, far worse than the first battlefield I'd seen. As far as the horizon there were bodies, not hundreds, not thousands, but hundreds of thousands, far-off splats of blue and brown with great splashes of red staining the snow. They filled the icy fields as closely as the corn had filled them in August. A few German soldiers were walking amongst the fallen, looking for survivors.

'Then I saw a Cossack, still alive in the midst of a pool of dead German riflemen. I ran over to pull him out of the snow and back to our lines. Before I reached him, a German had his rifle at his throat. I dived low at the German's knees and toppled him over. The rifle fire hit high into the sky. As he lost his balance, I threw myself at him, managed to get his rifle and shot him at close range. I turned to the Cossack, who pointed a weak finger to the shivering flank of his steed where his weapon lay trapped.'

Mr Durban picked up the shashka reverently. Billy turned his gaze to it, shaking all over from tensing his muscles rigid for so long. He'd never ever heard such a scary tale and it was true, really awfully true.

'I could see how old and how precious this sabre was. The Cossack pointed to it, murmuring urgently, "Shashka, shashka lixodaika" and gestured at his stomach which gushed dark blood. Rifle shots rained around us, but my comrade ran up and we carried the Cossack to lie beside our vehicles.

'He was so weak, but spoke rapidly to my companion, then glared intensely at me with his black eyes, pushing the shashka into my hands. He fell back, shaking his head as if to say he was all done. I knelt and thanked him for his most precious gift. I wanted to express my total respect. He understood, and put a finger on my forehead like a blessing, saying words I had no way of understanding.

'A shouted command just then meant I had to run, a German rifle on one shoulder and a Cossack sabre in my hand.

'When we got to base, my rifleman comrade took the story of my wonderful shashka to my friendly captain.

'"You saved the Cossack's honour if not his life," he explained to me. "His dying words to you were: *Take this shashka, like a son of mine. Mind its path, protect it well. It will inflict the most terrible wounds.*"

'I was awestruck. The captain examined the shashka carefully. The fineness of the workmanship and engravings showed that it had once been the weapon of an important, perhaps even royal soldier. "You are honoured. The sabre which takes down a Cossack warrior is legendary in its own right, and is named shashka lixodaika."

'One of the Cossacks with us demonstrated how it should be used with rapid cuts and thrusts above and about his body. The captain told me not to try to use it unskilled, for it was a fearfully dangerous weapon.

'After this, because I owned the shashka, the men respected me, and any German soldiers who set eyes on me kept their distance. I never had a chance to use it, and perhaps as well. I'd seen enough violence and death to last a man many lifetimes. I'd been just a schoolboy in the summer. My eighteenth birthday was still some months off.'

Billy took in a breath. Not eighteen? That was younger than Uncle Ted!

'We reached the port and the captain arranged for me to be taken onto a ship bound for Finland, saying from there I could get to England. I made my sad Goodbyes, knowing it was very unlikely that any of my brave comrades would survive long. The Germans had far more forces and machinery.

'In fits and starts, I did get home safely, much to the relief of my poor mother who'd had no means of contacting me. She said she should never have agreed to my holiday. I told her the Russians had looked after me. I couldn't tell her how dreadful things had really been, that I had fought deadly battles and seen thousands of brave men dying. I hadn't the heart to put such images into her innocent mind.'

Suddenly Mr Durban stopped short, blinked and looked down at Billy as if Billy had just appeared. He took a little breath. 'How old are you, son?'

Why did he ask that? Did he want Billy to be his son right now? One day to give him the shaska? Billy stood up proudly, hands straight by his sides, head up, just like a soldier and said, 'I'm eight, sir.'

'Eight! Lord, I thought you were much older.' Mr Durban leant forward and took the shashka from him. 'You are a big lad. Eight! I shouldn't be telling you stories like this. I'm afraid I've been in another world. Whatever will your parents think of me?'

'I won't tell them.' They might be cross if they knew how scared he'd been. He felt his hands to see if they'd stopped being so shaky.

'Mm. Perhaps best not. I'll go and put this away.'

Billy's legs felt light without the shashka resting on them. He sat down again. He didn't want to go home yet.

When Mr Durban came back in he said, 'Sir, it was jolly good you did get back home safely. And with the shashka.'

'Indeed. My goodness, what a tale to tell you.' He looked at his watch. 'Just time for some fizz and biscuits, then you must scoot off home.'

Billy didn't rush his drink when it came and he took two biscuits with thick custard cream in the middle. He'd have missed his elevenses by now. 'Thank you, sir.'

'No, you tuck in.'

Billy really meant thank you for the story but perhaps, in advance, for the shashka.

He nibbled and sipped as slowly as he could, but Mr Durban thought he should get back.

When he got to the front door, Mr Durban said, 'That problem with your cousin, Billy. Remember the heroes book? They had huge problems but they stood up for what was right. Remember? Think of Joan of Arc or Spartacus.'

'I do. I have thought of them. All of them. I want to be a hero, but I'm not.'

'There's time. You're a good little lad. Just - always stand up for what's right.'

Billy bit his lip. It would be difficult.

'As for the shashka and its history. Not for others' ears now!' and Billy shook his head. He wasn't a tell-tale, and anyway, the shashka was his secret. His and Mr Durban's.

He set off home quickly but couldn't run fast, for all the scenes in his head seemed to weigh his feet down and anyway the street was now icy. He didn't know whether he was shivering from cold or from hearing about all the death and dying. There would definitely be punishment at home now, but that wasn't nearly as scary.

When he got to his road he could see there was trouble. Everyone made a big fuss. Kenneth and Aunty, holding Baby, were at the window. Mother

164

was standing on the doorstep in her coat, looking around wildly.

Dad was just coming up the road as Billy reached the gate. He glowered. 'So. There you are! I've been looking for you in the school playground. Where have you been? You were supposed to be upstairs with your cousin.'

Kenneth called out 'I searched downstairs and in the garden before telling.'

Mother's hands flew in the air. 'Going out without telling anyone! How was I to know where you were, please?'

'I wasn't far. I was just playing out.'

'You could have been miles away. Someone could have taken you.'

He was confused. They'd wanted him to be taken last September. Why wasn't it like being evacuated? 'But—before, I was miles away. Miles and miles away for ages. You let me.'

'That's different. Mrs Youldon was caring for you and it was in the country. She knew where you were. This is London, you can't just walk off when you like.'

Dad joined in, 'Completely out of line. You worried your mother. This simply will not do. Go to your room. Now.'

It could have been a lot worse. Dad hadn't gone for his slipper.

Billy went to his room and spent the rest of the day there with no dinner. It was meant to be a punishment, but he was really glad of the silent, safe space while he lay on his bed and thought about Mr Durban's terrible tale. The huge rank of cannons, hundreds of soldiers on both sides, the Russians thrusting forward, wave after wave against the constant cannon fire, the Cossacks riding up with their sabres against their hip. He especially tried to replay the moment when Mr Durban first saw the shashka under the dead horse.

When he imagined all the hundreds and thousands dead bodies he put the coverlet over his head. Then he thought of holding the shashka up high. He sat up and stared at the wall as if he were at the pictures. Although the war stuff was terrifying, when he had the imaginary shashka he felt braver and more able to face enemies. He practised swishing his arms in the air, like slashing with a shashka or two.

Down below, the sounds of home seemed suddenly silly: Kenneth being fussed over in the kitchen while Mother twittered about what cakes and biscuits to bring to Uncle Frank's on Christmas Day.

When he went to the bathroom he found that a plate of sandwiches and a drink of orange had been left outside his bedroom door. He was jolly glad to see them, and took them inside to eat and drink like a soldier after a battle.

CHAPTER TWENTY
December 25th 1939

Olivia De Havilland enchants in
'Gone with the Wind'

Billy woke early. He put his nose around the blackout and saw a few flakes of snow drifting past. Christmas Day was still sort of exciting even though they had to go to Uncle Frank's. He hadn't been there since summer. Would Uncle be bigger and fiercer, or nicer because it was Christmas? Had Mother had been shopping for presents? Would Uncle Frank still want to wrestle, and would he have a tree? He'd better not ask anything, because everyone would still be cross with him.

Breakfast seemed to take ages because of Jill fussing about her porridge and then having to be wrapped up in all her pram clothes, but at last they were off walking down empty roads sprinkled with white. He remembered last year's twinkly lights inside houses with curtains open to show the tree. That made things feel cheery at night- time. Everywhere, windows were blind and if there were decorations behind them, it was secret. Everything had to be kept dark now.

A bitter feeling was in the air and there was white on the top of hedges and bushes. His wellies made a crisp crunch when he stepped into the gutter.

'A great deal of frost, today,' said Dad. 'Any snow will stay put.'

He looked up at the low white sky. Billy expected a saying, but none came.

Mother and Dad strode along quickly. Billy hopped behind, watching their footsteps appear in the thin snow. The pushchair left its own little roads behind. They'd make marvellous marble runways if only he was allowed to play on pavements, but 'playing out' was probably gone for good.

Mother said, 'I do hope their place is warm, Herbert. I'm like ice right through.'

Billy counted to four hundred and seventy two before they turned the corner into Uncle Frank's road.

'Thank goodness, we're here.' Mother parked the pram inside the gate and picked up Baby with all the bedding. Aunty's hall had no room for prams.

Dad knocked and Kenneth let them in from the cold. He was wearing brown corduroy shorts and a jumper with a yellow tractor knitted into its front. It was such a dark day that the curtains were drawn and the light on.

Aunty Doreen, red-faced in a floral pinny, welcomed them in to sit beside the smoking fire. 'The goose isn't nearly cooked yet, so excuse me all of you. Sit yourselves down and Frank'll entertain you.'

There was a Christmas tree in the corner with little candles on the branches. Aunty had sprinkled talcum powder so that it looked snowy, but Dad said there might be real snow outdoors soon. 'It was certainly cold enough on the walk over.'

'I'm the Christmas Spirit. Treats to come.'

Uncle Frank came round the door dressed in a Father Christmas suit, his beefy hands around a large sack. It was difficult not to look at him. 'And here's our little darling and her not-so- big brother, if I'm not mistaken.' His cheeks curved round and his range of teeth showed. 'Hello, kiddies.'

Kenneth fingered a set of dominoes. He looked at Billy from under his eyelashes, waiting.

There was a lot of grown-ups' talk about what had happened to them since War had been declared and whether both sides would have a cease fire today. Billy put his head between the velvety curtains and watched in case snowflakes fell. He perched up on the windowsill making sure all of him showed, even his feet, so that Kenneth couldn't do anything sneaky without being seen. It was a good place to stay.

Every now and then Aunty popped her head in and out of the kitchen door, reporting on the progress of the goose.

Uncle said, 'Sit down, Doreen, for Heaven's sake. It won't cook quicker for you looking at it.'

'Oh all right.' She flopped into a chair. 'I wonder what'll be in the King's speech this afternoon.'

'Progress of the war, bravery, what else?' Dad said.

Billy wondered if he'd have to listen to the speech. It might be longer than a sermon. He and Kenneth might be sent upstairs while the grown-ups listened and by tea-time, he'd have bruised shins or worse. He couldn't stand up for what was right on Christmas Day.

Baby toddled about touching everything.

'Not that, darling, it could break.'

'Don't touch. NO! Here, have dolly.'

After she'd explored the room and been passed from lap to lap, Baby got restless. Then Uncle Frank, not at all like Father Christmas, gave his toothy smile and lurched forward with his hessian sack.

'Ho ho ho. All little kiddies who have been good can have their toys off Rudolph the Reindeer's sleigh.'

There was no sleigh. Uncle knew Billy was eight and Kenneth was nine, so he must have meant this silly talk for Baby. He held out the bulgy sack. But she didn't know what to do, and it was Aunty who had to lean forward and pull out a present for her. Kenneth showed her which one, and stayed close to the sack.

Baby pulled at the crackly paper and played with that, while Mother looked at the present, six blocks in a box.

Kenneth lifted his lip to Billy, his hands on the sack. 'You can have first dip, Billy.'

Billy hesitated, it was so surprising. Could it really be that Kenneth was standing up for what was right, like Mr Durban said was the thing to do?

Aunty pushed him forward. 'Go on, Billy. Kenneth's giving you first go, bless him. You can take three things each.'

Billy unwrapped a Bakelite dog with brown spots, a book about Jesus and his disciples, and a colouring pad. Kenneth pulled out a pop-pop gun, the Radio Fun annual, and a chocolate ball filled with fruit jellies. He displayed his goodies on two open palms. Billy stared at them and then at his own presents.

'They're what you picked out, Billy,' said Mother.

'Lucky boy!' said Aunty Doreen, nodding at the book of Jesus as she unfolded a pink petticoat Mother had given her.

Dad said, 'Who could guess what was on top?'

Billy saw Kenneth's lip twitching. Something wasn't right.

Then Baby pulled out a present, and it was the last one. Just a doll made of that hard stuff that cracked.

Mother handed Billy another parcel from the big pram bag. Kenneth looked over keenly as a striped spinning top came out of the brown paper. 'It's from Uncle Ted,' Mother said. 'He sent it from abroad last month.'

'Abroad!' Billy held it very close. It would never fit into Dad's coat pocket.

Aunty peered at it over the table and said, 'Kenneth got a wonderful train set from my parents. I don't know how they afford it. I reckon it came from Harrods. They know I get worn out going shopping. He's got it in his trunk.'

That meant Billy wouldn't get to play with it, for sure. He slid the top under the table between his feet as Kenneth opened the present Mother and Dad gave him. It was a set of drawing pencils and a sketch pad, really boring. But Kenneth seemed pleased. His lips curved upwards and he took out the first pencil very carefully. He drew a large T on the first page, and decorated it, then turned it into a fancy *Thankyou*. Billy knew that should be two words but none of the adults minded. They all clucked and admired what he'd done. It did look good.

'Good choice, you two,' Uncle Frank said, as he went towards the kitchen. 'Just the job. Our boy's like you, Bert. Always with a pencil in your hand, I remember.'

Dad grinned and pushed at his beard.

'Do you like drawing, Billy?' Aunty asked, nicely.

'No. I hate it.'

'He shows not a jot of interest in it,' said Dad, and bent over the drawing book as Kenneth started on a large bird.

Aunty handed over their present to Billy. She had knitted him a stripy scarf.

'That'll come in handy right now,' said Dad. 'Snow's on its way.'

'Thank you, Aunty,' said Billy.

'How nice,' Mother called over to Aunty, then turned her head to mutter to Dad, 'I was hoping for a jumper.'

'Now. I am On Duty,' said Uncle Frank coming back from the kitchen with a tea towel tucked into his Father Christmas trouser fronts. 'Do you want to see this fine bird before I carve?'

Everyone crowded round him in the kitchen. The browned carcass cowered on a carving board as Uncle raised a hairy forearm and offered the knife. Aunty put parsley on the stumps where feet had once been.

'Ooh,' squealed Mother.

'Superb,' said Dad.

'You all get sat down while I deal with this,' Uncle ordered, bending his muscly frame over the goose.

Everyone deserted the bird and went to the dining table. It had its leaves pulled out so no-one could quite squeeze by the chairs. If only they'd had the dinner at home. There was plenty of space there, and it was a proper dining room.

Aunty came in and out with dishes of food. 'Are we all in?' She took her pinny off. Under it was a purple dress with red flowers mashed into it.

Dad looked at it a lot. 'Shall I turn the gas fire up? You've no sleeves.'

She shook her head. The shiny roll across her forehead slid forward. 'I'm warm enough with all that cooking, don't you worry. Now I'll bring the plates in. Help yourselves to greens, everyone.'

Aunty brought Baby's plate out first so that Mother could cut everything up and turn it to mush for her. Baby was already turning her head away and saying 'No, no.' But then when the other plates came out and they all started eating, she forgot and put her spoon in her mouth.

Billy got the darkest bits of goose. He found he didn't much like the meat and Aunty's gravy was thick and lumpy.

Dad said, 'What a treat, Doreen. These potatoes!'

Mother said, 'So kind, all this work, Doreen. Hope you haven't worn yourself out. Lovely, isn't it Billy? Tell Aunty how lovely it is.'

'It's lovely, Aunty,' said Billy before he put a sprout in his mouth. Kenneth put his napkin to one side of his face and mouthed a mocking, 'It's lovely, Aunty,' to Billy from behind it.

'And guess what I've brought! One can't come over empty-handed.' Dad bent down and brought out from under the table a bottle of ginger beer and two golden brown bottles with shiny corks. *A man hath no better thing under the sun, than to eat, and to drink, and to be merry. Ecclesiastes.*'

'You and your sayings, Bert! But that one'll do.' Uncle Frank rubbed his hands.

'Ooh, all that merry sherry,' giggled Aunty and rushed into the front room where the ornament cupboard was.

She came back with four glasses. Kenneth had already prised off the wire clip on the ginger beer bottle and poured himself a glass, and Billy half of one.

Uncle Frank poured the golden drink into the four glasses. Mother lifted a pale pink hand, then stood up.

'Wait everybody! A toast to those who aren't having a lovely Christmas dinner like us.' Her face was serious, so did this mean him, and was his Christmas dinner going to be taken away for a punishment for playing out? His hand left his glass and landed on his lap rapidly. But then she said, 'To Ted, and all our serving soldiers. Let's pray they'll soon be home.'

Everyone stood up then and drank to Uncle Ted, and all soldiers. Billy felt a little shiver go through him. Was there all that fighting and bombing in places where Uncle Ted was right now? He wanted Uncle Ted to come home more than anything.

'Drink your ginger beer then, lad. It's meant to be a treat,' said Uncle Frank.

'I'll have it if you don't want it,' said Kenneth, his hand halfway across the table.

Billy drank it down with a gulp ready to ask for seconds, but the words got mixed up with the bubbles and he spluttered all over the table. Lucky the grown-ups were so busy talking and drinking themselves that they only tutted at him. He left it a minute before risking a sideways plea to Aunty.

'Seconds, dear?' she said vaguely as Kenneth's hand shot out and upended the bottle into his own glass. 'Oh dear, looks like Kenneth's beaten you to it.'

The adults' bottles lasted right through the goose dinner until the gravy had a skin on it. Then it was time for the Christmas pudding.

'It's Billy's first time with Christmas Pudding,' Mother said. 'So rich. We always thought it best to keep him to rice pudding.'

'This has been boiling away for hours,' said Aunty, as she took a bandaged lump the size and shape of a bum from the steaming pan.

She unwrapped the white cloth carefully. Billy was shocked to see that the pudding was black, but no-one said it was burned. It made him think of his bad knee being unwrapped by the hospital nurse. It had hurt because his skin was stuck on the bandage. Quite a lot of the pudding stuck to Aunty's cloth, but there was still enough to go round.

Mother had made the custard. She'd brought the Bird's Eye tin with her. 'Better to save the rest of this for special times,' she said. 'Harder times after Christmas is over, so it's said.'

'Now, Marcia! You're here to enjoy yourself, remember. Or do I have to help you have fun?' Was Uncle Frank tickling Mother? She certainly laughed a lot, in her way. It sounded like an owl 'Oo, oo-hoo, oo-hoo.'

Mr Durban always had pinky-red cheeks but today Dad had them too. The grown-ups finished the pudding and cleared the table. Aunty put her feet up for a moment because the others told her she'd done her bit, cooking the dinner. And anyway, she had the hiccups. Baby stood very close and watched Aunty's body jerk.

Then they all had a jolly game of musical chairs that ended with Dad being cross with Mother. 'Honestly, Marcia, you could move a bit quicker.'

She'd landed on Uncle Frank's lap, fighting for the chair he'd won. Dad pointed a finger at her. 'You're out, anyway. Out you stand.'

Aunty Doreen hadn't done too well either, as she had Baby by the hand. Luckily Baby was happy to plump down on the floor every time the music stopped and other times as well, so she didn't have a tantrum when the others got the chairs. Billy let Kenneth win so that he wouldn't get Chinese burns when they were sent off to play with their new toys. They soon were.

'Enough fun, you boys. Don't want you over-excited. Off you go upstairs with all this clip-clap,' said Dad motioning to their presents. Mother took Baby to have her sleep on the reclining chair in the parlour.

When the boys reached the little bedroom, Kenneth said, 'I've put all my toys away so I can play with my new ones. I can't share when they're new. You play with your spotty dog.'

Billy held the hard thing that was only any good as an ornament. It didn't even have a nice face. 'It doesn't do anything.'

'I know. I watched Daddy pack the sack.'

'He let you!'

'Through the crack in the door, soppy.'

Billy sat on the bed. It wasn't fair. Kenneth wanted him to be upset so he wouldn't let it show that he minded. 'I think I'll read,' he said, opening the Jesus book.

'I think I'll eat these jellies,' said Kenneth. He began to chew and suck. 'Oh, yum, yum.'

Billy turned a page, trying not to listen. There were no pictures, apart from the one on the cover.

'Now I'll try out my gun,' said Kenneth. 'See if this hurts,' and he tried shooting pellets against Billy's arm and then his leg.

Billy read about Jesus turning the other cheek but he wasn't going to let Kenneth try the gun on his. He put both hands up against his face.

Kenneth looked around the things on the bed. 'You don't like that spotty dog much, do you?'

'Not really. I might give it to Jill when she's older.'

'I don't like it either but it'll make a good target.' He put the dog on the chair against the far wall and knelt on the floor, shooting it.

With Billy reading and Kenneth's mouth full of gummy jellies, they were loads quieter than the grown-ups downstairs in the front room. A lot of shouting out and laughing and hooting rose up the stairs.

Billy asked, 'What are they doing?'

'Playing housey-housey. Bet Daddy wins,' said Kenneth.

'He always does.'

Billy went to the landing and hovered near the stairs, trying to enjoy the game from above. The grown-ups didn't notice and Kenneth was busy behind him. Suddenly, Kenneth's arm curved round Billy. 'Something for you.' He was holding a folded piece of card.

Billy took it cautiously. Was there a spider or something inside it?

'It's all right. It's for you. I did it for you, for Christmas.'

Billy unfolded the card. There was a little picture in poster paint on each of its four sides: a boy snowballing, a holly bough, a present with a striped bow, and a smiling Father Christmas. The pictures were ever so, ever so good. On the back it said 'To Billy from Kenneth.'

Billy held it so hard that his fingers hurt. 'It's smashing.' He hadn't done anything for Kenneth. He hadn't even thought about it. 'I'm sorry I haven't done one for you. I'm no good at drawing.'

'I know. It's all right. I've got those pencils Aunty and Uncle got me.' He looked down at the pictures. Do you think they're good paintings?'

'They're really smashing. No-one in my class can paint like that.'

'Good. I'm going to be a painter, that's what.'

'Are you? Like pictures on the walls, painter?'

'Yes. Now you're supposed to say *Thank you*.'

'Thank you ever so. I do like it. I'm going to keep it.' It was suddenly the best present he'd had.

176

Now Christmas Day was all over and Billy was saying his Goodbyes and Thank yous. Aunty wrapped the new scarf around Billy's neck as Mother bundled Baby into the pram with loads of baby blankets. Then they were out in the bitter cold, feeling their way home in the unlighted streets and he was very glad of the scarf.

He hugged his new spinning top to his chest. Hiding it under the table had worked perfectly. But he felt mean, now. At least he could have shared spinning it with Kenneth when he hadn't done any present for him.

There were other people struggling home in the cold, heads down, a flickering torchlight in front of each of them. You could smell the frost in the air, but a gritty, mean frost waiting for snow to blanket it.

'My word, I shall be glad when this blackout business is over,' said Dad.

Mother was shivering. 'And I never remember winter being this cold. I wish we could have stayed longer, Herbert. It was such fun.'

'You're quite fuelled up enough for one night, Marcia. High time we were home, given your carryings-on.'

Billy was behind them in the dark. All he could see was the snow, not even a chink of light from any building.

'Come on, Billy, one, two, one, two,' and Dad led the way, his big shoes faintly gleaming where that morning they'd been polished like a guardsman's.

Billy was sure the sky hadn't been so very big before the evacuation. There were so many stars and he could see nobbles and clefts on the moon's surface like never before.

'Why is the sky so big now?'

'Don't be silly. The sky's as big as it ever was,' said Mother. 'Hurry up do, stop standing and staring. Aren't you cold enough? I know I am.'

He wanted to ask Dad, but he was striding ahead, his ears covered by his scarf, snowflakes on his trilby.

This is how it had been for the Cossacks fighting, fiercely cold, white and dark, field after field until they marked the snow with their blood. He wouldn't have been able to stand it, fight in it. He couldn't wait to get indoors to a fire right now. He wasn't a hero.

Dad turned back and started to pull him along. 'Come on, Billy. You'll freeze to death if you don't hurry up. Quick march, that's the way to get home.'

It was so good to feel some warmth when their front door opened to Dad's key.

'Better run straight up to bed, Billy. Very late for you.'

Billy took up his top and Jesus book and the paintings from Kenneth. He'd left the Bakelite dog behind on purpose, just to show it didn't count for anything. To help the shivers away, he counted while he undressed for bed – eleven, twelve, thirteen. The bedroom was always very cold and Mother had forgotten to put any hot water bottles into the beds before they went out, so when Billy slid into bed he felt like an ice sandwich.

He fell asleep dreaming he was a Russian soldier, a brave Cossack, dying in the snowy field that was splattered everywhere with blood.

CHAPTER TWENTY-ONE
December 26th 1939

Londoners cheered by the King's
Christmas Day Speech

Boxing Day seemed to begin very late. Billy felt very
hungry before he could hear any sound from his
parents.

He waited quite a while, but the house remained
silent. Did he dare sneak down and find some food?
First, he had to brave the cutting cold that lay
between his bed and the door where his dressing
gown hung. He rushed to snuggle into it and crept
downstairs. There was an uncut loaf in the larder. It
was best not to touch that. He cut a piece of cheese
from under its white cloth cover and tried to make a
smooth edge like it had before. There didn't seem to
be anything else unwrapped or half ready.

Mother had brought the rest of the custard home
in a jug. He lifted the edge of the skin and spooned
up a few mouthfuls. The custard was set hard, so
although he carefully replaced the skin, the curved
dents in the surface showed horribly. He was scared,
but Mother surely wouldn't look at custard until well
after breakfast.

When they did get up, Mother and Dad didn't
seem in a very good mood and because he'd been
so recently in trouble, Billy cleared the table
without being asked and then went to play in his
room, happy to have it to himself.

He tried out Uncle Ted's top, setting it to spin so
that the stripes became one splodge of colour, just
like his whizzer. It went ever so well and with a
cheery whirring sound. If only he could thank Uncle
Ted for such a lovely present. He wanted to see him;
he wanted him home. He was a soldier somewhere

179

and there were cruel Germans around. But at least Uncle Ted wasn't in Russia.

Kenneth must've messed with his home-made planes because there were breakages. He got out his glue and matchsticks.

Cross voices sounded downstairs. He heard Mother's snappy voice at Baby when she whinged. A freezing blast shot up the stairs as the front door opened extra wide.

Dad's voice stated, 'I shall go out to clear my head.'

'All right for some,' Mother said loudly before the door shut with a whoosh.

Billy kept out of the way, lost in repairing his aeroplanes.

Dad must have come back later, for wireless sounds floated up the stairs, but Billy had been too busy to notice Dad's return.

Lunch was silent and the dining room table seemed bare; only a sandwich of hard cheese with the custard to follow. Mother removed the cover and looked at it closely. 'Have you been at this, Billy?'

He hung his head and nodded. 'Sorry, Mother. I was hungry this morning.'

'You helped yourself? How dare you!'

Dad didn't look at her, or at Billy. Even Baby was quiet, eyeing each of them as she sat in her high chair, squelching mashed carrot between her teeth.

Eventually Mother said, 'Well you needn't try that again.'

She spooned the custard into the four dishes, splat, splat, splat, splat, the skin sliding silently into Billy's dish like a bit of dead body. It would be his punishment to have to eat it. Surely everyone hated skin?

Dad was looking at the dishes. 'I think I'll have a spot of jam with mine.'

Mother tutted and click-clacked into the kitchen. Dad swapped the dishes and put his in front of Billy, frowning as Billy gasped with surprise. 'Mouth shut, son.'

The click-clacks returned, and the jam pot with the lid like a flower, banged down on the table. Mother wagged a finger. 'You needn't think you're having jam, Billy.'

He lowered his head and ate up his skinless custard, gladly.

In the afternoon, Baby was dressed up and put in the push chair. Nothing was said, but they all wore their best clothes with extra cardigans on top and walked towards Nightingale Lane. Walking behind Mother, he saw her seams were a bit crooked but he didn't dare say so. He hoped Dad would notice and put them right, but he didn't. This road led to Grandad and Nanny's so his tummy had a happy butterfly feeling. It was ages since he'd come here. Also, Mother wouldn't want to show her crossness there. Dad walked forward and rang the bell.

Nanny and Grandad came to the front door with smiling faces that seemed as foreign as France. It was so long since he'd seen them. At last he had someone he could tell all about the evacuation –the playing out, the hip bath, the privy and running in the wood in old, torn clothes.

They both opened their arms and Billy ran forward. Baby had forgotten them and hid behind Mother's knees. In the end, Mother had to carry her inside.

'Well what a palaver, this evacuation,' Nanny began. 'And all for nothing, wasn't it? I've had your letters, Marcia, we've read them all so many times. Your kind vicar, the dear little village. But I don't know anything about how Billy got along. You tell us, dear. Come and sit here between us, and your little sister can get used to us gradually.'

As Billy opened his mouth he caught Mother's eye. It was narrowed by furrowed brows. There was a 'don't' message here. What was it he mustn't say?

'I was in a tiddly village with country round it.' He looked at Mother. All seemed well. 'I can't say its name because it's secret.' He looked at Mother again for approval.

Grandad gave it. 'Learned your lessons well, bright lad. Now then, were they good to you, then, those people you stayed with?'

'Yes. It was just a lady and her little children and they didn't have—'

Mother pushed a flat hand towards him. 'I'm sure Grandad doesn't want to hear about someone else's children, Billy.'

He wanted to talk to Grandad. Was it just about Timmy and Sally he couldn't speak? He tried again. 'There was another boy there like me, Grandad. He was called Alan, only he wasn't from my school. I didn't know him before.'

'That was nice, then,' said Nanny. 'A new friend. Another boy evacuated like you to share your room.'

'Yes, and we had to share a —'

'That's enough, Billy. Go and find Nanny's old dolls-house for Baby, please.'

'You're not letting him talk, Marcia. We want to hear all his news. He's been away weeks and weeks, after all.'

'Best he doesn't think too much about it,' said Dad. 'If it comes to it again, we'll look for a re-billeting. It wasn't a suitable place.'

Billy didn't know what 're-billeting' meant, but he understood 'billet' and 'not suitable'. Was coming back home, 're-billeting'?

If only Mother and Dad would go in the garden or upstairs or something, so that he could tell Nanny all about the train, the crocodile around the town, even being left till last, as well as the forbidden stuff of Mrs Youldon's home, the little ones and everything.

As he came back with the dolls' house and set it down before Baby, Nanny leaned forward to Mother. 'You started your family late, Marcia. So you're slow to understand children, what they're needing to do or say.'

Mother's lips formed a straighter line. 'My goodness, Mother, I'm bringing up two. I do all right. Very well, I'd say, under the circum-stances. Billy's been allowed to run a bit wild while he's been away. He needs a bit of correction, now he's back with us.'

Grandad turned to the mantlepiece, sighing. Then he picked up some letters and put them in Nanny's hand. She waved them at Mother. 'Did you hear from Ted as well? We've kept all his letters.' She held them out. 'He sounds cheery, but we dread what he might have to go through, now or later.'

'If it's like the last war...' Grandad muttered. 'I wouldn't wish that on anyone, let alone my son.'

Nanny looked over and Shh'd him. Mother was reading the letters closely.

Billy felt a thump in his stomach. Whatever it was Uncle Ted was doing, it must be horrible if Nanny dreaded it, and Grandad wouldn't wish it on him. 'Are there cannons where Uncle Ted is?'

Nanny quickly put the wireless on and there was Christmas music playing, although Christmas had ended. She turned to Billy. 'Know this one, pet? Jingle Bells, Jingle Bells.' She didn't sing in tune, but she waved her pinny in time to the music. Baby chortled and tried to copy. Nanny held out her hands, and with a little push from Mother, Baby took them. Nanny danced her around the room. The men went outside.

Looking through the lounge window, Billy saw them walk down the garden path together, smoking. It was very, very cold but they stayed there, talking with churchy faces. Grandad was tracing a sort of map on the bird table, jabbing his finger from time to time. Dad hunched his shoulders and rubbed his chin lots of times. The smoke from both of them made pretty twists in the air. It was ages before they came in again.

'Just as well to keep all that smoke out of here,' said Nanny following Billy's gaze. She'd never grumbled about Grandad's pipe before.

Mother was looking at a magazine. It was last year's. 'Now we're home, I just don't want to think about any of it,' she said. 'Anyway, it doesn't seem like war is going to be actually *dangerous,* here. Just think— we went all that way, had all that nuisance and here we are back at home. All for nothing.'

'Keeping your children safe isn't for nothing, Marcia, and now you're home, perhaps you can nag Herbert into seeing about a shelter.'

'Oh, we keep seeing notices about shelters. I see next door haven't bothered. They're going to the park one, if there is a raid. Herbert hasn't put in the Anderson yet, and just as well. It would ruin the garden.'

'Well, I wish he would. Think what's happening in other places. Try to persuade him, Marcia. Better be safe than sorry. It's quite a long way to the park shelter and you've got Baby to carry. I hate to think of how it would be.'

'There's our cellar if we really did get a raid. Sitting beside a heap of coal. That will be jolly! Anyway, we'll surely get warned if there's going to be bombing, so we'll worry about it then. The newspaper says Hitler's busy in Norway just now and anyway Herbert reckons Britain's too tough a nut for him to crack.'

Nanny made a face. Was Mother right, or Nanny? Beastly Hitler. War and sheltering from it. It all seemed very gloomy.

The afternoon cheered up when Grandad came in and collected Christmas presents for them all from upstairs. Billy's was extra special because it was for his birthday too. They hadn't had an address for him.

184

He opened the brown paper, letting it crackle to slow down the surprise. Inside was a large and shiny red car with opening doors. 'Super, super, Grandad! Thank you ever so much.' He held it on his lap to keep it safe until he was allowed to play with it somewhere.

'Let's have some tea, everyone.'

Mother went out with Nanny to the kitchen and brought back a tray with the teapot, milk and cups. Nanny passed round bread and butter, with a spot of jam on each slice.

Then she brought in a jelly in the shape of a fat rabbit. It squelched loudly as it was spooned into dishes, which made him giggle. She poured on thin custard and it had no lumps or skin. Afterwards, there was Christmas cake for the grownups and little cakes with white icing smothered with coloured dots for him and Jill. *Hundreds and Thousands*, Grandad called the dots. It was a good name because you really couldn't count them. Billy bit into his cake and watched the colours melt into the white, bit by bit, like little dead bodies in the snow.

'Good job that's not ice-cream, young Billy,' said Grandad, 'or it'd just be water, the time you've been gazing at it. Don't you like icing?'

'It's yummy. I'm just waiting for the hundreds and thousands to disappear like they've never been.'

'Funny little lad,' said Nanny. 'You take your time, dear, enjoy it. And I've got another one for you to wrap up and take home.'

It was sad that there was no chance to say anything private before it was time to go home, but the great fuss his grandparents made of him made Billy feel the happiest he'd been for a long time.

CHAPTER TWENTY-TWO
January 8th 1940

Finns make huge captures.
Another entire Soviet division killed

'Guess what?' said Kenneth, standing on Billy's bed, one hand on the hanging aeroplane. 'We're not going to be able to have butter, or bacon and all sorts of things. There's going to be ration books so you can't just go shopping and get what you like, even with lots of money. There's a thingy— shortage.'

'No butter? What'll we have on our b-bread then?'

'P'raps we won't get bread. We might have to eat dog biscuits.'

'Aunty Doreen would never give you d-dog biscuits.'

'But your Dad might give them to you. Because you don't need building up. And Mummy always says I do. So if there's any butter, I'll get it. They'll probably give me yours.'

Billy bit his lip. It could be another of Kenneth's tales. He waited until they went down to tea, until Mother brought in the scones. No-one had ever stopped him from ladling on the butter. He did so now, waiting for a moment when Kenneth had his nose in his mug of milk.

'You won't be able to do that, in future, Billy.' Mother had her eyes on his knife. 'Put some back. Bacon and butter, and probably other things, are going to be rationed.'

'What's rationed?' Best to try to get the truth.

Kenneth brought his lips out of his mug. 'He already knows because I just told him upstairs. Why does Billy ask questions when he knows the answer, Aunty Marcia?'

'I d-didn't understand. I'm not as old as you,' said Billy, playing the game.

Mother's eyes swivelled between them. She took a breath and explained all about rationing.

'I knew that, Aunty. We're all going to have to be very careful not to take more than our share, aren't we?' said Kenneth, his eyes pointedly on Billy's scone.

'Yes, Kenneth, that's right. Let's hope *you* don't have to go without too much,' and there was a definite edge to Mother's voice.

Billy held his serviette to his mouth so that he could peer at her face without being noticed. Was she cross? With him or with Kenneth? He wasn't sure. It might be worth trying to tell Mother a bit more about Kenneth if only he could make her pleased with him.

'Shall I b-butter this scone for Jill, Mother? Jill, do you like scones?' He bent over her as she held her sticky hands above her plate. 'You like jam, don't you?'

'Yum yam,' she nodded.

'I expect jam will be rationed, won't it, Aunty?' said Kenneth.

'Perhaps. Put your napkins in their rings, when you've finished, boys. Then you can listen to Larry the Lamb on the wireless.'

Billy smiled. He always looked forward to that.

Kenneth muttered, 'That's just for babies.'

Mother heard. 'Kenneth, I've seen you listening to it before'

When she went out, Kenneth made a little noise like a growl. Mother had caught him out and he'd hate it that Billy had been there to hear. Good.

It was six in the evening when the door-bell rang. Billy rushed to open the door before Mother could stand up.

'Put that light out!' bellowed the Air Raid Warden. But it was all right, because it was Mr Durban, Mrs Durban and Angela standing behind him. Dad had invited them to spend a jolly evening.

Mr Durban was wearing his ARP band but not his helmet. 'Never off duty,' he grinned.

'Oh, you gave me quite a turn,' said Mother bringing them all inside quickly and shutting the door tight behind them as a searchlight swept up and lit the heavens. 'Happy New Year. Come right in, there seems no end to this icy weather.'

Dad said, 'Next time, just wait until I say, Billy. Don't just take it on yourself to open the door.'

Mrs Durban put a hand on Billy's shoulder as the light went back on. 'Safely back, dear? And you, Marcia, you must be so glad to be home? Good evening, Herbert. Is it still busy at the Courts?'

'People don't change, war or no war, sadly. Let me take your coats.'

As they put their coats on the hallstand, Angela smiled at Billy. 'You can tell me all about evacuation.'

She was wearing a blue flowered dress and a little cardigan, fluffy like an animal. Billy went to stroke it.

'It's called Angora,' she said.

'Bit like you. Angora. Angela.'

She laughed and went down the hall after the women.

Mr Durban followed slowly, looking hard at Billy. He raised his eyebrows. Billy shook his head. He knew Mr Durban was asking if he'd told about the story. They were like two secret friends, men who knew the shashka.

'Good lad,' said Mr Durban, slipping half a crown into Billy's hand. 'A late gift. Go and post it in your money box. You can buy something later.'

Billy looked at it, and then at Mr Durban. The shashka story was thrilling enough, without a reward too. Angela was so lucky that he was her father.

'Th-thank you very much,' he breathed. But Mr Durban was saying Shh at the same time, so the *thank you* got mushed up with the *Shh* and sounded like *shashka*.

He fetched the Ludo set to play with Angela while the grown-ups talked. He felt rather shy of her. It seemed a long time since she'd put her arm round him and told him about Evacuation. She beckoned him over to the little table at the other side of the room and they set out the board and pieces.

Mr Durban was saying, 'You are going to join us ARPs, Bert? You're a long time nailing your colours to the flag.'

Dad's face was grim. 'For defence, maybe. Not offence.'

'He's a bit of a pacifist, on the quiet,' Mother said.

'Even so, wherever I can, I shall do my part. Fire-watching, I expect.'

Angela slid her white piece towards Billy's row of blacks. 'I didn't go away.'

'I know.'

'So tell me how was evacuation?'

No-one else was listening, so he told her about the village, the nature walks, Alan, Mrs Youldon and the party at the Grange.

'Like an adventure,' she breathed. 'I've just stayed here, knitting grey pieces for soldiers and sitting in the Anderson for practice. Some of our best teachers have gone to war and loads of my friends are still evacuated. I was sorry for you when you went, but now I think you had the luck.'

'Not really,' Billy said. In a whisper he told about being the last child to be chosen, the hip bath and the privy. 'But it's a secret like the— you know.'

'Sabre, yes. Sh.'

She looked over at the grown-ups but they were still busy with war talk.

'An outside lavatory? Ugh! Poor you. I'd hate that. I was supposed to be evacuated to my Aunty's in Wales, but I begged Daddy not to go. We were just going to start learning Shakespeare at school.'

'Shake spear?'

She laughed. 'Nothing to do with spears. It's a man who wrote plays long ago. I love English lessons and I don't want to miss any. The English teacher's quite old, so she won't go for war work. Daddy says even if there is bombing now, we're all staying or all going, and I think it'll be all staying because he's got to stick at his job and his ARP work. They depend on him.'

Mother called them over to the tea trolley. Billy handed round the plates and serviettes while she poured the tea. Angela passed the ham sandwiches and iced tarts.

Afterwards, Dad moved everyone to the front room where he'd pinned a white sheet on the far wall and set out the magic lantern. An open wooden box with white glass squares sat beside it. They had the special pictures on them.

It was so exciting sitting in the dark as the light flickered onto the white sheet, and scenes of iced mountains and great wide rivers and castles and jungles and Spanish dancers in long frilly dresses with black lacy fan things on their heads flashed up one by one. There were loads of scenes and by the time it was all over the scenes were mixed in Billy's head and he couldn't think whether the dancers lived in the jungle or the castle.

'That was a super show,' Mr Durban said as Dad collected their coats.

Mother turned off the hall light and opened the front door onto the freezing night. A searchlight swept right across the sky ahead and then everything went black. Billy gazed up at the stars in their strange patterns.

Mr Durban looked down at him. 'Star-gazing, my boy?'

Billy knew he wasn't Mr Durban's boy, not really, but he could ask him questions. 'Why does the sky look so big?'

Mr Durban didn't laugh or sneer. 'It's the black-out, no lights spoiling the view of the sky. I've never seen it like this in previous years, Billy.' A searchlight swept past again. 'Or those, I have to say.'

A light snow was falling as they walked away, smattering Angela's green school mac and pixie hood. She looked like a pine tree as she turned to wave. Mr Durban sent a smile specially at him. Billy felt the half crown in his pocket, all ready to join Uncle Ted's shilling. He knew where the ARP hut was. He'd visit it if he was sent to the shops and then he could ask Mr Durban anything, even about the shashka.

It hadn't stopped snowing for days. They all sat with their chairs close to the stove. Bandwagon was playing on the wireless. Mother took up some grey socks to darn and said, 'Early night tonight, Billy. School starts again tomorrow.'

Billy jerked his head up. 'Aren't I going to be evacuated then? Am I staying here?'

Dad said, 'While things are quiet in London. You can go to school, meantime.'

Billy rubbed his hands together. That was good, he'd see Jim, Andrew, Reg and everyone. There'd be games of football in the playground. He hadn't played since last term in the country school. 'I'll be able to see my friends.'

Mother stroked back a grey thread before plunging her darning needle back into the heel of the sock. 'Yes, you will. And Kenneth will be there of course.'

It was a funny feeling running towards school. He hadn't even thought about those roads for months and he knew them so well. The bitter morning made him rush along, the wind whipping round his knees like a punishment. He reached the dirty cement wall with 'Wot no Dads?' chalked on it and followed a crowd of children through the school gate. He didn't recognizemany faces.

He looked for anyone he knew. Sonia was back, and she waved, but there were loads of children he'd never seen before. When the whistle went, he moved towards his old class line and at last he saw Jim and Reg.

'Yahoo, I'm back.'

They grinned but as he started over towards them, an elderly lady teacher pulled him back in line. Wasn't he going to be in the same class?

Inside was different. The men teachers were all gone except Mr Hendrick. Miss Johnson and Mr Finlay were still back at the village. The old pair of classrooms had its dividing doors open, so there weren't two classes now, but one big one. Mr Hendrick stood at the door waving his walking stick to anyone not walking in quietly. He looked greyer and couldn't remember Billy's name. That felt horrible.

The most rotten thing was Kenneth, standing there at the middle desks, still with his gloves on. It was very crowded, three to a desk. Jim and Reg were in the back row, and there was no room for him. Mr Hendrick pointed to an empty seat by two smaller boys. One of them smelled like bad wee.

Billy looked all around. There was Andrew! They made silent signs to each other. There were so many in the class! Billy counted forty-two, and when it was register, some were absent. They all had to call out their names and ages. Some children were younger than Billy, and others were more than two years older.

'Now settle down,' said Mr Hendrick. 'I know you've all got lots of news about Christmas. Welcome back, those children who were evacuated. We're very happy to have you here safe and sound. But we must work all the harder because there are lots more of us. Older ones help the younger ones;

good readers help the strugglers. Understood? And no talking.' He handed out the exercise books, cut into three.

After everyone had written a page about Christmas, and chanted times tables that Sir had pinned on the wall, it was time for Reading. There were only six copies of the reading book and so everyone had to read from the same one, reading round the class.

The book was far, far too easy for Billy, but some children staggered over every word. It was very boring, so when it was his turn, he tried to make it more interesting by doing the voices of the different characters. Behind him, he heard a snort. It was Kenneth, nudging his neighbours and encouraging them to snigger.

'Don't be silly, boys,' said Mr Hendrick. 'Go on, Wilson, please.'

But now every word threatened to trip him up and the beastly stutter came back. Some of the girls tutted and sighed. Kenneth and the boys beside him snorted as loudly as they could without getting caught.

Luckily, the milk bottles were put inside the door at that point, so everyone lined up while Sonia handed out the straws. Mr Hendrick spooned out cod liver oil and malt at the doorway before they drank their milk and went out to play.

Outside, he was just joining Andrew, Jim and Reg when Kenneth ran up with a crowd of boys. They surrounded Billy, calling him soppy and mimicking his reading.

'What ab-bout you then?' Billy complained. 'P-people might laugh when it's your t-turn to read.'

'M-m-my t-t-turn.'

'M-m-my t-t-turn.' The boys copied and laughed.

Billy's face got hot and he raised his fists.

'Don't,' said Sonia, her new hair tied up neatly with a pink satin ribbon. 'Sir'll come out and you'll be for it if you fight.'

'Can't fight, Weakie. Girls say so,' taunted Kenneth.

'He m-might get into t-t-trouble, s-so he c-can't f-f-fight,' joked a fat, toothy boy and the whole lot fell about laughing.

They all needed bashing. Billy looked wildly around for his friends. They were at the edge of the crowd, looking awkward. Jim took a ball from under his arm and nudged the others. They ran away down the playground, kicking it between them as they went.

It was freezing and many of the girls were huddled in their coats under the protruding roof. Sonia pointed to them as she ran off. 'Come up here, Billy, with us lot.'

He shook his head, miserably. He couldn't sit with the girls, and if he hit out at the teasers, Kenneth would tell and if he was hit, perhaps he'd be ill again. Then there'd be Uncle Frank's punishment. Why couldn't Uncle Frank be a soldier and go to war, and Uncle Ted come home again?

Uncle Ted would know how to deal with Kenneth.

The boys jumped up and down around him making stupid faces and putting their tongues out. If only he had the shashka to whistle round their heads. That'd shut them up.

As soon as their attention wavered, Billy ran off down the playground to join Andrew, Jim and Reg. He'd always played football with them at playtime before. As he reached them, Reg kicked a whopper and it hit the sheds with a twang.

Everyone cheered. Kenneth put his foot on the ball. 'Kick it back, Kenneth,' said Jim. 'Give us it.'

Kenneth did, and so was then in the game. Jim gave Billy half a glance. Billy hesitated, then walked off. It was too risky playing any game with Kenneth in it. As the yards grew between Billy and the football, he heard Kenneth say, 'You weren't going to let old B-b-billy play, were you?'

This was too much, especially when the others, his friends, just shrugged. As Kenneth ran past, putting his tongue out, Billy grabbed hold of him. The school wall was nearby. Kenneth was backing towards it but Billy held on to his coat lapels.

He pushed Kenneth against the wall, saw his beastly eyes with their long lashes and skinny throat all white and smooth. He hated him, his hands itched to squeeze and strangle the throat.

'You better not hurt me. I shall tell Daddy.'

'I feel like killing you. I could put Hitler onto you.'

A crowd of children ran up. 'A fight, a fight. Go on Wilson, bash him.'

They were both Wilson, so which of them was meant?

Kenneth smirked at him, looking confident that Billy would never dare hit him.

Billy pulled back his fist ready. He wouldn't think about Uncle Frank. He just wanted to bash Kenneth into the far away.

'Fight-ing, fight-ing,' the girls were chanting.

Billy held firmly onto Kenneth, who was looking hard at Billy's fist. The other boys closed round them in a ring.

'Go on, Wilson, get him,' someone yelled from the back of the crowd.

Kenneth leant forward with hard staring eyes. There was a spot of malt just near his stupid mouth. Spit came out of it, he spoke so fast, 'You're being sent away to the country. If you hit me, they'll give me your toys and you'll never come back home.'

Billy's fist went slack. Was it true? He'd been sent away before.

Kenneth wriggled out of his grasp and ran through the circle of children, punching the air as they yelled 'Aw, Kenneth! Fight him.'

'Not worth it, the soppy stammerer!'

Billy could have chased him, pushed him to the ground and pummelled him over and over. He knew he was stronger. But then Aunty would hate him, Uncle Frank would beat him and Mother and Dad would send him away. Were they really planning it already? Or was it one of Kenneth's lies?

He leant against the wall, warm where Kenneth's body had just been, and folded his arms in front of him, holding the hate safely inside. The circle mooched away, leaving him alone.

After the whistle went, Andrew ran into school beside him. 'You should've fought him. Otherwise, Kenneth'll do it again.'

'You didn't stick up for me.'

Andrew hurried ahead.

In the classroom the inkwells were being filled up. The teacher had chosen Kenneth as the class monitor because he was clean and reliable. Some inkwells had fresh ink. People who got those could write fairly neatly. Others were clogged with bits of blotting paper so that pens made blotches even with the most careful of writers. Billy knew he would get a clogged one, and he did.

Sir had been busy in playtime. There were loads of sums written up on the blackboard. There were some groans. Kenneth looked around and frowned, as if he was the teacher.

Everyone leaned over their desks, some with the tip of the pen in their mouths. Billy was one of the first to finish.

'You boys who've finished, help these boys on the front row, please,' said Mr Hendrick. 'I see you've not forgotten your lessons after all those weeks away, Wilson. Well done.'

'Well done,' mimicked a quiet voice.

Kenneth's head wagged from side to side, a stupid grin on his face. Boys near him sniggered, and so did some girls. Mr Finlay didn't see. He had his head down trying to explain pounds, shillings

196

and pence to the back row. Billy hunched his shoulders. It was a beastly day, and his knees burned ever so badly. When Mr Hendrick paced down between the rows he noticed how red Billy's knees were.

'You've got chaps, Wilson. It's very cold weather, everyone. Turn your socks up so that they cover your knees when you go outside.'

Billy glared at Kenneth as they lined up, hoping to scare him but Kenneth just mouthed 'country' to him. Aunty always collected him at the school gate so Billy couldn't risk doing anything. He turned his socks over his knees and ran home.

He was out of breath when he got through the front door and it felt good to see Jill in the parlour with her toys.

He sat down to play with her and put his freezing hands and knees to the fire. The coals were red but his knees were even brighter. Mother put her head round the door.

'You're back sharpish, Billy. Was it nice to be back at your old school then?'

He wanted to tell her. 'I d-didn't like it with Kenneth in my class.'

'He's older than you, so of course he's going to be able to do everything quicker and better.'

'Not that. He's p-playing with all my friends, Jim and Reg and Andrew.'

'Of course, everyone's mixed in. You have to share, Billy. Share your toys, share your friends.'

'But he laughs at me and things.'

'That's nothing. Ignore it.' She wiggled a toy at Jill. 'Just poke the coals a bit, Billy. Put the poker back well behind the fire-guard, then go upstairs and wash your hands. I've got some jam sponge for tea.'

'And spam sandwiches?' 'Yes.'

'Goody.' Was she really sending him to the country? He'd test her. 'I was always h-hungry when I was evacuated, Mother.'

'That's in the past. At home, you can always have more bread.'

In the past? So Kenneth had been lying.

He hadn't eaten much at lunch-time, that horrible pale mince and wet cabbage and ucky junket afterwards. It would be super to sling the lot at Kenneth.

He slid back from the fire, a bit warmer now, and put the hot poker well out of Jill's reach.

CHAPTER TWENTY-THREE
March 18, 1940

Hitler meets Mussolini.
Will Italy join the war?

Billy was zooming in the garden. That meant being a spitfire, speeding across the sky.

He stopped when Kenneth arrived with Aunty and Uncle and followed them indoors. Mother had a flowered dress she'd finished with, and Aunty thought it would fit her.

'Will you excuse us, Frank, while Doreen tries this on?' 'Go on you girls. I'll take care of these lads.'

They giggled, went up to the bedroom and shut the door. It reminded him of Mrs Youldon when her sister Mary visited, except that *they* were young, more like Angela; Mother and Aunty Doreen were proper mothers.

Uncle Frank took Billy and Kenneth into the parlour. 'Stand back to back, you two.'

The back of Kenneth's head pressed against the top of Billy's neck. Uncle turned them both to face him. He was scowling.

'Put up your arms, Billy. No, roll up your sleeves first. Ha! Call those muscles! I've felt worms firmer.'

Kenneth leant against the wall, smiling quietly, although his arms were probably like threads of cotton.

'Now then, push against my arms, boy. Harder, try to get my arms down. No, no. Hopeless. Like this, like this,' and he pressed Billy's arms back until they felt they would break.

'Phew. Ow.'

'Take it like a man. Pain. Growing up. That's what it's all about. You wait till you get in the army.

199

Sergeant Major'll make mincemeat out of you. You've got to toughen up.'

'W-what about Kenneth?' It wasn't fair.

Uncle removed his beefy hand from around Billy's arm and placed it gently on his son's curls. 'He's an artist. He'll be exempt. His paintings will be on the walls of every fashionable house in London, in Paris, everywhere. Ah, yes. You, though. You're no drawer, are you?'

'No.'

'You'll be infantry. Marching your boots off. Cannon fodder, no doubt.'

'What's that?'

Uncle laughed. It wasn't a nice sound. 'Secret. You'll find out if this war goes on long enough. Eight, aren't you? Only six more years, then territorials. My bet is that this war'll go on and on. You better build up those muscles. You want to be able to fight Hitler off when he comes, don't you?'

Hitler? Coming here! Dad should come home. Or Mother come downstairs. Now Uncle had freed his arms, he could turn round. Kenneth didn't have a frightened face. He was looking at Uncle as if he was an ice-cream.

Uncle liked painters. Hitler might like painters, might save them, even.

Uncle Frank shook his sleeves down. 'I've got to be off, boys. I'm on blackout watch. Upstairs to play, now. And I'll be back soon for your training, Sonny Jim.' He poked a finger in Billy's chest and went into the hall. 'Back later, girls,' he bellowed upstairs, before shutting the front door behind him so firmly that the house shivered.

Billy led the way upstairs, rubbing his arms. Even playing with Kenneth was a relief.

Kenneth took his shoes off and stood on the bed, looking around. 'Hey, you've got a new car!'

'Grandad gave it me for Christmas.'

'So! Reg Parsons is having me to his party next Tuesday.' He bounced a bit on the bed.

'He's *my* friend, why hasn't he invited me?'

'Ha ha. You're a left-out.'

'Why are you so nasty?'

Kenneth bent down. His face was so near that Billy could smell the cod liver oil spooned into him that morning. 'Because you've got everything.'

Billy stared at him. 'What?'

Kenneth stood up again. 'And you're never ill. Anyway, you don't live here any more and Reg is my friend now.'

'I do live here.'

'Not really. I told you, you're going back to the country. I heard Daddy say.'

Billy went to his window and looked out at the washing on the line. His trousers weren't there. Mother would have washed them if he was going away. Kenneth was jumping lightly up and down on the bed, his hands like palm fronds in front of him. He wanted to be annoying.

'It's not true', Billy said. 'One of your fibs. I'm staying here now, like you.'

'No. You're going back to that country place. Like before. And I'll stay here with all your friends and play with your toys.'

'I'm not going. I'm not!' Billy plucked his pillow from his bed and pressed it round his ears.

Kenneth bounced up and down higher, chanting, 'You won't have your toy-oys, you won't have your toy-oys, I will play with the boy-oys, I will play with the boy-oys.'

Mother's voice streamed from her bedroom, 'Billy! Don't you dare bounce on the bed! Stop it at once!'

Kenneth slid down rapidly and went to the window where three little planes stood on the windowsill. He was pushing them along sweetly as Mother opened the door.

Billy was smoothing the coverlet that Kenneth had rucked up.

'Billy! You know you mustn't bounce on the bed.'

'It was Kenneth.'

Kenneth looked up from the planes with a hurt expression. 'Billy!'

Mother took hold of Billy's arm and smacked his leg.'Naugh-ty-Boy-Pass-ing-The-Blame,' she said, in time to each smack.

Billy swallowed hard several times. 'Is that w-why you're s-sending me away?' he asked in a wobbly voice.

Mother dropped her smacking arm and glanced at Kenneth just as his smirks disappeared. 'I am not sending you away,' she said.

'Kenneth told me.'

This time it looked as if Mother believed Billy.

'Kenneth?'

'I thought I heard Daddy say he was going back to the country, Aunty Marcia,' Kenneth managed a bewildered expression.

'Only if the war steps up, that's all we've decided. And then you may have to go too, Kenneth.' She tossed her head as she shut the bedroom door again.

'And it was Kenneth bouncing,' Billy muttered as loud as he dared.

'Grrrrrrrrr,' they both said, hunching their backs and going for each other, arms flailing, pulling hair, kicking and thumping. Billy put all his hate into it.

'Shhhhh,' they both said, not wanting the mothers to return and find them fighting.

Billy ended it by sliding out to the bathroom and locking the door.

When the six o'clock news started, they went downstairs. Kenneth hung about, half listening to what had been shot down or sunk.

Billy leant on the window-sill, peering through the coloured bits in the panes of glass. It was very dark.

Enemies of all sorts could be out there, and no-one would know. He said, 'It'll be t-time for you to go home soon, Kenneth. No p-point in going upstairs again, is there? Shall we just play draughts?'

'All right. I'll be white. You're black, ha ha.'

Halfway into the game, Kenneth said, 'Anyway, bet you do go back to the country soon. Then I'll take these draughts to school.'

Billy folded the board up with all the pieces inside, ignoring Kenneth's outraged wail. He put the draughts in two piles, then pushed the black pile so that the whites collapsed in a heap. He pointed to them.

'That's you, that is. White. Black's vanquished White, see. Now I'm putting the draughts away and I hope you're ill in bed again soon, so there.'

It was only a week ago that he'd quarrelled with Kenneth and wanted him ill. Now Kenneth was ill in bed and it was Billy's fault for wishing it. This was scary.

He piled up Jill's bricks and let her knock them down again. She giggled. He liked her when she was happy. Her cheeks were like little bouncy balls, pink ones. Not marbly white, like Kenneth.

He bent his head, pretending he wasn't listening to Mother and Dad talking about helping Aunty.

'It's little enough, Marcia.'

'But we've only just finished tea. Do we have to go now?'

Dad said, 'Doreen needs some support.'

'Doreen and Kenneth are a pair, always sickly.'

'Yes, they're very unlucky.'

The voices moved to the hall, Mother's getting a bit shrill. 'It is a nuisance, sometimes. We don't cause *them* any.'

'So I'm blessed with my healthy trio. Just go and relieve her for a couple of hours. You should be charitable to Frank's wife and child.'

'I am. Don't I have him here week after week?'

'He's a charming child.'

'Mm. He has the looks; those eyes and lashes, I'll give you that. But— there are things about him that aren't— oh I don't know. I just don't want the bother of look after him so often, and really not now.'

'Just do your bit. *The only gift is a portion of thyself*— Emerson.'

'I do wish you wouldn't quote at me. All right, I'll take Billy to keep Kenneth company while I do my best to cheer Doreen up.'

Dad came back into the parlour and lifted Jill onto her chair. 'Looks like you're going to be a Daddy's girl for the evening, so none of your nonsense. Billy, Mother's going to take you to see Kenneth. Run upstairs for some books or games you could lend him while he's stuck in bed.'

Billy went to his bedroom. At first, he pulled out the Jesus book. That would do. He looked at its hard white cover, sniffing its horrid shiny smell. Jesus on the front was its only picture. He dangled the book in one hand. He'd never been ill for more than a day himself. It must be awfully boring to be stuck in bed. He got some Beanos off the bottom of the pile and a magic painting book.

'Time to put your coat on,' Mother called.

'Oh, am I pleased to see you,' said Aunty when they arrived. 'Kenneth will be thrilled, Billy.' She waved him upstairs straight away and took Mother into her kitchen.

He padded upstairs, one step at a time, and put his head round Kenneth's bedroom door. There were drawings all over his walls, people and buildings and aeroplanes and whole scenes with things happening in them.

'Cor,' Billy said. 'These are super. Just like the real dog fights. We lot've been watching them at school. Two of them flew right near. You should've seen them.'

The bedroom was stuffy and the windows misted over, so Kenneth couldn't even see the clouds let alone aeroplanes outside, even when he was sitting up. His hands lay on the covers like pale seaweed. Billy hadn't noticed before that although Kenneth was smaller than him, his fingers were longer and very white at the tips.

A half-finished jigsaw of some horses in a stable, spread on a piece of thick cardboard, lay on the foot-end of the bed.

'Do you want us to do your jigsaw?'

Kenneth shook his head. 'You do some.' He leaned over sideways to turn on the bedside lamp. It was getting dark.

Billy did the sky pieces and the muddy ground so that Kenneth could do the horses and all the interesting bits. Kenneth put in a few pieces, slowly.

He looked over the picture. 'I'm sure pieces have fallen under the bed,' he said in a crotchety voice. Billy bent right down, but he couldn't see any.

'Put the jigsaw away. It's uncomfortable on my legs.'

Billy wandered round the bed. 'I've brought you some things to read.'

'My eyes hurt.'

Billy started to draw the curtains. 'Come to the window, Kenneth. See all the stars and the moon.' It had been hanging halfway out of the sky Christmas night. Now it was skinny and mean.

Kenneth said 'It's small, not worth drawing.'

'But you always draw.'

Kenneth slid back into bed and shut his eyes. 'Just talk to me.'

He lay back and Billy pulled the curtains to, crossing over the blackout sheet in the middle. He told the best of what he remembered from the stories in his heroes book. Kenneth liked the stories and said 'More', even though he'd surely never ever do anything like discovering a new land, or bravely fighting the Normans like Hereward. It was lucky Billy hadn't brought the book with him, because Kenneth might want to keep it. He jolly well mustn't because the boy on the cover looked like Billy and Mr Durban had specially given it to him. It was a book to keep always, like the secret about the shashka.

When Aunty called him downstairs so that Kenneth could rest again, she said he was a life-saver. 'Kenneth needs you more than ever.'

Billy didn't say anything. He pretended to look at a ginger cat on her calendar.

Mother was looking at him with her head on one side. She picked up her hatpin and felt its cruel point before skewering her hat with it. 'Time to get back, Billy. Your father's probably going potty trying to put Baby to bed. Bye, Doreen. Let's hope Kenneth's fit again soon.'

CHAPTER TWENTY-FOUR
June 5th 1940

Dunkirk rescue – Churchill defiant

The skies had been blue for some time and Kenneth had been well for ages. Sometimes he had to come home from school with Billy and stay for tea because Aunty did work at the Mothers' Union.

Everyone had got very excited at school when Mr Churchill became Prime Minister. They were allowed to bring their flags and wave them and cheer after Mr Hendrick read them Mr Churchill's speech about having 'nothing to offer but blood, toil, tears and sweat,' and that Britain wanted 'Victory. Victory at all costs. Victory in spite of all terror. Victory, however long and hard the road may be, for without victory there is no survival.' They all wrote those words down and the top set learned them off by heart.

At home, Billy told Dad about it proudly because he'd been one of those to memorise the words.

Dad said with a long face, 'Mr Churchill may be a warmonger but at least he doesn't pretend the price will not be paid.' Dad didn't look to the ceiling or say a name afterwards so that must have been his own saying.

Today Mother had a special meeting at the town hall. Everyone was looking grim so it was probably important.

'I'd better go to it, Billy. You can walk to Nanny and Grandad's and I'll collect you from there.'

Nanny met him at the door and took him in for milk and fruit buns. 'I'm sorry there's no cake, Billy. I just haven't the sugar, you see.' She didn't chat and didn't bring out anything for him to play with. Mother had told Dad that the war was getting

Nanny down. He ate up hungrily and looked round for Grandad.

'He's in the garden waiting for you, my dear.'

Billy ran out. It was warm and lovely, just right for playing ball with someone. But Grandad said, 'Come along, Billy. I'm going to teach you how to grow vegetables. It's very important now.'

He showed him all the planting in rows, then how to weed round the carrots.

Eventually he said he'd go indoors for a cup of tea and sit down. 'I'll see how Nanny is. You finish those last two rows yourself, now.'

Well past tea-time and still sunny, it was such a happy feeling. There was no Jill to whine or Kenneth to bully him and he'd just learned how to make a whistle sound. He practised as he pulled out the weeds and put them in a little wooden trug by his side. He did a whole row then held out his hands, really black with mud. All the fingernails were too. That was rather shocking but Nanny wouldn't mind and there was plenty of time for cleaning up before Mother came for him. Perhaps her meeting would be long, and she might ask Nanny if he could stay the night. That would be topping. He finished the last row and stood up to admire his work.

Down the road he could see someone dragging along. It was a sort of scarecrow man, all dirty and hairy in a big long coat and he kept coming nearer. Billy backed towards the house as he watched the boots all cracked and green, with only bits of lace, slop, slop, slop, coming right towards the gate. Billy scampered round to the back door.

'Quick, Grandad. There's a scarecrow man coming to your gate. He's going to come in. Stop him, stop him!'

Grandad pushed Billy gently towards Nanny, and went through to the front door. They heard him open it and start down the path. There was a pause, then hoarse voices.

Grandad put his head round the front door and called to Nanny, 'Send Billy next door for an hour or so. Then run a hot bath.'

Nanny looked confused, then gestured to Billy towards the gate. But as he went he heard Grandad whisper to her, 'It's Ted, love. It's Ted.'

The neighbour had to give Billy a tin bowl to soak his black hands in, with a nailbrush and carbolic soap.

There was something bubbling on the stove and it smelled horrible. 'Don't mind my cooking, duck. It's a pigs head. Hubby loves it, see.'

He shuddered. He didn't want to see.

The lady put gramophone music on for him while he sat there trying to work things out. Did Uncle Ted come after the scarecrow man, chase him away? He scrubbed at his nails. The dirt wouldn't come out. Was the scarecrow man really Uncle Ted? It didn't look a bit like him. The man on the record sang on, *Nice work if you can get it.* It took ages for his nails to get clean and soon the needle was just scratching round the record. He didn't want to listen to singing anyway.

It seemed a long time before Mother came for him with Jill in the pushchair. She didn't even look at his hands. She walked back home slowly, ignoring Jill's jabber. Although Dad said she was a late talker, Jill could say several words now, so she said them over and over, 'cup, dinner, dinner, cup, cup, mama, cup, cup, cup, cup, cup, mama, mama, cup.'

When they were well away from Nanny and Grandad's, Billy asked, 'Did Uncle Ted come home, Mother?'

She loosened her silky headscarf and shook her fringe from her forehead, looking to left and right as if she was going to cross the road, but they weren't near any crossing.

'Yes, he did. He's safe, isn't that good? He's back from France and needs to rest. So it may be a while before we see him.'

She wasn't going to say any more. He could tell.

As usual, it was Kenneth who told him more. At school playtime, Kenneth ran over to him. 'Your Uncle Ted's home.'

'Mm.' Billy didn't want him to know about the scarecrow man.

'Came home filthy. Nothing on except his underwear and a greatcoat. I know all about it, Aunty Marcia rang Mummy last night. Then she told Daddy, and I was there.'

Billy hunched his shoulders so that his neck was hidden by his jumper. Why couldn't Aunty be like Mother and not say anything in front of children?

He glared at Kenneth. 'Uncle Ted couldn't help it.'

'I know. Taken off the beach, like the others. Rescued.' Kenneth raised himself to full height, looking important. 'See, France has gone.'

'Gone where?'

'Nowhere, stupid. Hitler's fighting there and we've lost. Daddy says Hitler's won France now. He's doing Belgium and he'll come for England next. He'll bring thousands of soldiers and they'll all come to London.'

'They w-won't.'

'Will. Defeated, your uncle. De-feated by the Germans.'

'Germans are ENEMY!'

Kenneth danced around singing tunefully. 'Defeated by the Germans, defeated by the Germans.'

Miss Keaton, an old teacher who had come out of retirement, was on duty. 'Lovely singing voice, Kenneth. It's good to see you have so much energy after being ill so often.'

Kenneth lowered his head, his eyelashes too. 'Thank you, Miss Keaton.'

Miss Keaton blew her whistle hard and Billy ran as fast as he could to sit in his desk far away from Kenneth at the front. The sums were easy, but he couldn't concentrate and for once he was nearly the last to finish instead of one of the first. He'd wanted Uncle Ted to come home so much and now he had. But he wasn't Uncle Ted, but some dirty man like the ones people put notices on their gates for *No Hawkers.* He screwed up his eyes but couldn't get those greeny cracked boots out of his mind.

He ran straight home before Kenneth could get to him or shout out things to all of the others. This time, he was jolly well going to ask Mother.

'Mother. Was Uncle Ted on the b-beach? Was he d- defeated? Is England d-defeated?'

Mother sat down on the sofa in the parlour. She hadn't laid the table and Jill was still in her high chair from lunch, kicking the foot rest and banging a board book up and down on the tray, just like she'd done when she was a proper baby. Mother sighed and put her hands round her face.

'England isn't defeated yet. Our armies just had to withdraw. That means, get away for the moment. They'll go back again.'

'To France? Where the Germans are?'

She shook her head. Did this mean No, or she didn't know, or to stop asking her? 'Mother. Please tell me what happened to Uncle Ted.'

For once she didn't wave him off. She just looked tired. 'He was with his regiment but they got split up when they were fighting. He had to wait on the beach with all the other soldiers who needed to get back to England. Rescue boats came out but they were mostly small. He waited for his turn three days and nights standing in the sea. They had no food, he was exhausted. So he's resting now at Nanny and Grandad's. I told you that.'

'Is he a hero?' Billy could hardly hear his own quiet voice.

'Everyone's a hero who fights in the war. Or no-one is,' Mother said to herself, standing up at last. 'Jill, stop that banging.' She lifted her out and muttered, 'There's a nursery on the common now. I could sign up for war work, though I don't know what— make phone calls for the officer class?'

Jill trotted over to Billy and held up her book. 'Read me.'

'Do I have to, Mother?'

But Mother had gone out to the kitchen. He opened Jill's book. It only had six pages. It really was very boring. Cup. Doggie. Pussy. Chair. Bed. He could do much better if he wrote books for little children. He took Jill by the hand and went upstairs to his room with her. He found her one of his old books with a story about a bear who ran away to sea. He read it to her and she really listened. She was growing up, getting to be a proper person at last.

'Again, more,' she said.

He looked at her fat little face. Perhaps she'd grow up to be nicer than Kenneth. 'If you're good,' he said, 'I'm going to give you my animals.'

'Amimas.'

He found her a bear that fitted into her chubby hand very well and they went downstairs for tea. Mother only had bread and jam, no cake, but he didn't say anything.

No-one said anything. If there had been cake, he'd have saved it for Uncle Ted.

After tea, he said he was going out for a run, just nearby. It was still light, so Mother let him. It was Jill's bedtime. He ran really fast until he got to Mr Durban's ARP hut. He was lucky, Mr Durban had just come on duty.

'My Uncle Ted's back,' Billy had to stop to take a breath, 'and he's resting. From France. Mother said he had to wait three days and nights to be rescued from the sea. I saw him come up Nanny's road all dirty like a tramp and his boots had no laces and had gone all green.'

'Now slow down, Billy. Thank the Lord our good lads are home safe from Dunkirk. Tell me, is your uncle all right?'

'He's resting and Kenneth says England was defeated.'

'Defeated? Never! Mr Churchill says the withdrawal was a masterful success.'

'Success?' Billy looked at him hopefully. 'Was it? But Kenneth says France has gone. Where's it gone?'

'It's still there, my boy, but the French let Germany take over. Our brave soldiers couldn't fight the Germans alone. They went back to the French beaches to be collected. Your uncle needs his rest now. A couple of days' then he'll be back at the front.'

'Back! But he's done his fighting.'

'He's still needed. Britain needs all the soldiers she can get. But not your father, Billy. He's needed here.'

'What about my Uncle Frank?'

'Tax inspector, isn't he? Retained. So don't worry.'

Why couldn't Uncle Frank fight Hitler? He'd be just right. Hitler needed bullying. It wasn't fair. Billy fidgeted with his feet.

'Sit yourself down.'

He sat on a wooden stool underneath the poster of Hitler looking sneakily behind some nice English people to hear what they were saying.

'Now, Billy. I was just about to have a bit of tea. I've got chocolate here that I won't be able to manage. Can you help me out?'

Billy nodded. Probably he could. 'Thank you,' he murmured with his mouth full.

There was a map of Europe on the table beside him. Mr Durban pointed out Dunkirk and where the Jerries were. 'Doubt if it'll be France your uncle goes back to, don't worry.'

213

Then another warden arrived and Billy had to scuttle off home.

Nanny would look after Uncle and make him clean and strong again. He wouldn't let Kenneth sneer about Uncle even if he had to bash him and get punished. If only he had the shashka he could wave it and Kenneth would shake. Or it would be magic, and in a moment Uncle Ted would be just the same as he always used to be, laughing and teasing him, even doing handstands. He had to be, otherwise, how could he be sent back soldiering?

Uncle had been five days resting when Mother said to hurry home from school so that they could see him again.

Jill was already in her pushchair when he got back. She waved a toy at him, smiling, because she didn't understand they were going to say Goodbye to Uncle Ted.

On the walk to Nanny's, Billy didn't try to tell Mother about school that day. It didn't seem important, even though this air raid practice they'd all had to run their fastest and Andrew had tripped and fallen and blood came down and down from his knee. It couldn't be seen to until the pretend All Clear came. There'd been another *Run Rabbit, Run* game with teachers joining in too. It was like grown-ups growing down.

He watched Mother's feet marching along behind the push-chair. Her shoes weren't shiny and the heels rolled over at the sides. Everything was getting wrong.

Nanny gave Mother a special look when opened the door and hugged Billy to her side while muttering something to Mother over his head. Jill was happy in her pushchair so they left her in the hall.

'It'll be quieter for Ted if she stays here,' Nanny said.

Grandad was in the sitting room with a pack of cards dealt out on the card table. Uncle Ted was sitting the other side of it with his back to them. Mother went forward and bent over him to say Hello.

He turned round slowly and then noticed Billy. 'Hello, Billy,' was all he said.

Billy stared. Although his shirt and trousers were clean and his face too, his face was hollow where his cheeks had been and the front of his hair wasn't right. A great chunk of it was white, whiter than Grandad's.

'Hello Uncle,' Billy muttered and quickly stood back by Nanny. When she went into the kitchen, he followed. He found lots of helping to do while Nanny put things on trays for tea.

She said, 'We're keeping things nice and peaceful for your Uncle Ted so he can set off in a calm way, you see.'

He nodded, then when Jill whimpered, went into the hall to keep her company until Nanny came to lift her out, one finger on her lips.

She put Jill up at the table on a big cushion to make her high and gave her an iced bun, which kept her quiet. She didn't seem to notice Uncle Ted and he didn't seem to notice her.

Grandad went on with the card game while they all had tea and cake.

As Billy was carrying the dirty cups to the kitchen, a snatch of conversation escaped from the sitting room. Mother was saying, 'Thank God you managed to get on a boat, that's what I say. You got back safely, and you will next time.'

And Uncle's low voice, 'I did. But some Frenchies with us didn't.'

Billy edged nearer the kitchen door.

'They wouldn't let them on. "Britons only," they said. We'd fought beside them a few days before, and I had to leave them. Just standing in the sea, bodies floating all around them, and the Jerries still coming over, plane after plane, kerchow, kerchow!

None of us were firing, we weren't in a state to do anything. And they still bombed us. I can't stop thinking about it.'

'You've got to put it out of your mind, Ted. There was nothing you could do.'

Billy rushed past for a wee. Grandad cleared his throat at that point and they all stopped talking. It was lucky Nanny was in the kitchen so she hadn't heard. She would've been very upset.

When he came back from the downstairs lavatory, she was collecting up the left-over cake from the table, saying, 'We're going to sort stuff in a moment, Marcia, so that Ted goes back with what he needs.'

Mother kept her hand on Uncle Ted's shoulder, shaking her head.

Billy sidled back into the kitchen. Nanny was muttering, 'Though I can't believe they're sending him back in his state.'

He piled the plates and saucers up neatly on the draining board. It was such a high pile that it would topple if he didn't stay there, holding it all up. Nanny took over. 'Good boy. You go back and sit down now.'

Grandad was holding one of Uncle Ted's arms as though he'd just fixed it on. 'See, they need you to get back, lad. The longer you stay, the harder it'll get.'

'I can't face it.'

'You can.' Grandad put a cigarette in Uncle's mouth and flicked his lighter. The flame caught the end of the cigarette with a little flare. In a moment, the end glowed and a line of smoke crept out of Uncle's nostrils. 'Stiff upper lip. We all have to do our duty. I'd go for you if I could, son, but I'm no use to them.'

Uncle drew again at the cigarette.

'Gee-up, son, let's stop upsetting the womenfolk.'

They stayed by the spread-out cards, but not playing any more. Grandad puffed at his pipe. They were both looking down at the carpet.

Billy wanted to speak to Uncle Ted so much. He wanted to ask him what wild animals there were in France and see him do a cartwheel again. But he couldn't. This was a strange man sitting and sending out puffs of smoke. He wasn't like the scarecrow, but he wasn't like Uncle Ted, either. Uncle didn't even see Jill wagging her doll up and down in front of him, and he didn't say anything to Billy.

When Mother said it was time to go, Uncle Ted stood up and she hugged him hard. 'Good luck, Ted, I'll be thinking of you. Stay safe.' She pretended not to, but she was crying. Grandad and Nanny stayed in their chairs, looking at the floor.

Billy opened his mouth but didn't manage to say Goodbye. Uncle Ted didn't seem to notice. His eyes were bleak and his lips gripped the cigarette.

Jill was bawling as they reached the hall. Billy opened the front door. Mother took the pushchair and moved away down the path quickly. She didn't talk all the way down St James' Rise. At last, he risked saying, 'Is Uncle Ted going back to France, Mother?'

She was a long time answering. Then she said, 'Not France. They're all coming out of France. I don't think his regiment have told him where it's to be next.'

Billy watched a soldier on the other side of the road go into a pub. Had he been rescued?

They crossed the big road and turned a corner. He wouldn't ask Mother any more. He'd go to Mr Durban's hut tomorrow and find out what other countries there were to fight in, now that France was empty.

When they got home, they found Dad was back from Lincoln.

'Thank goodness, Herbert.' Mother almost ran to put her head on his shoulder.

She was going to tell Dad about Uncle, so Billy took hold of the pushchair. He heard her whisper 'Ted—' in a quavery voice.

Dad put his arms round her and turned her away, 'Ah, I feared that.' After a moment, he let her go. 'Let's see to these children first and then we'll go in the parlour.'

He came to help Billy with the pushchair. Jill was squealing with excitement to see him, so he picked her up and then patted Billy's back. 'You're a good helper.'

Mother sent Billy to bed right away, although it was early. He lay in bed and listened to her talking and talking and talking, and Dad answering. The voices stopped when they put the wireless on. The last thing he heard was something about towns falling. That was a very scary thing to think about. At least Uncle Ted hadn't been in a falling town and perhaps he'd be sent to a country with no sea this time.

CHAPTER TWENTY-FIVE
September 7th 1940

Luftwaffe target London.
Civil Defence responding admirably

Dad's puffs of smoke danced down the hall as he went to the front door. 'Kenneth has been nervy since that air raid, Billy. I want you to be especially thoughtful when he comes today, please.'

Billy swallowed his last sweet. *He* hadn't been frightened in the air raid. There'd been a torch in the cellar. He'd always watched the coal falling through the hole when the coalman came. Now the coal hid behind shelves, and two camp beds filled the space. The air raid didn't last long and it was rather exciting, and it'd been fun everyone swapping notes on their first day back at school after holidays, especially as now he was a *junior,* not an infant schoolboy, and had to line up outside the Junior Boys entrance.

Luckily, Mother wasn't there to see the evacuation notices on the school gate. Perhaps she wouldn't know.

Now Kenneth was at the door. He watched him coming down the hall, white and thin in his short sleeved shirt.

It was flipping hot so Mother put out a tub of water in the garden for them. 'Yippee! Come on, Kenneth!'

They both pulled off everything except their pants and took it in turns to pretend they were swimming. It was even quite fun splashing around with Kenneth until water went on his hair.

'Stop it, Billy. I don't want my face wet. I'm getting out.'

'Cissy. You get scared of everything.'

219

'Don't. Anyway, air raids are scary.'

'I'm not scared.' Billy stood up and looked down at his bare chest. It was strong-looking besides Kenneth's body, which caved in a bit round the ribs. He felt proud, perhaps he was growing into a Cossack.

Kenneth pointed at him. 'You're stupid and— ignorant. Don't you know a bomb dropped right in the middle of London during that air raid? And it was on a church!'

Billy didn't know. Dad didn't tell him anything. He risked saying, 'Only one bomb. That's probably all the Germans have.'

Kenneth started dressing. 'Huh! Fat lot you know. Bombing's horrible.'

'We've got shelters.'

'I don't want to be buried in an Anderson thank you very much.' Kenneth walked over to the french windows. They were wide open because of the heat. He called through them, 'Uncle, I've brought my paints over.'

Dad stood up and gave him half a roll of wall-paper. 'Here you are, Kenneth. I thought you might need this. Got it from the cellar. It's nice and smooth on the back, so you can paint on that.'

Billy stayed in the pool finding ants to plop into the water and then rescue out of it. He stayed in until his feet were all wrinkly.

Kenneth was still painting a long time after they'd eaten their stew and dumplings. Dad kept coming in and looking over his shoulder. 'Well done, Kenneth. That painting's worth finishing.'

Billy came to watch. He was no good with a paintbrush, the powder paint at school made a horrible mess when he tried it at school. Nothing of his ever looked any good, so he liked to see how Kenneth did it. The long white fingers gently swished up and down and soon there was a WVS canteen, sky behind it, and little figures in front.

Dad sounded pleased. ' Excellent, Kenneth. Very good composition.'

Kenneth only said, 'I'm nearly out of blue.'

Billy said, 'I haven't got paints.'

'I know.'

If he had paints, he would have let Kenneth have the blue so that the picture could be finished.

Dad went into the parlour and turned on the wireless. It must be time for the news.

The large jam-jar beside Kenneth was full of brown water.

'Whatever colours you paint with, Kenneth, the water ends up brown.'

'That's because it's a tertiary colour, stupid.'

Billy wasn't going to ask what *tirshy* meant. He'd ask Mother later, if he could remember the funny word.

Kenneth turned to him. 'You could get me some clean water. That'd be something useful.'

Billy took the jar out to the kitchen. Mother had finished making the scones. The lovely smell filled the room. The wireless, droning on in the parlour, got louder as Mother opened the door. 'Well, Herbert?'

'It's stepping up.'

That meant Hitler, war and bombing. He watched Mother flap her hands.

'Now don't mention the dreaded E word, please. I can't stand the thought of that disruption again.'

'Safety, Marcia. That's what I care about, for all of you.'

'Dal lalla, dalla lalla.' That's what Jill's babble sounded like as she put a block on the top of a tower shakily. She chortled. The tower fell for the umpteenth time, and for the umpteenth time Billy built it again. 'Lally da lal-lal.'

The doorbell rang. Billy shushed Jill because he heard Mr Durban's voice in the hall. 'I'm here to give you the nod, Bert. Got your cellar more organised?

The East End's been copping it and there's word of a convoy coming.'

Kenneth carried on painting. Tiny leaves decorated the border of his page and he was bending low over it.

Billy was just wondering if Mother would ask Mr Durban to stay for tea, when the air raid siren screamed out. Kenneth gave such a start that he knocked the paint water over, but Mother just said, 'Leave it, Kenneth. Come on, both of you.' She picked up Jill and made for the cellar.

Footsteps hurried up the hall and the front door slammed. Mr Durban was going out into the danger, like a hero.

'Quick sharp,' Dad shouted. 'Mr Durban says it might be coming our way.'

They scrambled down to the cellar. Kenneth sat himself on a little chair, saying nothing. Jill's eyes were wide and wet as she gazed around her. Mother started reading to Jill. Although the story was silly and only fit for a baby, Billy listened and kept listening until the rumbling started.

'It's some way off,' said Dad. Then it grew louder. 'Dad— Mr Durban's outside in it!'

'He's on duty, Billy. He'll be in the right place with his tin helmet on, don't worry.'

Dad brought a book out and some biscuits and a thermos flask. But before he could pass any over there was a huge thumping and thudding, and not so very far away. Kenneth slid forward and climbed into the bunk, covering his head with the blanket.

Remembering what Dad had asked of him Billy said, 'Isn't it lucky you're safe down here, Kenneth, and not in your Anderson?'

It was so good they had a cellar. Some people would be running for the underground station or the public shelter near the park. He hoped not anyone he knew. Then he remembered that Aunty and

Uncle would be in the Anderson. Kenneth wouldn't like that.

They all sat waiting for the next thump. Billy could hear everyone's breathing, even his own. He kept his eyes on Dad's large hands gripping the sides of his chair. He put his own hand on his hip, pretending he could feel the hilt of the shashka there. He must be the one to protect the others.

When the All Clear sounded, Dad hurried them all into the kitchen, then went out himself to find out the situation. Kenneth said he felt sick, so he was sent upstairs with a bucket to lie down.

Mother made sandwiches and tea, then saw to Jill. 'You read a book for a bit, Billy.'

Dad came back indoors and looked over at him as he had his tea. 'Reading. Good boy. Take your mind off. *What worries you, masters you—* John Locke.'

The air raid warning woke him with a start. He found he'd fallen asleep over the middle pages of his Wizard annual.

Mother was running down the hall outside, 'It's only two hours since the All Clear. Do you think it's a mistake, Herbert?'

Dad called down from upstairs, 'We won't risk it. Get Billy, I'm bringing the other two.'

This time no-one bothered with books or stories but just scrambled down the cellar stairs and sat waiting for the siren to stop wailing. As it did, there was a huge whooomph. Everyone jerked and gasped. Jill started whimpering.

'I should have got on with those arrangements,' Dad was muttering. He held a small torch over his notebook, making pencil ticks or crosses over his writing.

Thump. The house shook. Billy looked up at the black cellar ceiling. 'Is it a bomb falling?'

223

'Sit back, Billy.' Mother ducked her head and pushed Jill's into her chest. The whimpering went on and on. Mother couldn't stop her. She was all creased up herself. She said, 'Billy, I've got my hands full with Baby, look after Kenneth, please.'

Billy turned round and saw Kenneth on a little chair behind him, both arms wrapped around himself and shaking all over. He spoke in his nicest possible voice, 'We're safe down in here, Kenneth.' But Kenneth didn't stop shaking so Billy moved beside him and put an arm round his shoulders. 'We've got a thick ceiling, look,' and Billy tipped his head back to have a good look himself. It was curved, like a cave, with thick beams running along it. Surely no bomb could bash through that?

Every time there was a thud, Kenneth shook, and Mother jumped, squeezing Jill tightly into her chest.

Billy imagined the shashka was at his hip, lashed onto a wide leather belt. No one could be scared while he had that.

Far away there was a fearful crash. Dad stopped his writing. 'Hope there's no one under that, whatever it was.'

It wasn't like other times when they'd sat for a while and then been able to go back into the kitchen. This time the rumbling, whistling and thumps went on and on and on, so no-one could sleep even though Billy's eyes felt so hot and droopy. Every time his head jerked down to his chest a bang or a whistling or a crashing brought him wide awake again.

Dad waved Billy and Kenneth towards the camp bed but it was furthest from the cellar door and it seemed safest to stay put. Dad leaned down a couple of times to unscrew the cap of the thermos. He must have made tea beforehand. He never quite got to pouring it. His hand would reach down, Mother would shake her head, the cups rattled and Dad would sit up again. It was truly a terrible noise outside, like hundreds of roofs crashing, loud aeroplanes too low down and a kind of roaring.

Billy wanted so much to sleep that he almost didn't care about the noise, but the rumblings and shakings kept him sitting up straight. Looking after Kenneth, and keeping his hand on his shashka, stopped him being scared for himself.

It was a long long night, but eventually they heard the All Clear. Dad spread his hands wide. 'It's over for now. Come on, boys.' He took Jill from Mother's arms. 'Thank the lord we're all safe.'

Mother pushed them towards the stairs and when the cellar door opened, the hall was still there and it was morning.

She went straight to put the kettle on, Kenneth close beside her, while Dad took a quick look out of the front door. Billy took a few steps towards him. As the door opened, Dad was silhouetted against a distant blaze of red and orange going far up into the sky. It looked beautiful but there was a stink of brick dust and smoke.

Dad said, 'Stay inside,' and pulled the door to behind him. In a while he came back, grey-faced.

Kenneth whispered, 'What about Mummy and Daddy?'

Mother put four cups of tea on the table and a mug of milk for Jill. 'They'll have been in the Anderson, Kenneth, don't worry, but I'll ring them up. Look after Baby a moment. I'm going to check on my parents too.'

'Is Nanny and Grandad's house bombed, Mother?'

Dad sipped at his tea. 'We must certainly hope not. But some poor folks have been bombed, that's for sure.'

When Mother came back from the phone, her face looked relieved. 'No problems, Kenneth. They're all safe. Nothing came that near them.'

'That's good,' said Dad. 'Now, I think these children had better make up on their sleep.'

225

Mother bustled Billy and Kenneth back to bed, carrying Jill up too.

Kenneth was still silent. He looked so white and his eyes so sore that Billy gave him the best pillow for his camp bed, before sliding into his own bed. He tried to settle down, Dad's voice rumbling on down below and a strange glow outside seeping under his curtain. He pulled the blackout until it touched the windowsill so that not even a tiny plane could see in.

In the morning, Dad said the situation in London had got really serious. He was going to take Kenneth home and talk to Uncle Frank, and 'discuss matters with people.'

Billy went with them as far as the end of the road. He was surprised to see people going to church. Surely no-one had time to go today, even if it was Sunday. It seemed very wrong to be bustling along the in the normal way, but just everyone was going along the same as always.

'We don't want another night like that!' the lady opposite called to Dad as he passed.

'Indeed not! Let's hope that's the end of it for a while. I gather the Jerries lost twenty-two planes in it. Punishment enough, I should think.'

Billy waved Goodbye to Dad and Kenneth, then ran home to amuse himself in the garden for as long as he was allowed. He went to the far end of the garden behind the toolshed to practice kicking and catching his tennis ball. He listened hard to the aeroplane sounds and whether they were turning into dangerous dronings, ready for the squeal that would mean rushing indoors and down to the cellar.

There was a thick soup for lunch, and Dad still wasn't home. 'Is that the end of the bombing, Mother?'

'How can I know? I hope so. I'll wait to hear what your father says. He's seeing several people and making phone calls. Go and tidy your bedroom as best as you've ever done before. Then you can keep Baby occupied for me.'

He saw that Mother was twisting her hands and not really looking at him, so he didn't argue. Dad would calm her down when he got home.

He wanted to run down to the warden's hut to see what Mr Durban thought, but he didn't dare.

After he'd done a really good job on his bedroom, he came down to the parlour to play with Jill. He piled up a few bricks and let her topple them down. She seemed happy doing that on her own, so he sat at the table and played patience. Uncle Ted had taught him last year when everyone was happy and safe. He turned the cards over slowly, wondering what was going to happen.

Bombs sounded again in the night, so they spent another night in the cellar. It was really fearful like before. The noise went on and on, way past even Mother's and Dad's bedtime. Even though Dad wanted him to lie down like Jill, it was too scary to sleep.

In the morning, Mother was white and irritable, smacking Jill's hand when she grabbed things off the table.

He was going to get ready for school but Mother sent him to play with Jill, 'and don't come out until I call.'

He heard the telephone go, the crackle of the wireless and footsteps up and down the stairs.

When Mother did call, it was to send him for a bath.

'But I've only just washed!' Then he saw suitcases standing open in the front room. He screwed up his eyes. 'Are you going away, Mother?'

'We all are. Your father told you that you were only here while the going was good and now it's not. Aunty phoned. Kenneth's in a dreadful state, apparently, and you don't want to go through another night of bombing do you?'

'No.' Billy stood still, pushing a foot against the edge of the lino. There was going to be more going away. This was all Kenneth's fault. 'But *I* didn't make a fuss. Do I have to be evacuated again?'

He knew it was going to be *Yes* before he even looked at Mother. He pressed his hands on his tummy and twizzled around twice. He wasn't sure whether he minded dreadfully. He didn't like bombs. And Mrs Youldon would be happy to see him. 'Am I going back to the country?'

'Yes, but not to the same billet. We've been making the arrangements, so go and have your bath quickly. We need to get going and arrive well before dark.'

He went upstairs to run his bath, and had it slowly. It might be the last time he was in a bathroom. Tomorrow or the next day he might be shivering in a scullery, hunched up in a hip bath and it wouldn't even be Mrs Youldon's.

He'd be with another stranger. Suppose he was put with that awful woman who shaved Sonia's head!

He heard Dad come out of the parlour where he must have been making important telephone calls.

Billy dressed again and got his whizzer from the toy box. It would be 'only one small toy' again. He put a dinky car in his trouser pocket and picked up his whizzer, his heroes book and a comic. Downstairs he was able to push these inside the small case that was meant for him before Dad checked with Mother that everything important was packed. He was going to see them to the train.

They had sardine sandwiches and jam doughnuts before putting on their coats. Jill was surprisingly quiet. He held her soft little hand, and found she had a tiny rubber doll squeezed in it, as if she knew.

'Right then, everyone.' Dad put the gas masks out for each of them, then took two large suitcases.

Mother took a deep breath and looked around the room. 'I wonder how long we shall have to be away this time.'

She took the smaller case and the handle of the pushchair. Dad put Jill in it, where she sat very quiet, her mouth slightly open. The gas masks sat at her feet.

Billy held his small suitcase and a carrier bag of food. He hoped the new billet would be pleased.

Dad shepherded them through the door and locked it behind him. A light rain was falling. Mother pulled her scarf over her hair, and wrenched the pushchair hood up. Father couldn't use his umbrella because the cases needed both his hands.

They left their road behind, making for towards the railway station, the barrage balloons swaying in the damp breeze with no sign of sun shining behind them.

CHAPTER TWENTY-SIX
September 10th 1940

*Two waves of German bombers fly up the
Thames. 28 downed by RAF*

They were already on the station platform when
they saw Kenneth in his camel coat and hat, as
though he was going to a party or something. But
it was his gas mask he was carrying, not a present.

'Hello Billy,' he called, like a best friend.

Aunty stepped out of the waiting room, where
two large suitcases were standing. 'Frank says *God
Speed*,' she said to Mother. 'He was needed at the
first aid station for training.

Heaven knows how I'll manage without him.'

Mother shrugged slightly and raised her thin
eyebrows.

'And I'm having to do this all over again.'

Dad went down the platform to speak to the
station master.

Billy pointed to Kenneth's hands holding a bag
and the gas mask. 'Doesn't Aunty need you here?'

'Mummy's coming with me –we're right near the
vicarage where Aunty Marcia stays.'

Billy looked quickly at Mother. 'They've got room
for me at the vicarage this time?'

'No. It's too full.' She brushed away the wave
on her cheek. 'They've said they'll take me and Jill
again.'

'But— what about me?'

'Your father has sorted somewhere.'

Kenneth put his head on one side. 'It was
Daddy who phoned the vicar first. He found a lady
nearby who could take a mother and child. We
couldn't waste her billet on just you.'

Mother nodded. 'It was a decent billet for just one boy we needed.'

Aunty put a hand to her hair. 'Oh dear. It doesn't seem fair on poor Billy. I didn't mean it to work out like this.'

Billy looked at the floor. It wouldn't be Aunty's fault. Uncle was just quicker than Dad.

'Am I near you, Mother?'

'It seems there's a nice billet not far from where you were before.' She bent to rearrange Jill's curls.

Billy swallowed. So he wasn't going to be with any of them, or with Mrs Youldon. Bits of dust blew along the platform and he screwed up his eyes.

Dad came up to them again. 'Apparently, it doesn't make much difference where you wait on the platform. The station master said all the carriages are going to be crowded.'

'Purgatory.' Mother made a face at him and tilted her head towards Billy. 'I've told him about the billet.'

Dad put a hand on Billy's shoulder. 'I'm sorry you can't be with Mother and Jill. It's not that easy to get billets, especially arranging it privately. You were doing well at that village school. So you'll go there again. I've found you a billet with your own room.'

'Is it until Christmas again?' Billy kicked one foot against the other.

'Let's hope not, but I don't know. No-one knows. It's until we win the war and it's safe in London again.'

'Does Mr Durban know I'm going?'

'Yes he does. He's given me something to give you, a letter I think.' He took a hard envelope from inside his coat and slipped it into Billy's case. 'There. Something to look at when you arrive.'

Kenneth was dancing up and down. So he wasn't under the weather now. 'I'll be with Mummy and Aunty. I'll be like Jill's brother.'

Billy looked into the pushchair at the plump little face pressed into a blanket-wrapped doll. Jill wouldn't like that. How would she get on without him to play with her and mind her when Mother was busy?

Jill lowered her doll and peered both ways along the platform. As her gaze swept back, it reached Kenneth. A sunbeam momentarily blinded her and she grimaced.

'She's smiling at me, see?' said Kenneth.

'She's not.' The words slipped out so quickly they sounded like *snot*. Billy turned his back on them all and walked up the platform a little way.

Grandad and Nanny would need to check the carrots. They'd been nearly ready to pull. He hadn't even been able to say Goodbye. What would happen to Jim and everyone? And he hadn't been to Mr Durban's house to see Angela. They would all be staying behind and would be in their Anderson every night.

He closed his eyes. He could see the shashka. It would be shimmering in its scabbard. He would never forget it, waiting for him, until he was old enough to use it.

'Billy!' Mother pointed down the platform away from him. A chimney length of steam headed the train rolling in, smoke and grit with it.

He picked up his case and stood ready, as near as he could to Mother so that he wasn't put in a different carriage.

The station master strode alongside the slowing train. Crowds of soldiers, grinning, smoking, or slumped in their seats, showed at every window.

Dad stepped forward with the bigger cases as the station master opened a carriage door.

'Here you are, ladies, you can squeeze into the corridor, that's best. Fold that pushchair. You'll have to stow your cases on it. Perhaps the nippers can perch on top.'

Mother clutched Aunty's arm. 'Oh my goodness! We'll suffocate, Doreen.'

Dad hugged Mother. 'Keep calm, Marcia. Just a journey, then into safety.' He slid the cases into a gap while Mother folded the pushchair and Aunty took Jill, then he helped all of them up the steps where they stayed squashed against the door.

'Stay safe, Doreen. You'll all be best off down in the country.'

'And you get away from London, Bert, as soon as you can.'

Billy swallowed. 'Goodbye, Dad.'

'It's not forever, son. I'll get down to see you as soon as it's possible.' He put a hand on Billy's head then on Jill's. If he gave a quotation, Billy didn't hear it.

There was a great press of soldiers and rucksacks in the corridor. They squeezed forward into the train, stepping over the big black toe-caps of the soldiers. Some of them whistled at Aunty, and she blushed. Mother lifted her chin. They were still struggling to find even a foot space when the train started. Aunty lost her balance and nearly landed on a soldier's lap. There was a cheer and a lot of laughing.

Kenneth lowered his lashes at the soldiers and one of them pulled him into a space between them. Two others lifted Jill up high. She opened her mouth to bawl but a soldier put a sweet into it and her mouth turned into a smile.

The train lurched again, and Billy hung onto a door-frame. He peered through the spaces between soldiers' heads and arms towards a window. He caught a last glimpse of Dad's face shaded by his trilby, a blob of grey against the brown carriages, not moving.

It was a terrible journey squashed up against the soldiers, many of them smoking. Some of the men looked really sad but most of them were loudly joking and shouting to each other.

'Just boys, really,' murmured Aunty to Mother, but she was busy smiling at one with a ginger moustache. The soldier stood up for her and she squeezed into the seat behind him. Aunty took Jill from the soldiers, sat her on top of a suitcase and leant against it.

Nothing was easy. They needed to change train twice, struggling with Jill, pushchair and suitcases onto platforms and looking around wildly for information, before finally reaching the small station where Uncle Frank had arranged for the vicar to meet them. Mother had got herself into a state because the station names had been painted out, so almost screamed when she spotted the vicar on the platform.

He stepped towards them and seemed pleased to see Mother again and even Jill. 'What a big girl, now. You'll soon be able to come to Sunday school.'

Jill shrank back into Mother's skirt. The vicar wasn't a Daddy sort of person. He greeted Aunty and Kenneth and introduced them to a lady standing nearby. He opened his arms slightly, as if he was holding a hymnal and looked around at them all. 'My dears, you got out just in time. There's been a huge convoy of planes coming right down the Thames. In broad daylight! Dreadful bombing. Give thanks that you can all come here to safety.'

What about Dad and all the people Billy had left behind to face the awful bombing?

Aunty started chatting straight away, although her curls had started to droop with the stress of the journey. Kenneth stood near to her, brushing train smuts off his camel coat.

'And a matching cap. Fetching,' the lady said as she patted his cheek.

It was only a small station, the late summer sun still shining on its wet surface. Perhaps recent rain had washed it, but there was none of the dust of London or rubbish lying between the rails. There was a sweet smell, a grassy bank and clumps with red blobs. When Billy looked closer, he saw they were wild strawberries. It would be nice to pick them.

Mother took hold of his arm and checked his packages and gas mask. He looked around for the person come to collect him. No-one else was there except the station cat.

Meanwhile, the lady led Aunty and Kenneth away. 'The vicar's car is full. We shall walk. It's not that far.'

'Bye, Billy,' said Kenneth with a toothpaste smile, his hand firmly grasping Aunty's coat sleeve. 'We'll see you when we see you.'

Aunty turned and smiled sadly at Billy. 'Ta-ta for now. Hope to see you soon, dear.' She started to walk off, then suddenly dropped Kenneth's hand and ran back, pushing something into Billy's coat pocket. 'Here, ducky. You won't be that far away. We'll be visiting you, I'm sure.' She blew him a kiss before following their lady down the road.

The vicar turned to his car. 'I think we can squeeze everything else in,' he said, stowing the pushchair into the boot, 'if you have this little one on your lap,' and he held the car door open for Mother and Jill.

'And what about this boy?' said the vicar. 'Who is he?'

Mother said, 'It's my son, Billy. You met him, Vicar, remember.'

'Of course! You have a son, too, Mrs Wilson. I remember. My goodness. I didn't recognize you, young sir. You look so—different.'

'Yes, well he won't be going to that billet again.' Mother neatened Billy's collar. 'This is where we say Goodbye, Billy. You're not to worry. You've only a few miles further to go.'

He looked anxiously from side to side. It was evening, and now that the train had drawn out of the station the place was quite silent apart from Mother's voice. 'Someone is coming to meet you,' she went on. 'The billeting officer has arranged it. We said you'd wait at the station.'

He looked around for the someone. The vicar might drive off and leave him on his own. 'We didn't say Goodbye to Nanny and Grandad,' he said quickly.

Before Mother could answer, a farm cart clattered to a halt nearby. Mother went up and spoke to the driver, then came back to Billy.

'There, lucky boy. You're going to ride on this cart all the way to your village. Hand your suitcase up to the carter.'

He went to the cart with it. 'That's right. Now, say Goodbye to Jill.'

He saw her chubby face through the car window, damp lips open as she stared at Mother's back. He waved, but she didn't seem to notice.

Mother said in her anxious voice, 'We'll come and see you as soon as we can. Pull those socks up. Keep yourself clean and be good.' She bent towards him and he smelled her Parma Violets talcum powder as she gave him a small hug.

Then he was so busy scrambling up high to sit in the front of the cart that he hardly had time to say Goodbye, and when he turned to wave, the vicar's car was disappearing down the road.

He kept staring at the back of it until five rabbits hopping across the road surprised him, they looked so cheeky and carefree. He pretended they were family. *That's us, that is. Mother and Aunty, the big ones; Kenneth, Jill and me, the little ones. Running free in the country, leaving all the bombing behind. I am a lucky boy, riding on a cart.*

'Looks like I got you all to myself,' said the carter. His voice was rough, but sounded kind. He jerked the reins and the cart-horse plodded back the way he'd come. 'That your Ma, eh? And your baby sister. Off with the vicar. I know he. Been to one of his sermons. Keeps them short, he do. Very pop'lar.'

Billy took a look at the man. His face was leathery and browny red, not like Uncle and Dad at all.

He didn't quite manage a smile but his hand creeping into his pocket found the little bag that Aunty had pushed into it. Peardrops! His favourite. Aunty was nice. He popped a peardrop into his mouth for it seemed the right time to eat one. Then he remembered his manners. He leant forward and held out his bag. 'Would you like a sweet, Mr Carter?'

The man shifted his cap and smiled. 'No, no, you keep your sweeties, young'un. Coming out of that there London, you need all the sweetness you can get. I'm Jed Turnbull, I am, a carter but not Mr Carter, see. You call me Jed, right? I can see as you're going to get on real well with folks round here.'

Billy thought of the way the vicar looked at him that first time. And the teasing from the local children. Suppose the new billet people didn't like him? And he'd be living there till Christmas or even longer. He held onto his suitcase tightly.

Jed looked down, 'Have you got your favourite toy in that case to show me?'

Billy clicked open the latches. He could show Jed the special whizzer. Jed might not ever have

237

seen one, living in the country. Before his hand even got to the whizzer it felt the envelope Dad had given him from Mr Durban. How could he forget? He opened it and pulled out a letter and a photograph. It was the shashka! The shashka had come with him on this new evacuation to keep him strong as strong!

It was ever such a good picture. You could see all the letters along the blade and the decorations on the scabbard, which was lying on the table nearby.

Jed was geeing up the horse. Somehow Billy didn't want to share his shashka with anyone, not even the sight of it. He put it carefully back in the envelope and read the letter.

Dear Billy,

I am going to miss your visits to my hut, but you need to be safe and away from London. You will have a jolly time in the country with lots of boys you know from school. Your mother and baby sister won't be far away from you, I hear.

This photo will remind you of our chats and I know you will like looking at it. Keep it covered. One day you will be back here again, looking at the shashka for real. Until then, I know you'll be a credit to your family and that your foster family will be pleased to have you. Best foot forward, as they say. You are a brave boy.

I send you all good wishes from Mrs Durban and Angela, as well as from me. We shall be thinking of you until we meet again after the war.

Keep safe,

Peter Durban

Billy put the letter in the envelope with his wonderful picture. Both were something special to keep. He felt suddenly proud, and sat up a bit straighter. He put the pear drops in the case and pulled out his whizzer, then clicked the case shut. 'I've got a whizzer to show you, Jed.'

Jed turned towards him, 'You sit up by me so I can see it. And lookee— you need to see around proper. Come for'ard and sit up on these sacks so you're like a king, a king coming into his village. Right?'

His village? Billy scrambled over the rolls of firewood until his legs reached the pile of sacks next to Jed. A king might own a shashka; he probably would in far-off countries. He put his hand on his hip where the shashka nobble would sit in his hand. He was nice and high now, like an important person. He looked hard at the road ahead. 'Is that our church tower?'

'Yes it be, tallest thing in the village.'

Now he could see the church as well and that was only a quick run away from Mrs Youldon's. She'd be really pleased to see him. Timmy and Sally would shout out 'Billy!' and jump up and down.

'Jed, I've got friends here from last time.'

'Is that so? And now you'se a be making some more right enough, that's a' sure.'

The cart slowed and turned down a wide lane where there was a field and a brick house beside it with animal noises of all sorts: neighing, clucking, barking.

Jed stopped the horse and grasped hold of Billy's suitcase. 'Here we are, laddie. This'm the place, and the dogs already shouting a welcome, see.'

END OF BOOK ONE
but not the end of the story.

Was Billy happy at his new billet? To discover the dramas that both Billy and Kenneth experienced while they were evacuated for the rest of the war, read Book Two: INFILTRATION.

In Book Three: IMPACT, Billy and Kenneth are adolescents adapting to post-war Wandsworth. Now they face new challenges and share more psychological space. Tensions rise to a fearful crisis. After the worst has happened, somehow Billy must resolve the dramatic fall-out for them both.

If you've enjoyed INTRUSION please tell others. Do leave a review on the site where you bought the book. Did you know that even a sentence or two about your read is important to an author? Readers' opinions guide future writing as well as informing potential readers about the book. Thank you for reading about Billy's world.

Also by Rosalind Minett:

Me-Time Tales: tea breaks for mature women and curious men.
Satirical short stories with a dark edge. All kinds of women unlocked.

Crime Shorts, an e-book series:
No. 1. A boy with potential. *A choirboy's sinister discovery.*
No.2 Homed. *Who is guilty, child or adult?*
No.3 Not Her Fault *Why is she obsessed with a murder of a child she never knew?*

...and more crime coming your way.

Rosalind blogs at
www.characterfulwriter.com

. . .where you can sign up to receive her newsletter with more information about her writing.

24396140R00139

Printed in Great Britain
by Amazon